The Last Seduction

What Reviewers Say About Ronica Black's Work

Freedom to Love

"This is a great book. The police drama keeps you enthralled throughout but what I found captivating was the growing affection between the two main characters. Although they are both very different women, you find yourself holding your breath, hoping that they will find a way to be together."—*Lesbian Reading Room*

Snow Angel

"A beautifully written, passionate and romantic novella." —*SunsetXCocktail*

The Seeker

"Ronica Black's books just keep getting stronger and stronger. …This is such a tightly written plot-driven novel that readers will find themselves glued to the pages and ignoring phone calls. *The Seeker* is a great read, with an exciting plot, great characters, and great sex."—*Just About Write*

Flesh and Bone—Lammy Finalist

"Ronica Black handles a traditional range of lesbian fantasies with gusto and sincerity. The reader wants to know these women as well as they come to know each other. When Black's characters ignore their realistic fears to follow their passion, this reader admires their chutzpah and cheers them on. …These stories make good bedtime reading, and could lead to sweet dreams. Read them and see." —*Erotica Revealed*

Chasing Love

"Ronica Black's writing is fluid, and lots of dialogue makes this a fast read. If you like steamy erotica with intense sexual situations, you'll like *Chasing Love*."—*Queer Magazine Online*

Hearts Aflame

"Sleek storytelling and terrific characters are the backbone of Ronica Black's third and best novel, *Hearts Aflame*. Prepare to hop on for an emotional ride with this thrilling story of love in the outback. …Along with the romance of Krista and Rae, the secondary storylines such as Krista's fear of horses and an uncle suffering from Alzheimer's are told with depth and warmth. Black also draws in the reader by utilizing the weather as a metaphor for the sexual and emotional tension in all the storylines. Wonderful storytelling and rich characterization make this a high recommendation."—*Lambda Literary Review*

"*Hearts Aflame* takes the reader on the rough and tumble ride of the cattle drive. Heat, flood, and a sexual pervert are all part of the adventure. Heat also appears between Krista and Rae. The twists and turns of the plot engage the reader all the way to the satisfying conclusion."—*Just About Write*

Wild Abandon—Lammy Finalist

"Black is a master at teasing the reader with her use of domination and desire. Black's first novel, *In Too Deep*, was a finalist for a 2005 Lammy. ...With *Wild Abandon*, the author continues her winning ways, writing like a seasoned pro. This is one romance I will not soon forget."—*Books to Watch Out For*

"This sequel to Ronica Black's debut novel, *In Too Deep*, is an electrifying thriller. The author's development as a fine storyteller shines with this tightly written story. ...[The mystery] keeps the story charged—never unraveling or leading us to a predictable conclusion. More than once I gasped in surprise at the dark and twisted paths this book took."—*Curve Magazine*

"Ronica Black, author of *In Too Deep*, has given her fans another fast paced novel of romance and danger. As previously, Black develops her characters fully, complete with their quirks and flaws. She is also skilled at allowing her characters to grow, and to find their way out of psychic holes. If you enjoy complex characters and passionate sex scenes, you'll love *Wild Abandon*."—*MegaScene*

"Black has managed to create two very sensual and compelling women. The backstory is intriguing, original, and quite well-developed. Yet, it doesn't detract from the primary premise of the novel—it is a sexually-charged romance about two very different and guarded women. Black carries the reader along at such a rapid pace that the rise and fall of each climactic moment successfully creates that suspension of disbelief which the reader seeks." —*Midwest Book Review*

In Too Deep—Lammy Finalist

"Ronica Black's debut novel *In Too Deep* has everything from nonstop action and intriguing well developed characters to steamy erotic love scenes. From the opening scenes where Black plunges the reader headfirst into the story to the explosive unexpected ending, *In Too Deep* has what it takes to rise to the top. Black has a winner with *In Too Deep*, one that will keep the reader turning the pages until the very last one."—*Independent Gay Writer*

"...an exciting, page turning read, full of mystery, sex, and suspense."—*MegaScene*

"...a challenging murder mystery—sections of this mixed-genre novel are hot, hot, hot. Black juggles the assorted elements of her first book with assured pacing and estimable panache." —*Q Syndicate*

"Black's characterization is skillful, and the sexual chemistry surrounding the three major characters is palpable and definitely hot-hot-hot...if you're looking for a solid read with ample amounts of eroticism and a red herring or two you're sure to find *In Too Deep* a satisfying read."—*L Word Literature*

"Ronica Black's debut novel, *In Too Deep*, is the outstanding first effort of a gifted writer who has a promising career ahead of her. Black shows extraordinary command in weaving a thoroughly engrossing tale around multi-faceted characters, intricate action and character-driven plots and subplots, sizzling sex that jumps off the page and stimulates libidos effortlessly, amidst brilliant storytelling. A clever mystery writer, Black has the reader guessing until the end."—*Midwest Book Review*

"Every time the reader has a handle on what's happening, Black throws in a curve, successfully devising a good mystery. The romance and sex add a special gift to the package rounding out the story for a totally satisfying read."—*Just About Write*

By the Author

In Too Deep

Deeper

Wild Abandon

Hearts Aflame

Flesh and Bone

The Seeker

Chasing Love

Conquest

Wholehearted

The Midnight Room

Snow Angel

The Practitioner

Freedom to Love

Under Her Wing

Private Passion

Dark Euphoria

The Last Seduction

The Last Seduction

by

Ronica Black

2019

THE LAST SEDUCTION

ISBN 13: 978-1-63555-211-9

This Trade Paperback Original Is Published By
Bold Strokes Books, Inc.
P.O. Box 249
Valley Falls, NY 12185

First Edition: June 2019

Credits
Editor: Cindy Cresap
Production Design: Susan Ramundo
Cover Design By Tammy Seidick

Acknowledgments

Cindy Cresap, my editor, as always, it was a pleasure. Thank you! The entire Bold Strokes crew, you are all amazing and you continue to bless my life by taking my work and turning it into something incredible.

And finally, Cait. My one and only. Thank you.

Dedication

For the one. Eighteen years and counting. I love you.

PROLOGUE

"Ma'am, your bottle of Chianti Straccali." The waiter removed the cork and poured Sasha Bashton a glassful of the hypnotic, velvety red wine. It was one of her favorites, and her mouth watered in anticipation. She brought the wine up for a quick smell. Satisfied, she then swirled the wine and sipped it. She closed her eyes and smiled.

"Wonderful," she said, opening her eyes. The waiter pressed his hands together, seemingly pleased.

"Is there anything else I can get you while you wait?"

Sasha eyed the toasted bread that she'd been using to soak up the balsamic vinegar and olive oil. She'd heard that Italians didn't eat bread with olive oil or balsamic vinegar in Italy. But at the moment, she didn't care. She was starving.

"No, thank you, not now."

"Very well, then." He left her quietly, and she was once again alone with her thoughts. She plucked her phone from her purse and noted the time. Hannah was now a half an hour late. She debated calling, but she steeled her jaw, wanting to give Hannah the benefit of the doubt.

Hannah had been running late a lot lately. For the last two years, actually. And each and every time, she had an excuse. Some were reasonable, but most were her simply being absentminded and apathetic. Sasha blamed most of it on her attitude with life.

Hannah was ten years her senior, and she'd turned fifty with a very big chip on her shoulder. And four years before that, she'd battled breast cancer. Depression shrouded her, and instead of living life to the fullest, she began to act like she was ninety. She didn't want to do anything, go anywhere. She was just merely existing.

The whole thing had been wearing on Sasha, and she swore, to her friends and to herself, that she'd give her one more chance… just one more chance. This time there'd better be no excuses. Being a no show to happy hours and other events was one thing. But their fifteenth anniversary? A whole other thing altogether.

Hannah had sworn the evening would be the greatest ever and she'd been the one to make the reservations at their favorite Italian restaurant. The one where they'd had their first date, first smile, first laugh, first witty, flirty banter. Sasha recalled that date with tears in her eyes. It had been such a magical evening. So where had all the magic gone? It seemed it had gone right out the door with Hannah. Like an Arizona monsoon wind blowing through their happy home, only to wrap Hannah up in its embrace and sweep her out the door, leaving nothing it its wake but a lonely old tumbleweed.

Sasha drank her wine, taking in a couple of hearty swallows. Her heart rate was beginning to speed up. Sweat beaded along the nape of her neck. Surely Hannah hadn't forgotten. Not tonight. Oh God, she felt sick.

Around her, people laughed and glasses clanked. Waiters wove through tables. The heavy front door opened, and Sasha could no longer bear to look. She knew deep in her heart that Hannah would not be stepping through the door. She eyed her phone. Tears blurred her vision. It was pushing close to an hour now and no word.

She dialed Hannah and held the phone to her ear. Hannah answered on the third ring.

"Hey, babe."

Sasha inhaled sharply. "Uh, hi."

"What's up? You coming home soon?" A teardrop fell onto the wooden table as Sasha struggled to breathe. Hannah had forgotten. She'd fucking forgotten their anniversary.

"Uh, no. No, Hannah, I'm not coming home. Not tonight. And probably not ever again."

"What? Wait, why?"

"Happy anniversary."

CHAPTER ONE

Friday. Sasha knew Fridays were supposed to be fun, a day of celebration even, signaling the end of the workweek. Usually, she smiled right alongside everyone else and even had a little hop in her step on the way out of the office to happy hour. But today was not the typical Friday. For one, it was her birthday. And two, she felt like hell. Serious hell. To make matters worse, her brain fog was so bad she couldn't remember if it was her thirty-ninth or fortieth birthday.

She leaned into the bathroom counter mirror with narrowed eyes and tried to clear her mind to find the answer. As she examined two new slight wrinkles on her forehead, she did the math in her head. She pushed away and straightened.

"Fuck. I'm forty."

She sighed, thought about trying to cover the new wrinkles with makeup, and then rolled her eyes.

"Oh, what's the use?" She fumbled with her Coach purse, scrambling for her MAC Lipglass and quickly spread some on. Maybe somehow it would help to make her look less dead and zombie-like and more colorful and alive-like, able to move safely among the living. But she didn't hold her breath. Behind her, the restroom door opened and one of her coworkers entered. Karen caught her gaze in the reflection of the mirror and smiled.

"Sasha, hi. How goes it?"

Sasha thought briefly about telling her the truth. That her hands and feet were swollen and she felt dizzy and nauseous. And should she mention she felt like passing out? No, too much. She shook the thought and forced a smile.

"I'm okay. How 'bout you?"

Karen eased into a stall and locked the door. "I'm well, thanks."

"That's good."

Sasha braced herself on the counter and considered the walk to the parking garage. Could she do it? Could she make it? She would have to. She knew her colleagues would be more than happy to help if she asked; they all knew about her chronic kidney disease. But she preferred to keep her illness and its woes private. She didn't want to seem different from anyone else.

Karen emerged from the stall and stood next to her to wash her hands.

"TGIF, right?"

"You know it." Sasha zipped her purse and pretended to examine her eyebrows. She didn't want to leave until after Karen. That way, if she had to walk slowly or if she had to stop and rest, it wouldn't be noticed. Most of the day shift had cleared out, and the evening shift was already in production of the latest newscast.

"Say," Karen said, touching her shoulder. Sasha was certain she would mention her birthday just as others had. But she didn't. "You look a little…green around the gills. You okay?"

Again Sasha forced a smile. "Oh, you know, I'm just tired. End of the week and all."

Karen studied her for what felt like ages. Sasha felt her face burn from being scrutinized so closely. What all could she tell? Was it that noticeable? God, she should've gone to the doctor two weeks ago instead of cancelling that appointment. But she'd sprained her ankle, and she'd been told by her primary care to stay off of it as much as possible. So she had. Now she feared she was paying the price. Maybe her nephrologist could've seen this coming and prevented it.

"Okay, if you say so." She dropped her hand and gave her a sympathetic look. "Get home safely and enjoy your weekend."

She left Sasha at the counter and breezed out of the restroom. Sasha exhaled long and hard and gathered her purse. As she emerged back into the large office space, she wondered why no one had mentioned that today was her fortieth birthday. Had she done her math right? What was she missing? Did people not consider forty to be a milestone anymore?

A quick wave of dizziness washed over her, and she struggled to focus as she leaned against the wall next to the elevator. She stared down at her Gucci heels and had an urge to tear them off and walk to her vehicle in her stocking feet. Another wave came as the elevator door opened, and she walked carefully inside, glad to see it was empty.

"Oh, to hell with it." She slipped off her heels and stretched her toes. "Please help." But her free feet did little to rid her of the sickening feeling. She blinked and focused on the number panel. She felt like she had on the wrong prescription eyeglasses. Yes. That was exactly it. Only she didn't. She had in her contacts and they were fine.

The doors opened with a ding, and she hurried out of the elevator and into the dim parking garage. If she could just make it to her Jeep. Sitting inside her new Grand Cherokee would fix everything. The new car smell mixed with the cinnamon air freshener would soothe her and she would be fine. The sickness would be gone. A horn blared to her left, and she jerked as a taxicab screeched to a halt.

"Jesus, lady!"

"Sorry, sorry." She held up a hand in apology, but to her surprise he climbed from the car.

"You all right? You need a ride?" He was looking at her with concern under the sweat soaked brim of his Diamondbacks hat. "You look like you're gonna fall over."

She started to tell him no, to tell him she was fine, but she just suddenly deflated as if all the air had just vanished from her sails.

"Yes," she breathed. "A ride would be great."

He rounded the car quickly and cupped her elbow. "You want to go to a hospital or a doctor?"

"No, I just need to get home." He eased her in the back seat of his warm sedan. It smelled of hot vinyl and dirty carpet. But she didn't care. She just rested her head against the seat and spewed out her address when he slid into the front seat. He repeated it and asked about her cross streets.

Then the awful realization hit her again just as it did each and every day.

She no longer lived at her home. She no longer lived with Hannah, her partner of fifteen years.

She lived five long miles away with her best friend, Bonnie, in a small room with a clothes rack and an ironing board.

Sasha gave him the correct address and then allowed her heavy eyes to fall closed as a tear slipped down her cheek.

Chapter Two

The Bud Light was icy cold, and Hannah Carter grinned at the golden liquid that had sprayed her wrist as she cracked open the can and took a long, hearty sip. After she swallowed her fill, she leaned back against the windshield of her old seventy-six Chevy truck and crossed her ankles to stare at the soon to be setting sun and the vast desert before her. Next to her, on the side of the road, several kids screamed with delight as a fighter jet flew straight for them and then pulled up at the last second, soaring up into the rainbow sherbet sky. Hannah laughed at the enjoyment of the children and the rush the plane had brought on. She rubbed the gooseflesh on her arms and toasted the plane by holding her beer can up in the air.

"F-16?" her son, Casey, asked as he tossed her his unopened Coke and climbed onto the truck to sit next to her.

"Think so."

"Badass."

"Yep."

As he settled in, his short sandy hair blew in the breeze and his angled jaw flexed as his long fingers worked the Coke can, eventually snapping it open and shaking the excess soda from his hand.

"Blue Angels fly yet?"

"Not yet."

"Good."

He slurped his drink and relaxed just as two more fighters did maneuvers overhead.

Hannah watched in amazement.

"I never get over this. It gets to me every damn year." She'd been bringing Casey to the rehearsal for the annual air show for over ten years now. From back when he was just a little guy, all grin and ears. She glanced over at him and shaded her brow. He'd grown into his ears, but his grin was still as broad as ever and shit-eating to boot.

"What?" He'd caught her looking.

"You're a handsome devil."

He shook his head. "Whatever."

"You are. Eighteen and as handsome as all get-out."

Red plumed his cheeks, and she let it go, loving his modesty as well. Someday, he'd make someone very, very happy. And she couldn't wait to see it happen.

She stared off toward the towering purple mountains where the sun hung just above, wavering, trying to decide if it wanted to turn in for the night. Yes, the moment was perfect save for one thing. She cringed as the feeling of loss seeped in. That deep pain resonated in her gut, the one that always came when she thought about Sasha. She'd try to swallow against it, or cough or even try to outrun it. But it always remained until it had had its fill of slowly digesting her insides, leaving her feeling even emptier than before.

"I'm being eaten alive," she whispered before she downed the rest of her beer. A tear snuck down her face and she let it. She was growing tired of wiping them away. Let them run, let them drip, let them meander. She couldn't stop them, and what was the use? She was heartbroken.

Casey cleared his throat, and she somehow knew he'd seen the tear.

"Sasha?" he asked.

She didn't answer verbally, didn't need to. He nodded.

"Yeah, this is great and all, but there's definitely one thing missing."

"I don't want to talk about it." She followed another set of fighters for as far as she could see. One shot straight up while the others remained in formation. She prayed that focusing on the planes would quell the mad feast going on in her insides. But the pain kept on devouring. She touched her abdomen and willed it to stop.

"You never want to talk about it."

"Well, maybe there's a reason." She'd lost weight since Sasha had left. Twenty pounds. She swore it had all been muscle too, for she felt different, weaker. Like a goddamned sack of walking bones.

Casey sat up and fumbled in his bag. He pulled out sunscreen and tossed it to her. "We all have to talk about things that cause pain, Mom. It's how we get over them."

"There's no getting over Sasha."

He looked at her and patted her forearm, encouraging the application of the sunscreen. "Then go after her. Call her. Do something."

"I can't. She made it clear she needed space. She made it clear she doesn't want me around. Maybe she's right. Maybe it's better this way."

Casey scoffed. "My God, Mom, sometimes you are so much like a caveman. It's a miracle you won her heart at all."

"Hey, easy." She rubbed on the warm lotion and then applied some to her face. She was getting dark, and Casey was always commenting about how he preferred not to have a leather satchel for a mother.

"I'm serious. I feel for Sash. I really do. You're impossible sometimes."

"I'm doing what she wants."

"You're doing what you want. Which is not risking another rejection."

Casey offered her another beer, but she declined. She couldn't handle anything else in her stomach. Instead she sat back, inhaled the tropical scent of the sunscreen, and tried to find some soaring planes to focus on. At the moment, she wasn't having any luck.

After a long silence, Casey spoke. "Did you call her today?"

Great. There it was. The sword of all swords. He was bringing up Sasha's birthday. Her fortieth. He didn't know it, but he had just killed her, stabbed her right through the gut.

"I texted her."

"Oh my God."

"Casey, honestly, let up a little."

"It's her fortieth!"

"Yes, I'm aware. But I—I wasn't brave enough to call, okay? Besides, she was at work, and if the call pissed her off then she'd be at work all pissed off and it just wouldn't have been good."

"Did she respond?"

"She thanked me."

"Oh, how romantic. The two of you are a nightmare."

"Then leave us alone."

"I can't!" He tossed the sunscreen into his bag and sighed. "You two love each other. Like deeply love each other. That is so rare. Don't you know what you have? Why do you think all my friends wanted to hang out at our house growing up? Their parents were shitty; they fought all the time or they didn't speak. But you and Sash, you guys were just so easy. You fit together. You worked. And you didn't even have to try."

Hannah closed her eyes. She remembered those days. When things were easy and kisses were soft and embraces were long. She'd come home from work, and Sasha would be in the kitchen, sashaying to Led Zeppelin or Steppenwolf, wine glass in her hand. She'd make dinner while she and Casey did a few chores. Then they'd all settle in and eat and laugh and share. And there'd usually be a young boy or two joining them. Casey's friends. They'd talk for hours, clean the kitchen together, and then change into pj's and crash on the couch to watch television. Many a night she'd awaken only to find Casey and Sasha fast asleep. She'd carry first Casey, and then Sasha to bed. Her loves. Her little sleeping loves. Oh, how her heart had been full then.

The shrill of fighters forced open her eyes. She watched as one tore right by them seemingly tearing her heart from her chest as it did so.

"Things are different now," she said into the wind.

Casey heard her, but he continued to watch the planes. "Yeah, I know. But why? And why aren't you trying to fix it?"

"Because she doesn't want me to."

He shook his head. "Bullshit, Mom. I may be a man, but I know for a fact that is bullshit. You have to try." He dug his phone from his back pocket. "You've got to go tonight. You have to."

"I wasn't invited."

"So?"

She rolled her eyes. "So, I'd feel like an ass."

"I was invited. You'll come as my guest."

"I don't think that's a good idea, Casey."

"Well, thank God I never listen to you then." He hopped down from the truck and brushed off the back of his jeans. He began packing up. "Well, come on then. We gotta go get ready."

"Casey—"

"Don't argue, just do. Isn't that what you always told me? For once in your life you're going to listen to me. And we're going." He stopped to glare at her. "Go on, get your ass off of that truck."

She thought about arguing, about absolutely refusing. But Casey was determined, and she knew he was right. She should go. Despite it all. But the truth was she was afraid. How much rejection could she take?

She eased down off the truck and fished in her pocket for her keys.

One thing was for certain.

She was about to find out.

Chapter Three

"We're late," Hannah said as she slid out of her truck and smoothed down her jeans and button-down white shirt. She rolled up her sleeves as the warmth from the evening air settled on her like the baking heat of an oven.

"Doesn't matter," Casey said as he closed the passenger door and joined her to walk to the front door of Bonnie's house. "We're here and we're going in."

"Think Bonnie will let me in?"

Casey laughed. "That's why I insisted we bring this." He held up the expensive bottle of champagne they'd stopped to purchase.

"I always knew you were smart." She took a deep breath and opened and closed her fists. According to Casey, the surprise party started at seven. They were now pushing seven thirty. Truth be told, she was a little relieved. At least now most people would be busy mingling rather than silently waiting and looking around. She hoped she'd be less noticed.

"Nervous?"

"Hell, yes."

Casey squeezed her hand. "It'll be okay, Mom. This needs to happen."

They walked up the empty drive to the walkway leading to the front door. Music poured out, and the sounds of shrieks and laughter followed. A black fortieth birthday balloon stretched upward from a walkway light.

"I hope she's having fun," Hannah said. They stepped inside and walked sideways to maneuver through people. The house was warm and stuffy and smelled of potpourri and scented candles. Sweat broke out on Hannah's temple as she worked her way through, trying like hell to get to a better vantage point. At some point, she lost sight of Casey, and her heart sped up as she entered the kitchen. Caterers were busy moving hot trays of food, while others wove madly back into the crowd to serve more wine and beer. She managed to grab a cold bottle of beer before it was plucked and placed on a tray. She opened it and took several swallows before finding her way to the edge of the table in the nook.

The two-story house was jammed full of people, from the looks of it both upstairs and down. She recognized more than a dozen and gave nods and polite waves when they stared at her with their chins dropping. She knew it was only a matter of time before Sasha heard of her presence. She honestly hoped she wouldn't ruin her fun.

As a new song came on, and the young deejay spoke into the microphone, Hannah leaned against the wall, ready to wait the crowd out. She planned on just seeing Sasha and wishing her a very happy birthday and then slipping out. She wasn't there to cause a scene. She was there to show she cared. But as her eyes drifted to the second-story landing, her breath caught in her throat. Sasha was standing there in a tight skirt and form-fitting blouse, looking directly at her. Hannah pushed off the wall and called her name just as Sasha's hand went to her chest as if to catch her heart from escaping. She said something. Said it again. Hannah could've sworn it was her name. She moved toward the staircase, desperate to reach her, but she was blocked. And when she caught sight of Bonnie glaring at her from the top landing, she backed up and returned to her spot near the kitchen.

She sipped her beer and waited, debating whether she should leave. She eyed her watch and wondered what Sasha had said to her. Was she upset? Mad that she was there? Or was she calling to her? Should she try again to find out?

No, Sasha knew she was there. If she wanted to speak to her she knew where to find her.

She finished her beer. Eyed her watch. It had been fifteen minutes since Sasha had seen her. Plenty of time for her to come to her. Hannah pushed off from the wall. It was getting obvious that Sasha didn't want her there. She should go.

She began to weave through people once again when she felt her phone vibrate in her pocket. She managed to fish it out, and when she saw it was Sasha she was more than confused. She looked up the stairs, but Sasha was nowhere to be seen.

She answered, plugging her free ear with her finger, trying desperately to hear.

"Hello? Sasha?"

"Hannah! Hannah—"

Hannah grew alarmed at her tone. "Sasha, what is it? What's wrong?"

"Hannah—I'm sick, so sick. Come quick."

"Sash?"

"Need—help."

Hannah gripped the phone and shoved people aside as she headed for the stairs. When she reached them she yelled for people to move out of her way. She reached the top, but there was no Sasha.

"Damn."

She put the phone to her ear. Nothing.

But suddenly there was a voice behind her.

"What are you doing here?"

It was Bonnie. Hannah would know her scratchy nails on a chalkboard voice anywhere.

Hannah faced her. "I came to wish Sasha a happy birthday. I came with Casey."

Bonnie, who was wearing a tight silver shimmering dress, looked like hell. Her makeup was running and her hair looked like it had been windblown. "Do you really think that was a good idea?"

"Look, I didn't come to cause trouble. Where is she? She called me and she sounded really bad."

Bonnie looked at the bedroom beyond her and then back at Hannah. She gripped her arm and tugged.

"She called you?"

"Yes, now where is she?"

"She's sick, Hannah, and I'm worried. I just came out here to find my friend who's an EMT."

Hannah hurried after her to the master bedroom. Bonnie shoved open the door and then slammed it closed behind them.

Sasha called out from the bathroom beyond.

Hannah stiffened at the sound of her voice. She was crying.

"Sasha?" She took a step forward, but Bonnie held her back.

"She's sick," Bonnie said. "Really sick."

Hannah felt her world tilt. "Sash?"

"Hannah, oh thank God. Wait, don't come in here, Hannah. I don't—I don't want anyone to see me like this. Just let me clean up a little."

Bonnie collapsed onto the bed and ran her hands through her hair.

"She came home like this. Got sick to her stomach right after the big surprise." She looked over at Hannah. "God, what if it was too much? Did I do too much?"

Hannah stared at the closed bathroom door. She couldn't answer her, couldn't comfort her. All she cared about was seeing Sasha and making sure she was okay. But something told her it wasn't. Something told her this was more than the flu.

"Is it her kidneys?" Hannah asked.

Bonnie rubbed her face. "I don't know. She won't tell me anything."

"Well, how does she look?"

"Not good."

Hannah could wait no longer. She approached the door and knocked. "Sash?"

To her surprise, the door opened and Sasha looked at her with large liquid eyes. She reached out, but her hand trembled.

Hannah took it. "You're swollen." She examined the rest of her quickly. Sasha had changed into a bathrobe and tied her hair back, allowing Hannah to see her swollen feet and ankles and the pale color to her skin. She looked like she was going to fall over.

Hannah steered her toward the bed. "We've got to get you in somewhere. Last time, remember last time, Sasha?" She'd been in the hospital for two weeks with doctors scrambling to find an answer as to why her kidneys were failing.

"I'm not going," Sasha said. "It's not that bad." A tremor ran through her as she spoke. And then she grabbed her ears and a look of alarm came over her. "I can't hear you. It's all muffled. Oh my God, I can't hear."

Hannah reached for her again, but Sasha fell to the floor. Bonnie screamed and Hannah dropped to her knees and held her head.

Sasha looked sleepy, completely out of it. Her eyes were rolling closed.

"Call an ambulance," she said directly to Bonnie. "Now, Bonnie, go."

Bonnie hurried from the room and returned with a cell phone stuck to her ear. Hannah focused on Sasha while her own heart careened in her ears.

"Please, please. Make her okay, make her okay. Sasha. Sasha, baby, look at me."

And in that moment, Hannah knew without a shadow of a doubt that she'd do anything for her.

She looked up to the ceiling and gave all of herself to whatever being was beyond, promised she'd do anything to have her, to hold her, to love her forever.

But as she watched Sasha mumble incoherently as the paramedics rushed in, she wondered if all she gave, if all she had, would be enough.

CHAPTER FOUR

Sasha heard the squeak of shoes on a hard floor. Then the gentle swish of clothing as someone moved next to her. When she felt warm hands on her own, she heated and sank farther into the softness she was lying upon. A voice hummed, soft, safe, soothing. Then words, careful, gentle, kind. Light seeped into the darkness, kissing her face, encouraging her to open her eyes. She blinked against the yellow-white and focused.

"Hi, sugar," the sweet voice said. "I'm over here." There was a soft pat to her hand to get her attention.

Sasha blinked some more and moved her gaze to her left. A smiling face looked down upon her. A face she did not recognize.

"There you go." The woman smiled again and held Sasha's hand to her chest. The light from the window cascaded around her and lit her up like a heavenly figure. For an instant, Sasha thought she was from a world beyond.

"You're…an angel," Sasha said.

The woman laughed and Sasha could smell the subtle scent of lavender in the air. "No, child."

"You're real?"

"Mm-hm. My name is Cora. And I bet you're wondering where you are."

Sasha licked dry lips and swallowed against a tight throat. She glanced around at the small room, and the small television screen hung on the wall ahead. *Family Feud* was on mute as if someone had been watching it without wanting to disturb her. She looked at the bed with all the buttons and studied the cords that ran from her body. As if on cue, a blood pressure cuff beeped and tightened on her upper arm. She winced as it squeezed until she could hardly stand it and then released.

"Why am I here?" She had no memory of arriving at the hospital, or even why she needed to be there.

Cora eased into a chair and kept hold of her hand. "You were awful sick. Don't you remember?"

"No."

"You've been here for a few days now. In and out of sleep. I've been checking on you every day."

"Do I—know you?" Nothing was making sense, and her head was so cloudy it almost hurt to think beyond what Cora was saying.

"No, sweetie. I'm one of the chaplains here at the hospital."

"Chaplain?"

"Yes."

Sasha felt her eyes flutter. She tried to sit up as panic overwhelmed her. "Am I going to die?"

Cora patted her arm. "No, no, dear. You asked for me. When you first arrived. I'm just here for support. I've been praying for you each and every day. And so have others."

Sasha relaxed.

She gestured to the far side of the room where the sunlight barely kissed. To where plants and flowers and balloons sat keeping silent watch.

"I don't understand. I don't understand why I'm here."

Cora stroked her forehead. "I'll try to find the nurse. She'll be able to tell you more." She released her hand and backed away. "You be sure to rest. You've been through a lot." She left the room, leaving her calming scent behind for the faintest of seconds. Sasha almost called her back, not liking the feeling of being alone. What was happening? Why?

The door opened, and Bonnie rushed in with a flushed face and tousled hair. She looked dead tired and as if she'd been crying long and hard.

"Sasha, oh thank God." She nearly fell into the bed for an awkward embrace. One that nearly suffocated Sasha.

"Bonnie. Bonnie, you're crushing me."

"Oh, I'm sorry." She straightened and wiped tears from her eyes. "You don't know how good it is to see you awake and okay. I've been worried sick."

She rounded the bed, found a plastic container of water, and poured them both a cup full. But she hesitated in giving Sasha a cup.

"We better wait for the nurse. They are measuring your water intake and output."

"What?"

Bonnie downed her water as if it were a shot of whiskey. Her bloodshot eyes were heavy but frantic in the way they searched Sasha's face.

"Your mother is here and Casey has been in and out quite a bit."

"Wha? Really?" Panic tried to surface once again. "Bonnie? Why am I here? What happened?" She didn't feel bruised or sore, and nothing felt broken. There couldn't have been an accident. And something had to explain why she felt sick to her stomach with a head swishing back and forth like a stormy sea. And pee, she was dying to pee. Or wait, there was a pinch there, a pressure.

"Do I have a catheter?"

Bonnie's face fell. "It's your kidneys, Sash. They went kaput."

"What?" Couldn't be. They'd been fine for a while now. Her function was at thirty-eight percent and stable. Her blood pressure was good, her diet pretty clean.

"Yeah. You got really sick. I mean, really sick. Don't you remember your surprise party? Your fortieth birthday?"

"My birthday?" What the hell was going on? Was it March already? She rubbed her temples and tried to think, but nothing more came.

Bonnie sighed with obvious worry. "You can't remember can you?"

"No." But as she said no, brief flashes shot through her mind. She saw faces. Balloons. Champagne glasses. Loud music. And… Hannah.

"Hannah."

Bonnie shook her head. "She's not here."

Sasha stared off in thought. "Was she at my party? I can see her face. She looked worried. Scared. She was…" Begging God to save her.

"Oh God, it was bad wasn't it? Look at you. You're a mess. You all thought I was going to…die."

Bonnie squeezed her hand. "We were scared, Sash."

"I don't understand how this happened. I just don't understand." She tried to move, but Bonnie held her back. "I want to go home."

"You can't."

"Why not?"

But the sickness and the sloshing of her head stopped her cold. "Oh God, I feel like hell."

"You need time to recover."

Sasha eased back and closed her eyes. Slowly, the sickness passed, but the webs of her mind were still tangled, so she released them and allowed them to fall away. Her body grew heavy and her breathing slowed. Tired. She was so tired. She heard Bonnie speak, but she sounded far away. So far away.

And as she drifted off into a deep sleep, one image remained in her mind.

Hannah.

❖

When Sasha awoke again, her mother was sitting at her bedside, sipping coffee from a paper cup and watching the television on mute.

"That smells really good," Sasha croaked. The scent stirred her senses, and she suddenly wanted a cup, very black with no cream or sugar.

Her mother turned to her and squeezed her leg. "You're back."

"I guess so."

Her mother placed the cup on the bed table and inched closer. She brushed Sasha's hair from her forehead. "I'm so glad you're okay."

Sasha fidgeted with the bed buttons and raised herself a bit. "Am I, Mom? Okay?"

Her mother pressed her lips together in a gesture that let Sasha know she was nervous.

"Mom?"

"Yes, you're much better now."

"I do feel a little better. But I'd love to get this catheter out." She pressed the button for the nurse. "How long has it been now?"

"Six days or thereabouts."

Sasha winced. "When did you get here?"

"Oh, Hannah called right away, as soon as they had you here. And based on your condition, I took the next flight that I could."

"I'm sorry you had to do that."

"Oh, now don't say such a thing. You're okay and that's all that matters." She searched Sasha with her blue eyes, and Sasha knew she was hoping for answers. She was always able to bore a hole right through her when she knew Sasha was keeping something from her.

Sasha glanced away, unable to take the pressure. "I was going to tell you."

"When?"

Sasha closed her eyes. "When the time was right. And no, I don't know if the time would've ever been right."

"All this time and I didn't even know where my daughter was living? I had to find out in an emergency?"

"I know. I'm sorry. I just…I didn't know what to say."

"Well, you don't have to now. Bonnie told me the basics. What I could get out of her that is. Needless to say, it sounds like a big mess. A big, sad mess."

"It is," Sasha said.

"No wonder you're so sick. All that stress…"

"Can we please just drop it now?"

"No." Her mother stared into her. "I want to know my daughter. I want to know what's going on. Do you not love Hannah anymore?"

"No, I mean yes." Sasha grabbed her forehead. "I mean of course I love her. I just don't think she really loves me. Not like I need anyway."

Her mother sipped her coffee once again and crossed her legs. She was wearing gray slacks and a navy blouse. Both neatly pressed. Her manicure was fresh and her hair and makeup were impeccable. Even if things were rough and tough, you should always look your best. That was what she had always said. And Sasha had taken it to heart, trying to make sure she always looked her best. Though at the moment, it felt impossible.

"I don't know much about the whole lesbian thing."

"Mom."

"And you know I don't necessarily approve."

"Oh God." Sasha slapped her forehead.

"But I know that Hannah cares for you a great deal."

Sasha wanted to climb from the bed and bolt from the room. Her mother always had a knack for making her uncomfortable. It never failed. First when she was twelve and she called the entire family across the country to tell them she'd started her period, all the way up into adulthood when she'd asked Sasha and Hannah what vibrators were at a dinner party.

"That's the problem, Mom. I feel like we're just friends. Roommates. People who care for each other a great deal." Just talking about the situation with Hannah exhausted her, and she wanted it to stop. "I don't want to talk about Hannah, Mom. Not now."

"Why not?"

"Because." How could she explain? Her mother would never understand that the topic was emotionally draining because her mother could talk about anything to death. She'd talk to the walls if you let her. "Because I don't think you'd understand."

Her mother scoffed. "I was married forty some years to a man who damn near killed me with his ridiculous philandering, his secrets, and his manipulation. And you think I won't understand?" She shifted a little in her seat. "Marriage is a bitch, Sasha. No one knows it better than me."

Thinking about what all her mother had been through made her insides tighten. She wished she could take it all away, but she couldn't. They both had to live with the aftereffects. And as for her father? He was off living guilt free with wife number two. Somewhere in Florida. Somewhere where your past was the past and accountability was unlawful.

How could she be related to someone who lived completely guilt free despite how he treated people? It unnerved her, and every once in a while it crept up and made her wonder if she was being too hard on Hannah by walking away. But Bonnie and her other friends had assured her she wasn't, and that had been the nudge she'd needed to make a move. She didn't want to think beyond that.

Her mother started to speak again, but a quick knock came from the door and a woman in a white lab coat and pantsuit breezed in. She slipped on a pair of eyeglasses and came to shake Sasha's hand.

"Ms. Bashton. I'm Dr. Patel." She pointed to the other chair. "May I?"

"Of course."

The doctor pulled the chair over and sat, then tucked her long, dark hair behind her ears as she looked over her laptop.

"It's been difficult to find you awake," she said with a smile. "How are you feeling?"

"Somewhat better."

"Good."

"Can I go home?"

"Do you feel well enough to go home?"

Sash hesitated. She wasn't a hundred percent, that was for sure.

"Let's take one thing at a time shall we?" Dr. Patel pressed more keys. "You had a very serious infection and your kidney function was greatly affected. I'm afraid the infection caused your disease to act up and some considerable damage was done to your kidneys."

"Wait…infection?"

Dr. Patel met her gaze over the tip of her glasses. "Yes, you had a kidney infection. A very bad one. You were septic by the time you were brought in, and your kidney function was in jeopardy. You're very lucky you came in when you did."

Sasha's mind reeled. "But I hadn't felt seriously ill for very long. How could this have happened?"

"Sometimes UTIs can go unnoticed until they reach the kidneys." She typed more and studied the laptop screen.

"So what now?" Sasha asked.

"We finally seem to have the infection under control with the correct antibiotic. But you need several more days of it. That means you can either go to a rehabilitation center where they can treat you and help you get back on your feet or you can go home with a PICC line." She glanced up again. "An intravenous line would be placed in your inner upper arm and threaded inside you. Someone would then attach the container of antibiotic to that line and treat you. Usually insurance pays for a nurse to come to your home to administer the medicine and monitor your progress."

"Home, I'd rather be at home."

"She can't stay here?" her mother asked.

"I'm afraid not."

"What's this rehabilitation center you speak of?" her mother asked.

"Mom," Sasha tried to interrupt.

"It's where patients go to continue their recovery. There's a very nice facility down the road."

"No."

Her mother looked at her. "You might want to consider it, Sasha. Bonnie won't be home to look after you. She has to work.

She's already missed several days being here. And there's no room for me to stay there."

Sasha shook her head. "I'm going home."

"But where's home, Sasha?" her mother said.

Sasha glared at her and Dr. Patel caught the glance. "Just let the nurse know what you decide. You have until tomorrow morning." She closed her laptop. "You should feel better in a few more days, but you'll need to take it easy. You'll be weak. And I need you to follow up with your nephrologist. Your kidney function is down and it needs to be monitored closely. If it falls much more, you will need to start thinking about dialysis and transplantation."

Sasha heard her mother gasp. She closed her eyes, trying not to feel overwhelmed herself.

"Thank you, Doctor."

"You're welcome." She stood, shook her hand, and left the room.

"You need to look into the rehab center," her mother said, rising to pour them both some water. "You can't stay at Bonnie's on your own." She gave Sasha a full cup and then recorded something on a chart.

"Is that my water chart?"

"Yes," her mother answered without looking up. Sasha moved on, trying to push the thought of measuring her pee from her mind. But she would do it happily if it meant removing the catheter.

"I'm not going to any rehab center when I'm perfectly fine going home."

"But where is home, honey? Where will you stay?"

A voice came from near the door. One that both shocked and soothed Sasha all at once.

"She can stay with me."

It was Hannah.

Chapter Five

"With you?" Gladys asked, looking as if she'd just been slapped. She was gripping the sides of the visitor chair next to Sasha's hospital bed. "But I thought the two of you were…"

"We are." Hannah finished for her. "Separated."

Sasha was staring at her with a look that said "save me." It was a look she often fashioned when she was around Gladys.

"But I couldn't help but overhear that Sasha needs a place to recover for a while. And our place…ahem, my place is perfect."

Gladys fidgeted. "I think she'd better stay at the rehab center, considering your current situation."

"I'll do it. I'll stay with Hannah," Sasha said. "I'll be more comfortable there."

"But, Sasha, you two haven't been getting along."

"We don't fight," Sasha said. "Nothing like that. We just… exist."

"Can you take care of her, Hannah?"

"I'll have to work a few hours a day. But Casey is there, and he's often home between classes. We'll make sure she's okay."

Gladys stood. "I don't understand the two of you. I just don't understand it." She walked by Hannah and turned at the door. "I'm going for some more coffee so you two can figure this out." She shook her head as if confused and defeated and slipped through the door.

"Do you mind if I sit?" Hannah asked.

"You know I don't."

Hannah eased into a chair.

"So you were eavesdropping at the door?" Sasha asked.

Hannah blinked with surprise. "Yes, I guess I was."

Sasha scoffed. "I should be upset at that, but considering the circumstances I'm glad you did."

She struggled to reach for more water. Her hand shook as she grabbed the cup and brought it to dry looking lips. Hannah took it from her when she was finished. Her eyes thanked her, but her expression was one of ambivalence. She looked tired, weak, and gaunt. She'd lost weight, making her cheekbones more prominent, as if someone had sculpted them with a straight razor.

"I know I look like hell," she said, catching her gaze.

"Actually, I was just thinking how beautiful you still are despite everything."

Sasha stared at her for a long moment. "Liar."

"You know I'm not."

Sasha picked at her blanket. "You know this doesn't mean anything. My coming to stay with you while I recover."

"Sasha I think we should talk about it—"

"Good, because we're still separated and I'm still upset." She set her jaw and narrowed her eyes. Hannah knew better than to argue at that moment.

"Got it."

"So you understand we aren't together."

"Yes."

"Because I know you, and I know you'll try to get me back. It seems to take you losing me before you do anything for our relationship."

Hannah hung her head. Sasha, for the most part, was right.

"I want to try, Sasha," she blurted. "Seeing you that sick, seeing you in here…I don't want to lose you."

There was silence, and Hannah looked up to see Sasha wiping away tears. "Damn you, Hannah. Damn you. It shouldn't take something like this for you to want to try."

Hannah rose and handed her some tissue. Then she tried to hold her hand, but Sasha snatched hers away. "No, you don't get to do that. You don't get to touch me."

Anger flashed in her eyes, and Hannah knew she needed to back off. She stood at the foot of the bed. "I'll do whatever you want, Sash. Just focus on getting well." She left her and slipped quietly out the door.

❖

Hannah sank into the sofa with a bottle of water and propped her feet on the ottoman. There was a ball game on, one she wanted desperately to pay attention to, but she just couldn't seem to focus. She drank the water and stared through the television as the Tar Heels battled the Blue Devils. She heard the elevated voices of the announcers, but she couldn't even blink because her mind was back on that night just a few days ago.

The night she thought she was going to lose Sasha. The night Sasha lay limp in her arms with her eyes rolled back in her head and her body on fire with fever. It was a moment she'd never forget. Her nightmares made sure of it.

She'd thought of little else since. And seeing Sasha in that hospital bed, hooked up to machines and in and out of consciousness, she wasn't sure she'd ever get over it.

"What up? Duke winning?" Casey asked as he breezed through the living room with his large earphones on. He'd been playing video games. She'd heard him yelling and cursing across the house. He often unplugged to eat or drink and then he'd disappear again, back into his abyss of a bedroom. He opened the fridge and pulled out a can of Monster. He opened it and slurped like he hadn't drank for days. "Mom?"

"Hmm? I don't know."

She continued to stare.

Casey stood behind her drinking his energy drink. "Damn, we're down two." When she didn't respond, he nudged her shoulder. "I see you finished getting the spare bedroom ready."

She blinked but felt heavy coming out of her daze. "Yeah, just finished."

"It looks nice. Sasha will like it."

"I hope so." She'd cleared out all the boxes they'd kept in there for storage and moved the furniture around so the bed was the focal point of the room. Then she'd dusted, vacuumed, and spread on the new, freshly washed sheets and comforter. A warm scented candle was currently spreading its fragrance throughout the room, something she knew Sasha would appreciate. She'd also placed some photographs of Sasha and Casey and Sasha and their late dog, Freddie Mercury, on the dresser. Sasha adored Casey, and she'd adored Freddie. Losing him the previous year had been detrimental to them all. But the photos were so good and they reminded Hannah of happier times, and she knew Sasha would love them.

"She will." He took another loud sip. "The pics are a nice perk. So, what's the deal? She actually agreed to come here?"

"She didn't have much of a choice."

"Agh. That explains it."

"Explains what?"

"Why she agreed to move back under the same roof as you."

He nudged her again to let her know he was joking, but she didn't react. She felt like a slug, like she just might ooze off the couch in post-traumatic sadness.

"You okay?" He knelt, placing his elbows on the back of the couch.

She looked over at him and noticed he'd lowered his earphones. "I'll be fine."

He was silent for a long moment. "I'm scared too, Mom."

She felt her eyes widen with surprise.

"Scared she almost died, scared she's not here anymore, scared you two will never work it out."

Hannah nodded. He was so damned intuitive.

There was another long silence, and she could smell the berry flavoring of his drink. He was watching her closely.

"What do you want, Mom? Have you ever asked yourself that?"

Hannah met his gaze. "I thought I could live without her, give her the separation and see where things went. But now…I can't lose her, Casey. I just can't. I love her too damn much."

"Then you better figure something out and fast." He squeezed her shoulder. "Let's hope it's not too little too late."

Chapter Six

Sasha stood at the front door a little unsteady on her feet. The day was bright and beautiful and warm, bordering on hot. The queen palms she'd planted years ago blew in the breeze, as did the hibiscus and Mexican prairie bushes. They still had some fresh blooms, but they'd soon dry up in the fierce summer heat.

"You okay?" Casey cupped her elbow and stepped up to the door to unlock it. He'd been the one to pick her up from the hospital. Why Hannah hadn't shown, her guess was as good as any. She thought for sure after Hannah had offered to help care for her that she'd at least show to bring her home. But no.

Casey helped her step inside, and she swooned with dizziness as she did so. She leaned against the entryway wall and inhaled the scents of her former home. Her heart rate sped up and fluttered, and she nearly teared up. The house still smelled the same. Like fresh laundry, recently made meals, and candles.

"I smell toast," she said. "And candles." She'd always had candles burning, and Hannah had often teased her about it. But she liked her home to smell wonderful, inviting. Cozy.

"Yeah, Mom had toast for breakfast and she put candles everywhere on those warming plates for you. Thought you might like it."

Sasha swallowed hard. "I do."

He breezed back outside, grabbed her bags, and then closed and locked the door behind them. He led the way.

"I don't have to tell you to make yourself at home do I?" She followed him slowly beyond the living room to the hallway and down to the spare bedroom. He pushed open the door and motioned for her to enter.

"Wow." They'd cleaned out the room and made it into a proper bedroom. Even decorated it. "It looks so different."

He placed her bags near the closet. "You've been on Mom for years to do something with all of her junk. Well, she finally did." He placed his hands on his hips. "Looks good, right?"

"Yes." She'd known they'd have to do something to the bedroom to ready it for her, but this, wow, it was overwhelming. She couldn't have done a better job herself.

"Notice the candle," Casey said, pointing.

She eased onto the bed and held the photo next to the candle. It was one of Casey at age eight or nine.

"I remember this day," she said. "You had to wear a tie for a school tea party. And your mom and I didn't know how to tie one, so we had to ask a guy at the store to do it."

Casey laughed and sat next to her. "I looked damn good too. Suave."

She touched the photo. "Such the looker. You always have been."

He squeezed her hand. "I miss you, you know," he said.

"I know. I miss you too."

They embraced in a light hug, and she was touched and surprised at just how long he held her. When he pulled away, she could've sworn he wiped away a tear. They, of course, had continued to see each other after the split, but Casey had preferred to keep their conversations light. She could tell the separation was hurting him, and that's why he avoided bringing it up. But even if he had, she had no easy answers. Maybe, at the very least, her staying at the house would help them all find some answers.

"Want me to help you unpack?"

She glanced at her bags and groaned. "Maybe later. I think I'd like to nap."

He nodded, stood, and sank his hands into his shorts pockets. He still looked tall and lanky in his long shorts and v-neck shirt. But he was sinewy with muscle, and she knew he held a strength that couldn't be seen with the naked eye. Just like his mother.

She eased back farther onto the bed and settled into the pillows. Casey covered her with a light throw blanket.

"Fan on or off?" He stood at the door with his hand on the switch to the ceiling fan.

"Off."

"Okay then. Sweet dreams."

"Casey?"

"Yeah?"

"Where's Hannah?"

He seemed surprised at the question. "She, uh, she thought it would be easier on you if she wasn't here when you arrived and got comfortable. I think she's trying to give you some space."

Sasha closed her eyes in frustration. "Seems she's real good at that." She opened her eyes and found Casey looking crestfallen. "I'm sorry. I shouldn't have said that."

He didn't respond, just simply pulled the door partway closed.

And with that, Sasha stared at the ceiling of her former home, feeling like a stranger and an ass, and allowed her prevailing weakness to carry her off to sleep.

Sasha awoke to find an evening sun slanting at an angle through the partially closed blinds. Clattering came from the kitchen along with muffled voices. She rolled over to look at the bedside clock. It was after five. She'd slept for hours.

She stirred to sit up and found another blanket had been spread over her and a glass of water was next to the clock on the night table. She grabbed her heavy feeling head as her now bare feet touched the carpeted floor. Someone had cared for her while she slept. Covered her up, removed her shoes and socks. Most likely Casey. She'd have to remember to thank him.

She tried to stand but found it difficult. The walk from the car into the house had felt awkward enough, and her body obviously wasn't willing to do much more. She sank back onto the bed and groaned. And to her surprise, a knock came from the door.

"Yes?"

The door swung open slowly to reveal Hannah carrying a bed tray. "I brought you some soup and iced tea. May I come in?"

"Please."

She crossed to the bed, and Sasha positioned herself in a sitting position back against the headboard. "You didn't have to go to all this trouble."

"Nonsense. You need to eat and stay hydrated."

Hannah placed the tray in front of her and sat to fold a napkin.

"How are you feeling?"

"A little better."

"That's good." She set the napkin on the tray and watched Sasha with obvious nerves. She smoothed her tanned hands on her khaki shorts, something she did when nervous, and tucked her hair back behind her ears two times too many. Sasha tried to pretend she couldn't smell her coconut lotion or the way her skin shone against her white tank top.

"I see you still change into your tank tops when you get home from work." It was an odd observation, one way too familiar, and Sasha wished she hadn't shared it. Hannah looked down at her tank.

"I'm hot when I get home."

"Yes…I didn't mean anything by it."

"Days are getting warmer. Not sure how much longer I can work outdoors like this."

Hannah had been running softball tournaments for years for her business, and it meant she was outdoors on a daily basis. The heat often got to her, and she had to be careful.

Sasha sipped her iced tea. She nearly groaned with pleasure. "This is your mother's recipe isn't it?"

Hannah didn't even blink. "Of course."

"My God, how does she do it?"

"You know I can't tell you."

Sasha took another long drink, and memories and good feelings began to overwhelm her. The taste of the lemony tea, the smell of Hannah's lotion mixed with her pheromones, it was all stirring things inside her. Things she'd long forgotten. Things she thought she'd never miss. Her hand shook as she replaced the glass.

Hannah noticed. "I can put the soup in a mug for you if you like? That way you wouldn't need to use the spoon."

"Don't be silly, I'm fine. This is fine. This is really nice." She hesitated but then spooned a bite of what looked like chicken noodle soup. She tried to bring it to her mouth, but her hand shook worse than before and she dropped the spoon back in the bowl, splashing soup on her.

Hannah quickly dabbed her with the napkin.

Sasha stopped her by grabbing her hand. They stared at each other for a long moment, and then Sasha spoke, breaking eye contact.

"It's this damn PICC line in my arm. It hurts and it's a pain in the ass. I feel like I can't move my arm." She tried to cross her arms across her chest in frustration, but it hurt. Like someone was stabbing her in her inner arm twenty-four seven. She clenched her fist, hating that she looked and felt so needy, so helpless.

Hannah rose and took the soup. "No problem. I'll just put it in a mug."

"I'm not helpless, Hannah. I'm really not." She needed her to know that. She needed everybody around her to know that.

"I know, Sash. I know. You just need some help right now. So please, let us help you."

Sasha saw the softness on her face, and she leaned back and sighed. "Okay."

"Be right back."

Tears filled Sasha's eyes, and she battled within herself not to cry. She couldn't afford to. She didn't have time to feel sorry for herself. Nor did she have the capability. She'd always been a fighter, and nothing about that was going to change. Now or ever.

Hannah returned with the mug and a gentle smile, and Sasha thanked her. Then she asked to be alone. She needed to eat in silence and make sure no one saw her shaking. She couldn't handle the pity. Couldn't handle her own emotions in response to it. She sat and ate and stared at a black TV screen across from her on the dresser. She sipped her soup slowly, carefully, and with each swallow she willed herself to get stronger, better. She knew she could. But the thing that kept gnawing at her wasn't the shaking or the embarrassment or the feelings of inadequacy. It was the nostalgia she had felt with the iced tea and with Hannah.

That was the one thing she wasn't sure she could beat.

Chapter Seven

Hannah entered the spare bedroom quietly, trying to retrieve the bed tray without waking Sasha. But as she grabbed hold of the tray and moved it away, Sasha's eyes fluttered open. She blinked a few times as if trying to focus.

"Mm, what are you doing?"

"Just taking this so you can sleep comfortably." She hadn't eaten all of the soup, and it concerned Hannah. Sasha had lost weight and she still looked frail. She wished she would eat. "Can I get you anything else? A sandwich maybe?"

"No, thanks." Sasha struggled to sit up and swing her legs over the bed. She stood on unsteady feet, wobbling a bit. She stood before Hannah. "I can take that."

Hannah wasn't sure what to do. "That's not necessary. I got it." She smiled. Sasha looked as though she'd fall at any given second, and she didn't want the tray to fall with her, possibly injuring her more.

Sasha's face clouded, so Hannah walked to the door quickly before she had a chance to grab the tray. To her surprise and dismay, Sasha followed her into the kitchen, leaning on the walls as she did so.

Casey, who was making himself a grilled cheese sandwich, eyed Hannah with a concerned look. But when he faced Sasha, he was all smiles.

"You sleep well, Sash?"

Sasha eased herself onto a barstool. Her hair was mussed and she wore no makeup. Her sleep shirt and cotton plaid pants were wrinkled. She looked adorable, and Hannah's heart panged at seeing her sitting in the kitchen that way once more.

"Yes, thanks."

Hannah cleaned up the soup mug and glass and wiped down the tray. "Are you sure you don't want a sandwich?"

"No, I'm good."

Casey flipped his grilled cheese. "I've made two," he said. "Want one?"

Sasha groaned with a smile. "I suppose. It smells so good how can I refuse?"

Hannah felt herself heat. She hadn't missed the fact that Sasha wanted nothing from her. But Casey offering was a different story. She hoped she was only reading into things.

He placed the warm smelling sandwich on a small plate and handed it over. Hannah busied herself making her some iced water. When she placed it in front of her, Sasha merely glanced at her without a word.

"What time is the nurse coming?" Casey asked.

"Oh, I forgot about that," Hannah said, checking the clock. "She's due any minute."

Sasha took a mouse-like bite from her sandwich and scowled at her PICC line. "Maybe I can talk her into pulling this damn thing out."

"I wouldn't count on it," Hannah said.

"Oh, don't worry. I don't count on anything anymore."

Casey gave Hannah another look, and Hannah shrugged. It seemed she was in for it with Sasha. And that was fine. If Sasha needed to take digs at her so be it. It wasn't like she didn't deserve it. But still she wished they could get past it. Sasha would be there for a short while, and Hannah didn't want it to be uncomfortable for anyone.

The doorbell rang and Hannah crossed to the front door. She opened it to find the most obvious looking lesbian she'd ever seen. Her heart jumped to her throat and then crashed down to her stomach. She almost slammed the door. Wanted to slam the door.

She didn't want this woman anywhere near Sasha. Especially now. Not when things were so up in the air and Sasha was vulnerable.

Not now when she was trying like hell to figure out how to win her back.

God damn it. Not now.

"Am I at the right house?" the woman, who was wearing light blue scrubs and standing nearly a foot taller than Hannah, asked. Her blue eyes sparkled and her sizable muscles twitched as she maneuvered her bag. She was tanned, toned, and sporting a perfect dyke haircut with her black as night hair. Definitely Sasha's type.

"God damn it."

The woman turned. "Sorry, I'm looking for twenty-three oh three. Must be the next one over." She started to leave, and Hannah had to step outside to stop her.

"No." She grabbed her forehead in defeat. "You're at the right place."

"Oh." The woman turned. "I'm Charlie, the home care nurse?"

"Of course." Hannah shook her strong hand. *Of course it's strong. Aren't you just perfect?* "Forgive me, I was thinking of something else."

Charlie didn't seem sure what to make of her behavior.

"Please, come in." Hannah led the way into the kitchen after closing the door behind them. And she didn't miss the double-take Sasha did when she caught first sight of Charlie. It made her heart all the more sick.

"Sash, this is—"

"Charlie. Hi. I'm your nurse." They shook hands and both wore beaming smiles.

Hannah wanted to vomit.

Casey raised an obvious eyebrow. She elbowed him.

Then she stood behind the counter with her arms crossed, watching the exchange before her. Charlie had taken a seat next to

Sasha and was happily explaining the upcoming process. She was tenderly touching Sasha's arm, examining her PICC line, going over the antibiotic and the treatment. Then she gently touched her forehead.

"I think you might still be running a fever."

"I don't feel like I am," Sasha said.

Charlie fished out a thermometer and delicately moved Sasha's hair from her ear. It was such a sensual move it caused Sasha to inhale suddenly and blush.

Hannah cleared her throat at the sight of Sasha's red cheeks.

Sasha gave her a dirty look. "Would you mind giving me some privacy, Hannah?"

Hannah felt her chin hit the floor. She began to stammer, but Casey grabbed her arm and led her away to the living room. When they reached the couch, Hannah jerked her arm away.

"Thanks for the help," she sneered at him.

"If you get any more jealous you'll turn green."

"Yeah, well, so be it."

He cupped her elbow to stop her from returning to the kitchen. "Mom, stop. You're being an ass."

"Did you see that woman? Did you see Sasha?"

"Yes, I saw. But Sasha isn't with you anymore."

Hannah pulled her arm away again and let it drop. His words sank in, and she just about fell to the floor and melted into the carpet. She was totally and completely helpless. And Sasha might as well be as good as gone.

She sank onto the couch and ran her fingers through her hair. "Damn it, Casey. I don't know if I can do this. She wants nothing to do with me. Not a thing. I might as well not exist."

He sat next to her and placed his plate on the table next to the couch.

"I know, Mom. This sucks. But this is what it is."

"I just wish I could go back, take it all back. Do it all over." She heard laughter come from the kitchen and her stomach churned. "I've got to get out of here. I can't do this."

"Mom."

"I can't." She stood and hurried to the garage door. She took her keys from the hook and walked out with Casey calling after her.

❖

"I don't understand. Don't you want a beer or two to at least calm you a bit? I mean you just left Sasha with a tiger shark."

Hannah looked up from her Coke to her long time friend Mickey who was looking at her like she was absolutely out of her mind crazy.

"No, no way. I need to think. To strategize. If I drink I won't give a fuck, and that's been the problem."

"Suit yourself." Mickey poured herself another from the pitcher of Miller in front of her. She slid a piece of pizza onto her plate and smothered it with crushed red pepper until not a speck of cheese could be seen. Then she turned her ball cap backward and leaned in for a big bite.

Hannah watched still feeling sick, still seeing Charlie brush Sasha's hair from her ear. She gulped at her Coke, but she knew nothing short of a miracle would help.

"What can I do? I've got to do something."

Mickey shrugged. "If you ask me I don't think Sasha will care one way or another. Seems no matter what you do she's unhappy."

This wasn't the first time Hannah had heard such words from Mickey. She knew how she felt, and she also knew that Mickey had a bit of a thing for her. But still, she chose to be around her because she was fun and brutally honest, and she needed an honest friend right now. Even if she didn't sing Sasha's praises.

"She's who I want, Mick. So I'm not giving up."

"You're into masochism, my friend."

Hannah shook her head. "You don't get it. She nearly died in my arms. You don't know what that does to you. How it makes you see things. How it reaches in, grabs your fucking heart, and shakes all kinds of sense into it. I'll never get over that and I'll never get over Sasha. She's who I want to be with. I know it without any shadow of a doubt."

Mickey wiped her mouth and took several large swigs of her beer. She stared off for a long few moments, and Hannah knew she hadn't necessarily liked what she'd just heard.

"I guess I can't argue with that."

"No, no one can."

"I don't know what to tell you. You can't control people and how they feel. I'm just worried you'll do nothing but bang your head up against a wall."

"Well, if that's what it takes, that's what it takes."

"And if she never comes around?"

"She will."

"How do you know?"

"Because I know Sasha. Better than anyone. And I know she loves me. No matter how she behaves or what she says."

"And how do you know that? I mean no one can really know."

"I do."

Mickey met her gaze with her green eyes.

"She told me. When we were in the ambulance. She said so."

Mickey twirled her glass. "And you're taking that to heart."

"Yes."

"I don't know if I would. She wasn't in her right mind. She probably doesn't even remember it."

Hannah scoffed. "Man, you just don't get it."

Hannah knew Mickey had only had a handful of serious relationships and that she was younger than Hannah was and still playing the field. So she excused her lack of belief. She'd just never been in love like Hannah and Sasha. She'd never experienced that deep down, rip your guts out kind of love.

"My guts are certainly ripped out," Hannah whispered.

"Hmm?"

Mickey took another bite of her pizza.

"Nothing."

"Look, I guess I just don't get it. If she's the one, if you're so sure and she told you she loved you on her deathbed and so on, then why the fuck weren't you two happy?"

"We were. For a long time." She stared at the red checkered tablecloth and recalled better times. She smiled, despite her current situation. "We really were."

"Well, what happened?"

"Me. I fucked it all up."

"It couldn't have been all you, Hannah."

"No, I really think it was." She met her gaze. "I think Sasha's right. I'm depressed." She'd even seen a therapist at Sasha's request. And though she'd learned that her own illness and Sasha's as well, had deeply frightened her and caused her to pull away, she'd done nothing the therapist had recommended to help. Maybe it was time she put those suggestions into motion. It couldn't hurt could it? She could exercise. She could stop all the drinking and the running from her emotions. Would she though? Would she actually try and do it?

Mickey pushed her plate away and sighed.

"What?"

"You have been different lately. Like for a long time lately. But I thought it was because Sasha nagged you?"

Hannah thought back and remembered all the times she'd met up with Mickey and complained about Sasha constantly nagging her to do things. To do anything to show she had some life left within her. She'd taken it personally and blamed Sasha, treating her like an unhappy wife who was always looking for excuses to complain.

But now, looking back, she knew it was her. She'd shut down. Shut off.

Her battle with breast cancer. Losing her father. And then Freddie Mercury. It had all overwhelmed her and sucked any remaining life out of her, and she'd just lost her will to live. She'd just drank and merely existed.

"Sasha did nag. But that's because she'd been unhappy. Because of me."

"You have been pretty low. Even I've been concerned."

Hannah nodded. "I know."

"I'm still concerned. You look like hell, you rarely smile. I've tried to be a good friend. I listen and I try to get you to do things. I try to get you to laugh."

"You have been a good friend, Mick. And I appreciate that more than you know."

"I don't like you blaming everything on yourself. You went through a really rough time."

"Yes, but it wasn't fair of me to just shut Sasha out like I did. I should've handled things differently." She buried her head in her hands.

"What are you going to do? Is there anything I can do?"

"I don't know. I just don't know. One thing I do know though, is that I have to change on my own. I have to better myself. I just hope I can."

Chapter Eight

"Call me if you need anything before tomorrow," Charlie said, handing over a business card. "I mean it, day or night."

"Thanks." Sasha took the card and met her heavy gaze. Charlie had the brightest blue eyes she'd ever seen, and she couldn't help but want to stare. In fact she felt a little breathless, and she was beginning to wonder if it was her condition or something more. Something like Charlie. But she reminded herself that she had felt weak and a little off for days. And receiving the antibiotic did seem to wear her out. It took what felt like forever for it to completely drain into her, and the damn liquid was like ice going into her body because it had to be kept cold. She hugged herself as Charlie stood from the couch to spread a light throw blanket over her. She once again felt her forehead.

"Mm, I'm still a little concerned about that fever. So I'll be back before noon tomorrow." She smiled a brilliant smile, and Sasha felt herself blush. It had been a long time since she'd found herself attracted to anyone, and admitting that brought on a bag of mixed feelings. After all, they were in Hannah's home, and she was interacting with Hannah once again, where memories and feelings she'd long ago buried were trying to surface. Charlie, it seemed, couldn't have walked into her life at a more confusing time.

Was it wrong to be attracted to her? She knew it wasn't, but she'd seen the jealousy on Hannah's face. It was a look that had cut her deeply just before it burned her with anger. How dare Hannah be jealous when she had had her chance to prove she wanted to be with her? She'd had months, days, years. And the second Sasha found someone a little heart fluttering, Hannah reacted like someone tore her heart out? Acted like she still had a say. What gave her the right?

Sasha tried to put herself in Hannah's shoes. Would she be jealous in the same situation? Yes. But would she try to interfere? She didn't know. She just knew that Hannah had no right. Whether she was interested in Charlie or not.

She closed her eyes and clutched the blanket tight to her chest. She knew her interest was piqued. But what it meant, she didn't know. Could she honestly be with someone other than Hannah?

She prayed for warmth and thought back to Hannah coming home after her double mastectomy. Her heart had bled for her, and Hannah had fought her tooth and nail when she'd tried to comfort her or care for her. It had been a side to Hannah she'd never seen. She was so cranky and so lost she'd insisted Sasha sleep on the couch, and night after night, Sasha had heard her crying in her sleep. She'd tried to go to her the first night to wrap her arms around her and hold her tight, but Hannah had screamed at her to get out. Sasha had scrambled out, crying and confused and hurting so badly for the woman she loved. She'd often wondered if they'd taken her heart when they'd taken the cancer. Sometimes it seemed that way.

Sasha felt her body grow warm and heavy despite the chills that racked through her. She was just about lost in sleep when she heard someone enter and kneel next to her. Through heavy, blinking eyelids, Sasha saw Hannah's face. She looked distraught and as if she'd been crying.

"What is it? What's wrong?"

But Hannah shook her head. "Come on, let's get you to bed."

"No, I'm too tired."

"I'll get you." Hannah scooped her up before she could protest. Sasha wrapped her arms around her neck and buried her face in her shoulder. She caught her scent, and tears of her own formed in the corners of her eyes. She could feel her strength, her warmth. And she noticed something else. She didn't smell like alcohol.

"You didn't drink," Sasha said as Hannah set her gently on the bed and tucked her in. Sasha was sure Hannah had run out to go drink with Mickey just as she'd done the past two years of their relationship.

"I don't do that anymore," she said.

Sasha felt the surprise of the statement, but she was too tired to talk about it. Instead she drifted off to sleep, gripping Hannah's arm.

❖

Sasha awoke to the smell of bacon and maple syrup. She groaned, almost convinced she was dreaming. Finally, hunger churned in her belly and she sat up and pushed off her covers. She was so excited to have some real food, she nearly fell when she tried to stand too quickly to ease into her slippers. She half fell against the wall causing commotion but then was able to walk on her own. She winced at the pinch of the PICC line and thought how good it would feel to have a bath. She still felt like the hospital was on her, the smell of it in her hair and on her skin. Her hand and her inner elbow were bruised from IV lines, and blood still stained her in some of those areas. She was almost sure someone could scrape the film of the hospital off of her it was so thick. Yes, a bath would be wonderful.

Someone had obviously heard her dance with the wall because she could hear them hurrying down the hallway. Hannah appeared with a look of worry on her face.

"Everything okay?"

Sasha brushed past her. "Fine."

"I thought I heard you fall."

"I'm okay." She wasn't about to admit to losing her balance. She already couldn't stand being treated like a baby. For some reason Hannah was jumping at every little need, and it confused her more than anything. The Hannah she'd come to know recently would've cared, yes, but she wouldn't have gone out of her way to do so like this Hannah was doing. And if Hannah thought caring for her in this manner after all this time was going to heal things between them, she had another thing coming.

Sasha heard Hannah follow her down the hallway to the kitchen where the scents of a fresh breakfast came alive.

"This smells so damn good," Sasha said.

Hannah pulled out a chair for her at the table. "Please, sit."

Sasha did so. "Since when are you such a gentleman? You haven't done that in years."

"Oh, I don't know. Just felt like doing it is all." Hannah moved to the stove where she cracked eggs and whisked them quickly in a bowl. "I hope you still prefer scrambled," she said as she poured the liquid in the pan.

"It doesn't matter," Sasha said. "Right now I'd eat anything."

Hannah laughed. "Hospital food was pretty bad wasn't it?"

Sasha smoothed the handwoven placemat they bought together at Pier One. She swallowed against a tightening throat. "You have no idea."

"I actually caught sight of some of the stuff they served you. It looked and smelled pretty awful."

Sasha glanced up at her. "You…saw? When?"

Hannah stirred the eggs. "When I was there."

"And when was that?"

Hannah fell quiet. Then she turned and spooned the scrambled eggs onto two plates.

"Hannah?"

"I came at night, mostly. Knowing no one would be there. Other times I snuck in while you were sleeping and your mother was in the cafeteria."

"But why? Why not let someone see you? Why not say hello to me?"

Hannah replaced the pan on the stove and slid some bacon and small pancakes onto their plates. She carried them to the table, set them down, and then rounded the counter once again for silverware and juice. When she came back to the table, she sat and unfolded a cloth napkin to spread on her lap.

"I wanted to be alone with you. And as for not saying hello, you were sleeping."

Sasha wasn't sure what to think. All this time she'd thought Hannah hadn't been there as much as everyone else. What else didn't she know?

"So you came after all," Sasha said softly.

Hannah sipped her juice. "Of course. Wild horses couldn't keep me away."

"I thought—I thought you didn't care."

Hannah stared at her and then seemed to grow uncomfortable. "It hurts to know you thought such a thing."

"Well, maybe if you would've come at a decent time, like everyone else."

"And what? Sit there with your mother while she grilled me on our breakup and separation? Try to answer questions about our future and why you never told her we were separated? I couldn't do it, Sash. You know how she is, and God forbid I said something you didn't want said."

Hannah took a bite of bacon, letting her know she was finished with her response. And by the way she chewed, like an angry animal with fire in her eyes, she let her know she preferred not to talk about it anymore.

"You're right. I didn't think of that."

Sasha bit into her own bacon, but the wonderful flavor was lost as she thought about the stupid assumption she'd made about Hannah and then again when she'd accused her of not showing up at a decent time. Hannah had a point. Her mother would've given her the third degree, and Sasha would've had a fit if Hannah had answered without her input.

Sasha quietly studied Hannah as she ate. Her tight jaw flexed, and the sunlight played with her shoulder length chestnut brown hair. Her hazel eyes shone against the mint green of her shirt, and

Sasha could smell her freshly showered scent from across the table. She often used a men's body wash, and the scent was strong and fresh and spicy. It awakened her senses and it used to drive her mad. She took a sip of juice and realized that even though she wasn't being driven mad with desire, it was still affecting her.

She cleared her throat and willed her insides to stop spinning out of control like a crazy carousel. Hannah was off limits now. It was over. She'd told her at the hospital that her stay here meant nothing. It couldn't. She couldn't go through it again with her. Sure she cared and she was going out of her way to show it now, but how long would it last? How long before the depression overtook her again? How long before Sasha was once again sitting at a table in the Italian restaurant waiting for her?

It couldn't happen again.

Sasha swallowed another bite of eggs and finished her juice. Then she excused herself, no longer able to eat. Hannah called after her, but she ignored her. She couldn't look back. Not now or ever.

CHAPTER NINE

The doorbell rang as Hannah was finishing cleaning up after breakfast. She grabbed a dish towel and wiped her hands as she headed for the door. It was nearing ten, and she wondered who it could be. Casey was already at class at the community college, and Bonnie was probably at work. Hannah pulled open the door and squinted into the bright morning light. Charlie stood looking at her with a broad smile.

"Morning."

Hannah tried to focus through her shock and dismay. "What are you doing here?"

Charlie looked taken aback. "I'm here to tend to Sasha. Remember? I'm her nurse?"

"Yes, I can remember as far back as yesterday, thanks. I'm just wondering why you are here so early."

"I'm concerned about her fever. It was rather high yesterday. Can I come in?"

Hannah stepped back and pushed open the door. Charlie bypassed her without another word. Hannah closed the door behind her and followed her into the kitchen.

"She ate some breakfast," Hannah said. "I made her a homemade breakfast, and she really enjoyed it."

Charlie began to dig through her bag. Hannah watched her muscled arms move and strain against her dark purple scrubs.

"That's good, good that she's got her appetite."

"Yes. Well, she does."

Charlie retrieved her stethoscope and some surgical gloves. "Where is she?"

"She's in her room. I'll go get her."

"That's okay. I can do it. I need to examine her, and I'm sure she'll want some privacy."

But Hannah wasn't about to stop. She hurried down the hallway and stopped at Sasha's door. She cocked her head when she heard water running from the bathroom. Charlie showed up at her heels.

"She's in the bathroom," Hannah said, crossing to knock on the door. "Sash? I hope she's not trying to bathe alone. She's still weak, and with that PICC line she's really only got one arm." She knocked again. "Sash? Can you let me in?"

The water stopped running. Sasha called out.

"I can't. I'm in the tub."

"I think maybe I should go in and help her," Charlie said.

"No." Hannah blocked her access. "That's not necessary. I can do it."

"I need to make sure she doesn't get that arm wet. I'm her nurse. It's what I'm here for. "

Hannah laughed. "Right, and I bet you're just loving that aren't you?" Hannah opened the door a crack and Sasha quickly covered her chest.

"Hannah, what are you doing?"

Hannah stepped in. "I'm trying to help you. There's no way you can get out of there on your own."

Charlie stepped in after her. "Do you need help, Ms. Bashton?"

Sasha stared at both of them with her mouth open. "I'm fine. I can do it myself."

"Okay then. Just call me when you're ready to get out," Charlie said.

Sasha nodded and gave Hannah a dirty look.

"Thank you, Charlie. I'll do that."

Hannah shook her head and tried to argue, but Sasha stopped her.

"In fact, Charlie, why don't you stay? Hannah, we'll be fine."

Hannah backed away in disbelief. She gripped the doorknob as the feeling of nausea she'd felt the night before overcame her. She stumbled from the bathroom and hurried down the hall and exited through the garage. She climbed in her truck and collapsed against the steering wheel. She pounded it with her fists and cried. She cried for the first time in a very, very long time.

Sasha was gone.

❖

"Mom. Mom, oh my God." Hannah heard Casey's voice, but it sounded far away.

"Wha?"

"Mom, come on. Jesus, you're burning up out here." She felt him slide his arm around her and help her from the truck. She gained her bearings and leaned into him. They were in the garage, and it was stifling hot with the door closed.

He tugged on her and helped her inside. "What were you doing out there? Do you know how lucky you are that I found you?"

"No, I'm fine. It's fine." But she was weak and tired and so thirsty. She fell onto the couch and heard Casey rush to the fridge where he banged around. Then he was at her side in ninja-like speed, placing cold packs on her.

"Keep this on the back of your neck and put these under your arms."

She did so but winced against the icy cold feel of them. He handed over a cold bottle of water. "Sip it," he said.

"Okay, all right."

He stood before her and watched with his hands on his hips.

"What the fuck were you doing out there? You weren't like trying to kill yourself were you?"

She glared at him. “Of course not.”

“Then what the hell, Mom?”

“I went out there to…to get away. But I ended up falling asleep I guess.”

“Yeah, Sash filled me in on the bathtub brawl. She figured you got mad and left. So I went in the garage to look for your car. Thank God I did. We had a record high today, Mom. Over a hundred degrees. With these temperatures—”

“I’m fine.”

But really she was very tired and weak.

“You went out there and had a fit didn’t you? Maybe cried real hard like you do sometimes?”

She didn’t answer. She was embarrassed enough at the moment.

He ran his hands through his hair. “What is going on, Mom? Are you drinking again?”

She shook her head. “No. And as for what’s going on…I don’t know. The nurse. That asshole nurse.”

“She’s here to treat Sasha whether you like it or not.”

“I know. I have to accept it. That’s why I went out there and cried. I couldn’t help it because now I know what I need to do for Sasha and for myself.”

“What’s that?”

“I have to let her go.”

Casey sank down on the couch next to her. He squeezed her hand.

“I think you may be right.”

“Yeah.” She stared off into space. “That’s what I’m afraid of.”

CHAPTER TEN

The midafternoon sun highlighted Sasha's thick blond hair as she finger-combed it in the mirror for what felt like the twentieth time. Eventually, she sighed and dropped her hands and instead focused on applying her makeup. She wasn't doing much because she didn't want it to be obvious, so she settled with mascara, a little eyeliner, and some lip gloss. Then she sprayed a dab of her favorite perfume, Creed Love in White, on her inner wrists and neck.

"There." She smiled. Overall, she was pleased with her appearance even if she did still look a little pale and thin. She'd gained five pounds, which was good, but she definitely needed some color. She'd have to get some sun later on. It would give her color and vitamin D which her doctor had told her was really low. She relaxed as she imagined the warm sun caressing her skin and giving her body what it desperately craved. Though she'd been feeling better, she was still battling her poor kidney function, and she could feel it by the time evening rolled around when her body grew weak and her muscles burned and stiffened as if she'd lifted weights all day. She'd drift off to sleep at the dinner table, on the couch, or in the bath. Hannah had had to help her more than once to bed. And most times she could hardly remember their encounter by the time morning came when she assumed Hannah must've helped her. But Hannah never said a word one way or another.

Sasha gave herself one last look in the mirror and headed for the kitchen. She recalled how quiet and almost distant Hannah had been lately. She'd been polite but in a strange kind of way. As if they were mere acquaintances and Sasha was renting a room from her. Hannah would offer to cook for her, bring her drinks and fold her laundry, but she'd stopped trying to make conversation. The doorbell rang as Sasha reached the kitchen, and she did her best to hurry to it. She knew it was Charlie, and she couldn't help but grin. She'd grown quite fond of Charlie the past two weeks, and she knew her attraction was more than obvious. But she couldn't help herself. She'd been starved for attention, and it felt nice knowing someone else was attracted to her and that she wasn't an ogre after all. She knew the distance Hannah was showing had something to do with her and Charlie, but she was too scorned to be empathetic toward her.

Sasha pushed Hannah from her mind as she pulled open the door. Charlie smiled and whipped off her aviator shades.

"Hi."

Sasha heated as she caught her scent in the hot breeze. It was clean with a hint of an ocean breeze, and it set her insides afire.

"Hi." She allowed Charlie entry and they brushed each other as she passed by. A touch that didn't go unnoticed by Sasha.

"You look nice. Very healthy," Charlie said. The corner of her mouth lifted.

"Thank you. I think I need some color. I may get some sun before it sets today." Sasha closed the door and they crossed to the kitchen. The house was quiet with Casey at school and Hannah at work. Sasha was grateful to have Charlie to herself.

"Don't get too much," Charlie said, setting down her bag. "You're pretty perfect as it is."

"Are you flirting with me?"

"No, of course not. I'm still your nurse."

Sasha made herself comfortable on a stool and awaited her examination and the last application of her antibiotic. It was Charlie's next to last visit and to say Sasha was disappointed was an understatement.

Charlie retrieved her stethoscope and listened to her chest front and back. It was difficult for Sasha to control her breathing, and she knew her heart was careening despite her best effort to control it.

"I noticed that Hannah isn't around anymore," Charlie said as she finished. "Everything okay?"

"Not really, but it's not anything to worry about."

"I take it there's a history there?"

"Yes."

Charlie checked her temperature. "I don't want to cause you any trouble."

"You haven't. It's just something between Hannah and me."

The thermometer beeped. "Temp is normal. Great news."

Sasha smiled. "Thank God." A part of her had worried that the antibiotic wouldn't work. She was more than glad to hear it had. The hospital was the last place she wanted to be.

Charlie opened the refrigerator and grabbed the plastic ball full of antibiotic. She hooked it to Sasha's PICC line, and they sat in silence for a while as it dripped into her insides, chilling her to the bone.

"Cold?" Charlie brought her the blanket from the couch just as she often did.

"Thank you."

"Anything else? Maybe some coffee?"

"No, I'll be fine, thanks. I'm just ready for this to be over. Besides, I should be the one offering you the coffee. You're the guest."

"I'd hardly call myself a guest. And something tells me Hannah would agree."

Sasha nodded. "Yes." She sighed softly. "About Hannah. I didn't really want to get into it, but seeing as how I would like to keep seeing you, I think I'd better discuss her with you. Hannah and I were a couple for many years. And we've been separated now for a couple of months. She's…having a hard time dealing with that. She's trying to win me back."

"I can't say I blame her," Charlie said. "I know I wouldn't want to lose you."

Sasha leaned into her. "Oh, I don't know. I can be a handful."

"I think I can handle it. I know I'd like to try."

Sasha stared into her eyes. They were deep and vibrant with color, and they seemed to be pulling her in. They grew closer with lips a mere millimeter apart when Charlie's finger touched Sasha's mouth.

"Not quite yet. I'm still your nurse."

Sasha groaned. "That was mean."

"I'm just being professional."

"Of course."

"Doesn't mean we can't talk about it. I'd definitely love to see you outside of this house."

"God, yes, that sounds so good. I need to get out of here. For so many different reasons."

"How about you?" Charlie asked. "Do you still have feelings for her?"

Sasha wasn't expecting such a direct question. She cleared her throat and shifted a bit, not quite sure what to say. How could she explain what she was feeling and experiencing when she didn't understand it herself?

"Okay, I think that answers my question."

"No." Sasha touched her arm. "I'm sorry. I'm just so overwhelmed with all these crazy emotions when I think about my situation with Hannah. And being here right now is just adding to that."

"I can understand that," Charlie said. "But I don't want to get into the middle of someone's messy breakup either."

"Once I leave here…there should be nothing messy about it. I told her my staying here meant nothing as far as our future. That she was too late to win me back."

"Maybe so, but from what I've seen, she's not taking that to heart. She still seems rather serious about you being hers."

Sasha stood as she saw the antibiotic nearly completely drained. "I don't belong to her or anyone. And it angers me that she has the nerve to think that."

Charlie stood alongside her. "Okay, let's calm down. I didn't mean to upset you." She gently unhooked the PICC line and held her shoulders. "Let's forget it for now and concentrate on removing that PICC line shall we?"

"God, yes. Please."

"Good, lead the way to the bedroom. I need you in the supine position."

Sasha headed for the bedroom and lay on her back with her PICC line arm on the edge of the bed. She heard Charlie in the bathroom running the sink water, and soon she smelled the soap she'd no doubt used on her hands. When she entered the room with her bag she had on sterile gloves. She smiled as she spread out a towel and the instruments she'd need on the night table.

"Will this hurt?"

"It shouldn't."

"I'm still nervous."

She laughed as she set out scissors, dressing, stitch cutters, and solution. Sasha swallowed.

"You really need all that?"

"Yep."

"Oh, God."

"Shh, try to relax. You'll be fine. And just think how much better you'll feel."

Sasha closed her eyes and allowed her mind to drift. As she felt Charlie begin, her thoughts went to Hannah and the way she'd looked so torn and hurt in the bathroom that day with Charlie.

Can I really fool myself into believing that she doesn't care?

CHAPTER ELEVEN

Hannah pulled into the garage after nine and killed her engine and headlights in the darkness. She sat for a moment and took in the immediate heavy heat that settled over the stopped air conditioning. It reminded her of her stunt a few days before when she sat there crying so hard her body had shook. She'd cried and cried until a numbness overcame her and she was too tired to move. She'd fallen asleep on the steering wheel with hot tears trailing down her face. And still, despite it all, her pain was as fresh as ever, and it didn't seem to be going away anytime soon.

She crawled from the truck and entered the cool, quiet house. Dried sweat coated her from her workday outdoors, and she could almost feel the coating crack as she moved. She couldn't wait for a cold shower, but first she stopped for a cold bottle of water. She sipped it on her way to her bedroom on the other wing of the house. She assumed Sasha was home, but she resisted the urge to check in on her. They hadn't really spoken in two days, and the silence was killing her.

Nevertheless, she pressed on, determined to give her space. Though it hurt like hell, she stayed away.

She stripped as she entered her bathroom and turned on the shower. She faced the mirror and took off her ball cap to run her fingers through her stiff hair. She had white circles around her eyes from where the sun had baked her around her sunglasses. She'd once again forgotten sunscreen. She pulled off her shirt and examined her body. She was slightly toned and sinewy, but she couldn't get past the scars on her chest. They were dark red and looked a little like half circles, like somebody's joke of a smiley face. A fucked up pair of smiley faces.

She ran her fingertips over the scars and thought how funny it was that she didn't really miss her breasts all that much until she was nude. She'd always been a tomboy and an athlete, and she'd hated the large size of her breasts and the trouble of finding a proper bra, which she'd just rip off as soon as she walked in the door anyhow.

But when she was nude, like now, she noticed the emptiness, the void, and the last thing she felt was sexy or desirable no matter how toned the rest of her was. She hated the angry scars that left her feeling like half a woman. And a lot of times, if she admitted it, half a person. That was because she knew she was vulnerable now. She could die. Something could happen. The realization had terrified her, and she'd pushed everyone away. Mainly, Sasha. Now she had to pay for that. With her heart.

She stepped in the shower while refusing to cry. It was very rarely that she showed her emotions, and when she did, it often drained her and left her helpless and exhausted. So when she did cry, she preferred to do it alone.

She swallowed back her tears and soaped herself twice and rinsed under the cool spray. When she stepped out and dried, she was covered in goose bumps and trembling in the cold air. But the change felt glorious, and it was always the perfect end to a hot as hell day. She dressed quickly and headed for the living room on the search for Casey. She'd seen his car in the driveway and she wanted to, at the very least, wish him good night. But to do so meant she'd have to pass Sasha's room. She didn't want to admit it, but she knew it was a big reason why she wanted to check in on Casey.

She breezed down the hallway, heard Sasha talking on the phone, and hurried along to Casey's door, determined to leave Sasha alone.

She softly knocked, but Casey couldn't hear her. His door was cracked and she could see he had on his headset.

She pushed her way in and touched his shoulder as the television exploded with graphics. He jerked and tore down his head set.

"Mom, Jesus."

He paused his game and stood to retrieve a Coke from his night table. He was shirtless and in board shorts, toned and sinewy just like she was.

"Sorry, just wanted to say good night."

He drank heartily and saluted her.

"That's it?"

He lowered the can and softly burped. "You were expecting what? A cartwheel?"

"No, I was just hoping for a brief conversation is all."

He returned to his seat and dug into a small bag of Spicy Doritos.

"How's school?"

He shrugged. "Okay." He turned and looked at her. "You forgot sunscreen again didn't you?"

She rubbed her face. "Maybe. Your grades okay?"

"As if you have to ask."

She stumbled for words. Of course he had good grades. He always did. And he barely had to try.

"Okay, well good night then."

"Night, Mom."

She wanted to tell him not to stay up too late, but he was eighteen and had every right to do whatever he wanted. He excelled at school and any part time job he worked so she had no complaints. She stood at the door and watched his television flash with more graphics as he began to play again. She inched the door closed and stood in the hallway recalling how just yesterday he was five and having dreams about his favorite Pokémon.

She cocked her head as she heard Sasha laugh. Slowly, she moved toward her room and stopped. Sasha was packing her things and talking to someone on speakerphone. Hannah's heart clenched as she watched her pack, and then her heart fell as she heard Charlie's voice come through the phone.

"You're sure you feel up to a date tomorrow?"

Sasha laughed. "Yes, for the hundredth time, I'm ready. I'm dying to see you."

Charlie laughed and Hannah wanted to throw up. She moved away from the door, but Sasha heard her and ended the call. She pulled open her door.

"Were you spying?" She stood glaring at her in a threadbare tee and sleep pants. Her hair was in a ponytail and her PICC line was gone. She looked as though she'd seen a little sun. She looked good, the healthiest Hannah had seen her in weeks.

"No, just passing by." Hannah dropped her eyes. She couldn't bear to look at her; it hurt too much.

Sasha sighed and leaned back against the dresser. "I'm all packed."

"Yes, I see."

"Bonnie is picking me up tomorrow."

"So soon?"

"Yes, it's more than time to go, Hannah."

"Will you be okay?"

Sasha didn't answer right away. "I should be. I'll be seeing my doctor frequently, and I have people who will look after me…" She trailed off as if she'd said something she shouldn't have.

"Of course."

"I mean, you know, I have friends and stuff."

"Uh-huh, yes." But Hannah could feel herself burn with anger and jealousy knowing she was referring to Charlie. But there was nothing she could do. Not a damn thing.

"Okay, well, good night. And if I don't see you tomorrow, good luck with, you know, everything."

"It doesn't have to be like this, Hannah."

"Yes, yes, it does."

"No, it doesn't."

"Sasha, I have to let you go."

Sasha fell silent. She seemed shocked and unable to respond. She blinked quickly and pushed away from the dresser.

"That doesn't mean we have to act like strangers."

"For me, yes, I think it does. I, uh, can't handle it otherwise. And knowing you're seeing someone else…I shouldn't know about it. I can't know about it."

"Hannah."

"No, I have to go, Sasha. Just—good luck and all. I love you."

And with that she turned and left the room, leaving the love of her life behind.

Chapter Twelve

"Oh my God, nothing fits. I look like a kid too small for her hand-me-downs," Sasha said as she yanked off yet another sundress and tossed it on the bed.

"You look fine," Bonnie said from her position on the bed. She began folding the latest discarded garment. "For God's sake, she was your nurse; she knows you've been sick. I'm sure she'll understand."

"No, you don't seem to understand. This is my first date, in what, sixteen damn years? I need to look good. Not just for her but for myself."

"Okay, okay. Why don't you just try some jeans? Don't you have a skinny pair you always celebrate when you can fit into them?"

Sasha snapped her fingers and pointed at Bonnie. "Yes!" She dug wildly through her closet until she found them. She shook the folded denim and eyed the dark blue color and the cut of the pants. They were perfect.

"It's been two years since I could fit into these bad boys." She stepped into them and pulled them up with ease. "Wow. I really have lost weight." She buttoned them and turned to look at herself in the door mirror Bonnie had hung for her. "What do you think?"

Bonnie nodded. "You look good. What'd I tell ya?"

Sasha clapped her hands. "Okay, now a blouse."

"So where is this hotshot taking you?"

Sasha cringed at the word hotshot, but she kept digging in her closet, looking for the proper blouse. "What's with the tone? Charlie isn't a hotshot."

"No tone. She just sounds like a bit of a hotshot is all."

"Well, she's not."

Bonnie was quiet, and Sasha retrieved a lavender blouse and slid it on. She was buttoning it when she caught Bonnie's faraway look. "What's wrong? Is it too light? Should I go darker?"

"The shirt is fine."

"Then what is it?"

Bonnie looked at her and shrugged.

"Bons, come on, tell me."

"It's just—I think—"

"Yes?"

"I think you may be moving a little too fast."

Sasha felt her herself blink with surprise. "What?" She sat on the bed facing Bonnie.

"I wish you would give yourself some time is all. You just got out of the hospital a few weeks ago, you're just now feeling well, and you know, it hasn't been that long since Hannah."

Sasha shook her head. "Bonnie." She felt her face rush with heat and she stood. "I think you're wrong. I mean, I'm fine. And if anything I need to do this to get over—" but she stopped short of what she was about to say.

"See? You need to get over her. Meaning you aren't yet over her."

"That's not what I meant." She sighed with frustration and finger combed her hair in the mirror. Her makeup was done and her outfit on, now all she had to decide on was shoes. "I simply need to do this for myself. To move forward, to start my life anew. I know you can understand that."

Bonnie didn't speak. She just stood and walked to the doorway. Downstairs they heard a loud rumbling and Bonnie crossed to the window. She pulled back the blinds.

"Um, your not a hotshot nurse is here. On her motorcycle."

"Shit." Sasha scrambled for her brown ankle boots and hurried downstairs. She could hear Bonnie trailing behind her. "Don't wait up for me. I have no idea when I'll be home." She sat on the bottom step and slipped into her boots and zipped them up. When she stood she turned to look at Bonnie. "And don't think I didn't catch the sarcasm in your comment."

The doorbell rang and Sasha answered. Charlie was standing there in a tight black T-shirt, faded jeans that hugged her muscled legs, and big black boots. Her dark hair was thick and windblown, but easily stylish once again with the pass of her fingers. She was James Dean sexy and had a tilted smile that had no doubt brought dozens of women to their knees.

"Hi," Sasha finally managed.

"Hi."

Sasha turned to close the door but found Bonnie standing there staring at them.

"You two kids have fun," she said. "And I'm not sorry about my sarcasm." She closed the door, and Sasha clenched her jaw at Bonnie's rudeness.

"That was, uh, my friend Bonnie."

Charlie seemed unfazed. "Doesn't sound like much of a friend. You ready to go?" She held out a black helmet.

"Oh shit, the bike. I'm riding on it?"

Charlie grinned. "For now."

Sasha took her hand and followed her to the driveway. Her stomach rumbled in anticipation as she took in the metallic jade tank and khaki seats of the Indian motorcycle.

"It's beautiful." She loved the look of it. The dark green with the black engine and wheels. It looked beautiful yet fierce.

"It's a Scout. I just got it last month."

Charlie climbed on and put on a black helmet. Then she held Sasha's hand as she climbed on behind her.

"You ready?" Charlie asked.

"God yes," Sasha said into the grumbling and vibration of the bike. "I've never been so ready."

❖

Sasha released her hold on Charlie as they slowed to a stop in a busy parking lot. Charlie cut the engine and Sasha climbed off the bike and removed her helmet. She vehemently ran her hands through her hair, knowing the helmet had probably ruined the look she'd been going for. Despite Charlie already having seen her, she still felt the need for perfection, and her mother's words replayed in her mind. Always look your best.

Charlie laughed as she removed her helmet.

"Do you always worry about how you look?"

"Of course, don't you?"

Charlie swung off the bike. "Not overly so, no."

"Well, we can't all be a natural James Dean," Sasha said, checking her reflection in the side mirror of the motorcycle.

Charlie tugged on her hand. "I'm not sure how to take that," she said. "Come on, you look great." She pulled Sasha along after her.

"Where exactly are we going?" Sasha glanced around at the handful of restaurants they were near.

"This one. It's new and I want to try it."

Sasha hurried to walk next to her. She almost slid in her boots, and as she regained her balance she noted how she'd never had to run to keep up with Hannah.

"That okay with you?" Charlie asked.

"Sure."

She smiled and wove them between a dozen or so people waiting outside and pulled open the heavy looking door.

"We have reservations." She squeezed Sasha's hand and led the way inside. The restaurant looked to be like a roadhouse of sorts with peanut shells on the ground, country music blaring, and steer horns on the wall. The wait staff wore denim and boots and cowboy hats, and some danced to the music as they moved between tables. The atmosphere was festive, and Sasha breathed easy, hoping for a fun night.

Charlie gave the hostess her name, and they were led farther inside to a back area booth where a single candle burned in a red votive. The tablecloth was also red, and Charlie slid into the booth first and watched as Sasha slid in across from her. They took the menus from the hostess, and Charlie immediately ordered a beer.

"I can't serve you, ma'am. Your waiter will be with you shortly." The hostess seemed annoyed and walked away quickly.

"She's lucky I don't have to tip her," Charlie said with a smirk.

Sasha burned with embarrassment and looked around to make sure no one else had heard her comment. She was always very kind to restaurant staff and to everyone really. She didn't understand those that weren't.

Charlie reached across the table and squeezed her hand. "Are you going to look at your menu? I'm starving."

Sasha hurriedly opened her menu, getting the hint. She quickly focused on a grilled chicken meal and closed the menu. She sat politely, wondering what she should say. Charlie's behavior had caught her off guard and now she felt awkward.

"What are you having?" Charlie asked.

"The grilled chicken."

"That's it? I bring you here and you get grilled chicken? Not me, buddy. I'm going for the prime rib." She closed her menu and patted the table.

Sasha thought briefly about reminding her of her dietary restrictions, but she decided it wasn't worth the effort.

"Now if we could just get some beer life would be wonderful."

She apparently wanted Sasha to laugh by the look she was giving her. So Sasha did.

"This place is great isn't it?" Charlie reached for the pail of peanuts sitting next to the ketchup. She shelled one and popped it in her mouth. She tossed the shell on the floor and dug in the pail for another. She pushed the pail Sasha's way, but Sasha held up her hand.

"No, thanks."

Charlie shrugged and their waiter showed up all smiles and western attire. Charlie spoke before he could even greet them.

"I'll have the prime rib with a loaded baked potato and a side of butter for the vegetables. And I'll start with a bottle of Bud Light, ice cold, and some bread please. She'll have the grilled chicken—"

"With a side of vegetables only please," Sasha interjected. "And could you please bring me a box with my meal? I won't be able to eat all the chicken." She smiled sincerely at him and he returned it though obviously flustered.

"And to drink?"

"Water, please."

He wrote everything down and walked away when Charlie had nothing more to say.

"Hopefully, he's a good one," Charlie said. "We'll see how fast he brings our drinks."

"What does it matter?" Sasha said. "I mean aren't we here to relax and have a good time?"

"Sure, but I'm thirsty. And these waiters can take forever on a Friday night like this so you have to be aggressive."

Sasha fought closing her eyes. "Let's just ease up a bit on the aggression, okay? For my sake?"

Charlie grimaced but then smiled. "All right, for your sake. But don't tell me not to be aggressive later on when I get you alone." She winked.

Sasha stiffened. "What do you mean?" She'd planned on a good night. A very good night. But nothing about it was romantic so far, and Charlie's behavior with the staff had really turned her off. Now the thought of being alone with her unnerved her a little.

"I mean, we take the bike up a mountain trail, park, maybe make out a little under the moon. Then we go to my place and—"

But the waiter brought the beer and water, interrupting her. Sasha was grateful because she honestly didn't know how to respond. Sure, the mountain and moon sounded great, but could they make it that long without Charlie saying something asinine or rude?

"Good man," Charlie said to the waiter. "Now let's see how quickly you can bring my dinner."

Sasha cringed. "She's kidding," Sasha said. "Thank you for bringing the drinks so quickly." She smiled at him again and prayed he wouldn't spit in their food.

He gave a nod and walked away.

"I wasn't kidding," Charlie said. Then she laughed and took a long pull off her beer.

"I was afraid you weren't. I just hope he doesn't get too upset."

Charlie shrugged. "It's his job. He's used to it."

Sasha thought for a second about getting up to leave. But then she thought of the Charlie who'd cared for her those long two weeks and how sensitive and kind she'd been. She thought about how Charlie had closed her eyes when helping her up from the tub and then handing over a towel trying to make her comfortable. Where was that Charlie?

Then she thought of her mother and the way she always said you can tell a lot by a person by the way they treat others. She'd always found that to be true, and she swallowed hard forcing a smile at Charlie who was watching her closely.

"Have I upset you? I'm just trying to get us some good service. I'm good like that. I want tonight to be very special for you."

Sasha laughed. "I wouldn't worry about it so much. I just really want to relax and have a good time."

Charlie raised her beer. "Then here's to a good time. And to you, Sasha, may your night be special and may your coming days be healthy and happy." She winked again, and Sasha half-heartedly clinked her water glass with Charlie's beer bottle.

She closed her eyes as she drank her water and wished one more wish. She wished the night would go by quickly.

CHAPTER THIRTEEN

Another Friday night. Hannah sat slumped on a stool in a dive bar downtown spinning a bottle of Miller Lite around and around.

"You ever gonna drink that?" the beefy bartender asked.

She looked up at his shiny bald head and black goatee. He had scratches on his forehead and face, and she didn't dare ask what they were from. She hoped they weren't from a woman.

"Nah," she finally said. She pushed it away and rested her head on her arms. Drinking was what caused part of the problem with Sasha. She didn't want to play with that fire anymore. Sure, she could wallow in it, get trashed and try to forget her, but she knew it wouldn't work. She'd just be trashed and hurt, and that was no fun. Facing reality was what she had to do, and boy, what a bitch it was.

Her girl had run off with somebody new. A poster model for dykes that Charlie was. How could she ever compete? What's more, she couldn't compete at all. She had to let Sasha go.

So what now? What the hell was she supposed to do?

"Listen, if you ain't gonna drink or buy anything, you need to beat it. I got paying customers wanting your seat."

She raised her head. "Yeah?" She slammed cash down on the counter for the beer. "That's for your shitty beer. And this…" she slammed down a dollar bill, "is for the pleasure of your company."

She looked away and stood as he glared at her. He said something to her back, but she didn't care to listen. She just headed for the door.

What was wrong with a world that didn't let somebody sit and stew without getting hammered? She pushed out into the warm night and climbed into her truck. Tears nipped at her, but she refused to let them surface. What she needed was a plan. A way out of this pit. A pinpoint of light at the end of this damn tunnel.

Mickey had told her she needed to date. To meet someone new. Maybe that was what she had to do. She didn't want to, but maybe it would help to get her going half speed again. She plucked her phone from her pocket and texted Mickey. Then she put her truck in drive and sped over to the nearby gay bar. She walked inside the small hole-in-the-wall without waiting for Mick, and she was bombarded with dance music. Lights and strobes flashed, and men and women were yelling over the music trying to hear each other.

Hannah crossed to the bar and eased on a stool. She ordered a Coke and felt relief when the bartender was friendly. He slid her her drink and touched her hand.

"Don't get too wild on me now."

She cracked a smile, and she could almost feel the crumbling of her stone-set face.

"That's a girl," he said. "You keep doing that and they'll be on you like kids on candy."

She shook her head. "I'm not sure I'm ready for all that."

"Too late." He winked and moved away as a woman moved in next to her.

"Hi. Care to dance?" She was short in stature and looked almost cherub like with pursed pretty lips and pink tinted cheeks. Her golden hair fell around her face like it was gently caressing her.

"I, uh, don't dance." Nothing terrified her more than getting out on a dance floor and moving her body in strange ways for all to see. She'd even had nightmares about it when she was younger.

"Why is that?" She smirked. "Is it me or the dancing you're not fond of?"

Hannah struggled for words. "The dancing. Yes, the dancing."

The woman full-on smiled. She shook her hand. "Good. I can work with that. I'm Pauline."

"Hannah."

"Hannah, huh? Never would've pegged you for a Hannah."

"No?"

"No. You're too sporty." She rested her hand on Hannah's thigh. Hannah covered it with her own.

"I think we're going just a little too fast here."

"We are?"

"For me, yes. I just walked in the door and I'm waiting for a friend."

"What can I say? I go after what I want." She leaned into her and inhaled her scent. "You smell really good." She placed her lips gently on her skin, and Hannah jerked and stood.

"Okay. That's a little too much there." Her heart was careening, but it was out of panic rather than desire.

"I think you liked it."

"No, I, uh, it's too much. Too much too fast."

Pauline was staring up at her like a lover lost in the throes of passion. Like she should be on the cover of a romance book.

"I have to go," Hannah said.

"Wait, don't you want my number?"

Hannah hurried across the dance floor toward the door. But as she approached the exit, she remembered Mickey. Thinking quickly, she sidestepped and found an empty table. It was strewn with drink glasses and napkins, but she didn't care. It was out of the eye of Pauline and many other patrons, and she felt more secure. What had she been thinking in coming to a gay bar? Had she honestly thought she'd have more peace here?

And what was with Pauline? The woman was practically riding her leg. Was that how it was now? Women came on strong and expected one to just jump right in with them? If so, she had a lot to learn. A lot she didn't want to learn.

"What am I doing here?"

She palmed her forehead and wished for a beer. She pushed away the temptation and focused on the part of the dance floor she could see. Two blondes were dancing, one with long hair like Sasha. It panged her heart, and she wondered what Sasha was doing at that very moment. She wondered if she might walk in the door. What would she do? Speak to her? Leave?

She didn't know, and she pushed that thought too from her mind. Her leg jumped with nerves. She focused on the messy table and flagged down a cocktail waitress. The woman was friendly and offered to get her a drink while she cleaned the table. Hannah shook her head, too afraid to speak. She didn't trust her voice.

When the table was clean, she rested her elbow on it and rested her chin in her hand. Just then, she felt a hand on her shoulder. She jerked and prayed it was Mickey.

"Hey, handsome, buy me a drink?" Mickey rounded the table and sat with a shit-eating grin.

"Screw you," Hannah said, breathing easy. "You have no idea what I've already been through."

"Oh?"

"Yes."

"Do tell."

"I'd rather not."

Mickey shifted in her seat and turned to check out the crowd. She turned back around and whistled.

"Quite a crowd here tonight. Anyone strike your fancy?" She ran her hands through her short spiked hair and flashed her eyes at her. She was wearing a tight fitting gray tee with jeans.

If butch was Hannah's thing, she'd say she was attractive.

"Uh, no."

"Come on, have you even looked?"

"Not really." This time Hannah shifted. "I don't think I'm ready. Someone already approached me, and she came on really strong. I mean really strong."

Mickey leaned forward. "No kidding? Where? Is she hot?"

"That's not the point. It scared the shit out of me."

Mickey sat back. "I was afraid this might happen. I was afraid you might be gun-shy."

"I'm not gun-shy. I'm just...old-fashioned."

"Old-fashioned."

"Yes."

Mickey laughed. "I don't know where the hell we'll find you a girl who's old-fashioned."

Hannah blushed. "I'm not talking Little House on the Prairie here, Mick. I'm talking respect, personal space, easy smiles, and witty banter."

"Please tell me you're kidding."

Hannah looked away, defeated. She knew what she wanted, but she didn't dare voice it. She wanted what she'd had with Sasha when things were good.

"Okay, okay." Mickey held up her hands. "Say I found you a nice woman. Someone who was more your speed. Would you, what? Take her out?"

"Yes. A date would be nice."

"A date."

"Yes."

"Okay." Mick nodded. "I might can manage that."

Hannah had somehow given her the green light to find her a woman. How had that happened? "Wait, I'm not saying that I'm ready for that."

"Come on, Hannah. One date. You can do it. It would be so good for you."

The cocktail waitress returned and Mick ordered a beer. As she walked away, Mick leaned in once again. "I'm going to take my beer and patrol the crowd for a bit. Promise you'll stick around?"

"No, I'm gonna go. It's late and I'm tired."

"You're just gonna take off? I just got here."

"You're going prowling and I have no interest."

"I'm going prowling for you."

"Even so. I can't sit here on the edge of my seat while you do that. I just don't think I'm ready. I think I'd throw up with nerves the second I saw her."

"Oh, my God." Mickey dropped her head into her hands. "Okay, fine, go. But promise me we'll talk tomorrow. You've been isolating and it isn't good for you."

Hannah stood. "I don't know. I'll try, okay?" When Mick nodded, Hannah walked away and exited the bar. She headed for her car, relishing the silence and the darkness of the night. She looked up at the stars and once again thought of Sasha.

Chapter Fourteen

Sasha rolled over in bed and willed the voice to go away.

"Saaasha, I brought coffee."

"Go away." It was Bonnie and she was annoying the shit out of her. "I'm sleeping."

"It's nine o'clock. Wakey wakey, eggs and bakey."

"Fuck off."

Bonnie tsked, and Sasha could smell the coffee. Still, her body didn't want to budge.

"Tell me about last night," Bonnie pleaded. "How was it?"

Sasha was sprawled out on her stomach with half her face sunk into the foam mattress.

"It was a nightmare," she said. She pushed herself up and wiped away some drool.

She pulled the covers to her chest and eyed Bonnie who looked as fresh as the day was bright.

"A nightmare?" Bonnie handed over the mug of steaming coffee and sat.

"Yes," Sasha said between sips. "A nightmare."

"What happened?"

"She was a Neanderthal. End of story."

Bonnie looked perplexed. But Sasha didn't want to talk about it.

"You were right, okay? Feel better?"

"No."

Sasha scoffed. She placed the mug on the night table and rose with the covers wrapped around her.

"Where are you going?"

"For a shower." Sasha crossed the hall, entered the bathroom, and started the shower. The water warmed quickly, and she dropped the bedclothes and stepped inside. The water felt miraculous, and she relaxed her muscles under the spray.

"You have to tell me what happened."

Sasha jerked and yanked back the shower curtain. "Holy shit, Bonnie. What the hell?"

But Bonnie merely sat on the toilet seat and sipped her coffee.

Sasha pulled the shower curtain closed and soaped her hair. "She was rude. Rude to the entire restaurant." Just thinking about it made her want to cringe. "I've never been more embarrassed in my life."

"Oh, no."

"Oh, yes. She was rude, curt, and demanding. And worst of all, she thought it was turning me on somehow. Like she was putting on a show."

"Yikes."

"Yeah." Sasha rinsed her hair. "It was awful. And after we finally left there, I asked to come home and she wouldn't bring me. She took me to listen to this god-awful band. All I got was a terrible headache while she danced the night away with her biker friends."

"I thought you said she was nice?"

"She was! And I kept waiting for that person to appear, but it didn't happen. Not until the very end when she finally dropped me off. Then she was sensitive and caring and gentle. She suddenly cared about my wants and desires, and she seemed truly heartbroken that I didn't have a good time."

"Oh no," Bonnie said. "You didn't say you'd go out with her again did you?"

Sasha rinsed her body and then the conditioner from her hair. She didn't want to answer, but she knew Bonnie would keep pressing.

"I said maybe."

She heard Bonnie make a noise.

She killed the water and reached for a towel, which Bonnie placed in her hand.

"I don't want to hear it, Bonnie. I only said maybe."

"You have the hardest time telling people no."

"I told Hannah no."

"That took years."

Sasha dried herself and her frustration grew. "Can I have some peace please? I had a hell of a night and I still have a bit of a headache."

She heard Bonnie stand. "I'm sorry you had such a terrible time, Sash. When you're ready, I made breakfast." She closed the door softly, and Sasha stepped from the tub and stared at herself in the mirror.

She couldn't explain why she'd told Charlie she might see her again. The date had obviously gone way wrong, and she no longer had an interest in her. But there was something about the way they ended the night. She'd seen a glimpse of the Charlie she'd been attracted to. And if she was really honest with herself, she'd admit the real truth. That she didn't want her first date after Hannah to be a failure. If she did that then who knew what the future held. Here she was so determined to move on, so headstrong, turning Hannah away, and her first date was a bomb.

What would Hannah think when she heard? Surely someone would tell her. Would she gloat? Would she move in again thinking she had another shot?

Would that be so bad?

She groaned at herself for even allowing the thought to enter her mind. Hannah had manners, yes, and she would never act like Charlie did last night, but that didn't mean anything. She would just have to give Charlie another chance was all. It could work.

Charlie could show up all sexy and kind. They could have a good time. Maybe she just needed to talk to her.

She crossed to the bedroom and dressed in navy cotton shorts and a white tee. Then she lotioned up and headed downstairs. Bonnie had already made her a plate, and she gave her a big smile as she sat at the table.

"You've really been a good friend to me, Bons," Sasha said. "Thank you."

Bonnie sat across from her with another full mug of coffee. "Quit thanking me already. I'm getting a complex."

"I mean it. All you do for me. You're the best." Sasha took a bite of the turkey bacon and then spooned some homemade preserves on a piece of toast.

"How do you feel about returning to work on Monday?" Bonnie asked.

Sasha chewed and mulled it over. "I'm nervous. It's been weeks."

"I think I'd be a little anxious as well. But they said someone has been covering for you, and they are thrilled you're coming back, right?"

"Yes. But still, what if I have trouble getting back in the groove?" She'd had a nightmare about that a couple of days before. Now it was on the forefront of her mind. She'd always been great at her job, and the people at her station were wonderful. Being gone so long though…could she jump back in without feeling lost?

"Try not to worry about it. You're an old pro at your job."

Sasha continued to eat and think.

"Has my mother called the home phone?" She hadn't heard from her in a few days, which was a bit unlike her since the hospital stay.

"Yes. Four times." Bonnie rose and retrieved a paper from the fridge. "If you ever ate, you would've noticed your messages."

Sasha scanned through the names and her heart sank for a split second. Bonnie must've seen the brief look on her face.

"Hannah hasn't called."

She said the words softly, as if they were a confession she didn't want to voice.

Sasha shrugged. "Okay."

"Has she called your cell?"

Sasha shook her head.

"Does that bother you?"

"No, it's what I wanted." But still, she was more than surprised. "I guess it proves I made the right move."

Bonnie looked down at her coffee.

"Your silence speaks volumes," Sasha said.

"I'm just thinking."

"And?"

"Nothing. I think you did the right thing. Now you should move on from this Charlie."

"Actually, I've given it some thought. I think I'm going to go out with her again. Give her another shot."

Bonnie stood at the sink, and Sasha saw her shoulders fall.

"Sash."

"Please don't argue with me. I need to give it another shot. For me."

Bonnie turned. "You know things aren't automatically going to be perfect now. You know that, right? You aren't going to just ride off into the sunset with someone else."

Sasha pushed away her plate. She wanted to protest and tell Bonnie she was being ridiculous in thinking that Sasha expected such things, but no words would come. Because that was exactly what she was wanting. She blinked and stumbled out a sentence.

"How—you're—I don't think that."

"Maybe not, but you do want it."

"So? I can dream can't I?"

"Yes, of course. Just don't let your dreams cloud your reality. We can't all live in a romcom or a romance book, Sash."

"Me? What about you? You don't seem to have any dreams. You haven't dated in God knows how long, and you find an excuse about every man you meet."

Bonnie looked stricken, but she remained calm. “This isn’t about me, Sash. But if you need to deflect, I get it.”

Sasha shoved her chair back and stood. She pointed at her, but in the end said nothing. She just hurried out the door to her Jeep and climbed inside. She didn’t bother to wait for her vehicle to cool before she sped off down the street.

Chapter Fifteen

Hannah didn't sleep. Couldn't sleep. Her brain had been on overload, flashing images of Sasha and Charlie all night long. She groaned and finally crawled from her useless bed into the bathroom where she splashed warm water on her face. She groaned again when she caught sight of her reflection. She looked like over-tanned hell if there was such a thing. She had the dark circles under her eyes, deadness in her irises, and the deep abyss to nowhere in her pupils.

She was familiar with the look, but she'd never seen it quite so bad before. Unable to stand to look at herself any longer, she swept her hair into a ponytail and walked back into the bedroom to pull on mesh shorts and a sleeveless shirt. She slid into her Adidas trainers, grabbed her phone and earphones, and crossed the house to the stifling backyard. She didn't bother getting a water bottle; she'd make herself earn that.

She tucked the earphones into her ears and scrolled to the song that had been replaying in her mind throughout the night. The beat started up on "Hostage" by Nothing But Thieves, and she lay down on the weight bench under the patio and began pumping out reps. She started out low on the weight but lifted until her arms and chest quivered. The music pushed her and pressed her. She put the song on repeat and did more reps. Then she adjusted the bench, moved the bar back, and did incline presses. She worked until she was burning, until she was breathless, all the while thinking of nothing but Sasha and their life together. She worked until she was forced to stop, unable to do any more hammer curls. She set down the weights and rested her arms on her knees. Sweat dripped off her face onto her shorts. She didn't bother to wipe it away, for it was Sasha exiting her body. She was sweating out Sasha. Lifting away the past and all the love and laughter. And it felt wonderful. Painful. Agonizing.

She heard the Arcadia door slide open, but she didn't have the strength or the desire to see who it was.

"Here," Casey said, placing a hand on her back. He gave her a cold bottle of water. She promptly poured half of it over her head, causing her to gasp, and then she gulped down the rest.

"Thanks," she managed.

Casey leaned against the patio post and crossed his arms. He, too, was wearing mesh workout shorts and a tee. Only he was barefoot and his hair was messy from sleep.

"So, whatcha doin', Mom?"

"Working out." She pointed at another set of weights.

"I can see that," he said. "Question is, why?"

"I have to."

"You have to?"

"Yes. Hand me those will ya?"

He brought her the twenty-pound set of hand weights. "Don't you think you've had enough for one day?"

She grunted as she tried to lift one. She did three and dropped it. "Damn it." She stood on shaky legs.

"Why are you pushing yourself so hard?" Casey returned the weights to their holder. "You're killing yourself."

"I have to. I have to get it out. All this shit. I have to get it all out and I have to wake up my body. I have to wake up, come alive, and do better." She looked at her son who was staring at her full of concern. "If I don't I'll wallow until I die, Case. I'll just curl up in a ball and let the wind take me away. And I can't do that. You deserve better."

She opened the back door and entered the house with Casey close behind. They both sat at the kitchen table. And though she was worn out and spent, she felt alive and thriving for the first time in years. It gave her hope, and that was what she needed most. She smiled at Casey and covered his hand with her own.

"I'm going to be okay, son. I am."

He wiped away a tear and blew out a long breath. "It's just… I've been so worried since the cancer and now with Sasha—you really had me scared."

"I know and I feel awful about that. About all of it. But I'm going to pull myself out of this. I have to."

He nodded. "You want to work out together?"

"Sure."

"I work hard. I have to warn you. Crossfit got me ripped last summer, and I know all the tricks of the trade."

"Bring it on."

He laughed. "You'll regret saying that, you know." He rose and got them both another bottle of water. Hannah opened hers and sipped. She was chilled in the air-conditioned house and she needed to shower. But first she wanted to sit and enjoy the feeling of freedom she had, most notable in the twitch of her muscles. She felt good; she felt strong. And she felt loved. Her son was all she needed.

She smiled and patted his hand. "Let's make a schedule shall we?"

"Oh, yeah." He jumped up and grabbed the wall calendar. He was so excited and she couldn't help but warm at the sight of him so eager to work out with her. She'd kept him in the dark for too long, thinking she was protecting him. Well, no more. Things were about to change and she was starting with herself.

CHAPTER SIXTEEN

Sasha hung up the phone from yet another sponsor and looked at the date on her digital desk clock. It was only Thursday and she was exhausted. Her return to work had been brilliant, and for the most part she'd been very happy in being super busy again. She loved the hustle and bustle of the newsroom, and she thrived on adrenaline rushes like she'd get under tight deadlines. But she'd noticed that she didn't have anywhere close to the same stamina that she had had before. Now she had to close her office door and take breaks with her head down on her desk. She'd have to rehydrate and recharge with snacks. And by the end of the day, she was ready to be carried out to her Jeep. Others, too, seemed to notice, but they were very polite in the way they approached it.

A knock came from her door. It was Dennis, one of their new hires.

"You need anything before I take off? Coffee, soda, water?"

She smiled. "No, thanks, Dennis. But thanks for thinking of me." She suspected he had a little crush on her, and now that the department knew of her split from Hannah he'd been dropping by more and more. He was sweet in a teenage first love kind of way. The fact that she was a lesbian didn't seem to faze him.

"Sure thing. Oh, and I'll get those graphics to you first thing tomorrow."

"Wonderful."

He gave her a wave, hesitated, and then disappeared. She exhaled long and slow and debated staying late as she had done the previous two nights. She'd been back since Monday, and there was still a lot of work to catch up on. Her boss had stressed that she not bite off more than she could chew, and he'd assigned Dennis, Laura, and Katherine to be her right hands as she transitioned back. She'd originally protested, but he'd insisted and now she was glad he had.

The phone rang again, and she answered quickly despite it being well past six.

"Sasha Bashton."

"Hi, gorgeous. You ready for a fabulous night?"

She blinked, confused. "I'm sorry?"

She grinned, thinking one of the staff was playing a joke. She even stood to look through her office window for the culprit, but she could see no one.

"I thought I'd take you for a nice ride up to watch the sunset."

She sat and ran a hand through her hair. She was growing frustrated with the game. "Who is this?"

"What do you mean who is this? It's Charlie."

"Oh. Charlie, hi." She tried to cover. "I wasn't expecting to hear from you on this line."

"Well, I called your cell phone, but there was no answer. So I looked you up."

Sasha squirmed in her seat. She wasn't sure how she felt about that. It seemed a little intrusive. And aggressive.

"You didn't have to do that. I would've returned your call."

"I know. I just wanted to get a hold of you right away. So what do you say? How about that sunset?"

She turned in her chair to look out the window at the valley beyond. No doubt it was hot, but the clouds promised a smashing sunset. And she had been putting Charlie off. Partly because of work but also because she was a little anxious about the second date. Would everything completely go up in flames?

She decided she should put it off no more.

"Okay, let's do it."

What the hell she was doing she had no idea. But she was tired and feeling cooped up being in the office so much. She needed some fresh air, even if it was like a furnace blowing in her face.

"Great. I'm right out front."

"Out front?" Geez.

"Yes, I wanted to get you quickly."

"I'd say so. Can you pull into the parking garage and drive to the second floor elevator? I'm super exhausted."

"Sure. Meet you in a few."

They hung up and Sasha did her best to close everything down to leave the office. She almost grabbed her purse and satchel full of work to take home, but she decided she'd get them when she came back for her Jeep. She killed the lights, locked her office, and crossed to the elevator and exited to the parking garage. She heard Charlie's Indian before she saw it. The sound grumbled around the corner, and Charlie grinned wearing her helmet and aviator shades. She pulled to a stop in front of her.

"Hey, gorgeous. I was worried you were wearing a skirt."

"Nope." She glanced down at her slacks and flats. It wasn't the best motorcycle apparel, but at the moment she didn't care. She just needed to feel the wind in her face. Charlie handed over her helmet, and Sasha put it on like an old pro. Then she climbed onto the back of bike and hugged Charlie. She closed her eyes as they took off and concentrated on the feel of Charlie's muscles as they rippled beneath her tight fitting tee. The feel of her turned her on, and she felt her own body heat more than what the evening desert could cause. She hugged her tighter and wrapped her hands up and over her powerful shoulders. At stop lights she could smell her fresh ocean breeze scent, and it only made her heartbeat faster. By the time they reached the lookout on a nearby mountain, darkness was threatening and the sun had exploded with color. Charlie parked parallel to the sunset, switched off the engine, and turned around on her seat.

She took off her helmet and Sasha did the same. Charlie reached back and hung them from the handlebars.

"What do you think?" She swept her hand toward the sunset as if she'd painted the sky herself just for Sasha's enjoyment.

"Unbelievable," Sasha breathed.

When she looked back at Charlie she found her staring at her with obvious hunger. Sasha felt the desire, knew what she wanted, and she reacted before she could change her mind. Closing her eyes, she grabbed Charlie's face and planted a hot, firm kiss on her mouth.

She felt Charlie tense with surprise and then groan with delight. Charlie brought her closer and deepened the kiss. She teased with her tongue, seeking permission, and when Sasha welcomed her, she pushed into her with full force, causing Sasha to make a small noise herself.

Sasha clung to her as the velvet of their tongues danced and her body reacted. She began to thrust against the seat, her loins so hungry for touch, for caress, for release.

"Oh God," she mouthed quickly as Charlie attached to her neck. She raked her nails up and down Charlie's back. "Fuck," she whispered. "Take me. Take me, please."

Charlie pulled back to look into her eyes. She didn't ask if she was sure. She merely burned a hungry stare into her and then got busy unfastening Sasha's pants. Sasha looked around hurriedly, making sure there was no one nearby.

"Do people hike through here at this time?" she asked.

"I don't know. Probably not. Once it gets dark it's hard to see the trail." She undid her pants and scooted closer. Then she slid her palm down into her and Sasha jerked and groaned as she found her.

"I'm so wet," Sasha said, leaning forward to give her more access. She bit into her shoulder, and Charlie laughed and began to stroke her.

"Yes, you are."

"Oh fuck, it feels so good." She clenched her eyes and rode her hand, allowing the world to melt around her. She moaned and thrust, and when Charlie went up inside her she called out wildly and clung to her like a beast attacking a kill.

"You're so hot, Sasha. So hot and tight. Ride my fingers, baby. Yeah, just like that."

Sasha moved into her, crushing her hand, taking all she could, insisting, wanting, needing. Her mind exploded like the setting sun, and she thought of nothing and everything all at once. It only fueled her more, kept her dancing, going, fucking.

"I'm gonna come," she said, smothering her face in Charlie's neck. "Mm, God, I'm gonna come."

"Come, Sasha. Come on me, baby."

Sasha broke like a long swelling wave, cresting and crashing with ferocity. She screamed into the pink and black night and tore at Charlie's back like a mad woman. Charlie kept speaking, but she could not register the words; everything was muffled and melted into the strange canvas around her. Her body kept moving, drawing out as much as it could as if it were its own being. It fed like it was starved. And when she started to slow, her breath caught in her throat and she trembled. At last, she stilled and Charlie eased herself from her pants and held her hips. She was all grins and Sasha couldn't stand to look at her.

What was she so proud of? Did she think she was special?

Sasha hugged herself, feeling exposed.

"It was good," Charlie said.

"Are you asking or telling?"

Charlie laughed. "I don't know. Need I ask?"

Sasha glanced around, worried about hikers and other cars. A chill swept through her even though she felt like she could fall to the ground and sleep blissfully for years.

"I needed it, okay? It doesn't mean anything." She couldn't stand the grinning. How could she have let herself go like that?

"Okay."

Sasha closed her eyes and breathed deeply. "I'm sorry. I just feel…raw."

Charlie touched her face, causing her to open her eyes. "I get it."

"Do you?"

"Sure."

Charlie leaned in and kissed her lightly. But when she pressed for more, Sasha pulled back.

"I think I need to get home."

Charlie cocked her head. "Are we good?"

Sasha nodded. "Yes, I just need to be alone right now."

Charlie stared at her a moment longer and then turned back around on the bike. She handed Sasha her helmet and started the engine.

Sasha didn't hold her as tightly as she had on the way to the mountain. She held her as close as needed, and when she returned to her office she left Charlie without a kiss, grabbed her things, and drove home in a daze.

She hadn't known what to expect in coming at the hands of another woman. But it wasn't this. It wasn't this lost, exposed, and cranky feeling. It wasn't.

Would it get better? Would it be at the hands of yet another woman?

God, she didn't want to think about it. She didn't want to think about anything at all.

But Hannah's face came, and along with it a gut-eating guilt.

She drove home in tears.

Chapter Seventeen

Hannah popped U2 from her ears and slowed as she approached her driveway. The morning was fresh but she felt wilted in the heat. Sweat coated her body, and her legs trembled and throbbed. But the run was well worth the endorphins she was now experiencing. She punched in her garage code and ducked under the rising door. More stifling heat welcomed her, and she made a note to rise even earlier the next morning. Six o'clock just wasn't cutting it.

The house was a welcome wall of cold, and she paused in the kitchen to wipe her face and neck with her Nike towel. She grabbed an icy water bottle and sipped as she sank into a kitchen chair. She'd been running for over a week now, and her body was finally growing accustomed. She'd promised herself she'd give it five days before quitting from the pain and stress. But thankfully, her body had caught up and decided to play along. Now she couldn't imagine a morning without breathing in that chest clearing high.

She sipped more water and headed to the shower. Casey was no doubt still sleeping, and he'd passed on this morning's run, complaining about being up too late the night before. The price of being eighteen. Thankfully, Hannah was able to sleep some now, and she had a feeling it had to do with how hard she was pushing herself physically. The exercise also seemed to be helping her spirits. She was thinking more positively, even when it came to Sasha. She wanted her to be happy, and all she could do was be the best person she could be. The rest…she'd have to let it fall into place.

She showered quickly and dressed in khaki shorts and a light blue tee. She slid into her leather sandals and locked the door behind her as she entered the garage. She climbed in the truck, checked her watch, and drove quickly to the nearby coffee shop. To her surprise, the place was already crawling with people. What happened to sleeping in on a Saturday? She found a rare parking space and crossed the pavement to enter the shop. The strong scent of coffee smacked her in the face it was so rich. It made her want a cup all the more. But first she had to look for Mickey. She wove between tables and decided to sit. A quick check of her watch showed her she was early. Something she definitely wasn't used to.

"Are you early or late?" a woman at the next table asked. She flipped her auburn hair back over her shoulder and smiled. She gestured toward Hannah's watch.

"Oh. Early."

"Impressive. I'm early too. Always early. It sucks doesn't it? You always end up waiting."

Hannah smiled, unsure what to do. The woman was beautiful with dark hazel eyes and deeply painted lips. And she was staring at Hannah in a playful kind of way, letting her know the conversation was far from over.

"I'm usually late," Hannah confessed.

"Oh no. You're my pet peeve. Whatever shall we do?"

Hannah felt herself flush. The woman laughed. She stuck out her hand.

"Brandy."

"Hannah."

"Hello, Hannah. Habitually late Hannah. It's nice to meet you."

"You too."

The woman crossed her long legs and bobbed a sandaled foot. Her white shorts showed off her tan, and her linen blouse was loose, revealing a white tank top underneath. A sea tortoise charm rested on a necklace at the base of her throat.

"It's for protection," she said, catching Hannah's eye. She fingered the charm. "Got it in the Bahamas."

"It's nice."

"Thank you. My niece bought it for me. She thinks I need protecting."

Hannah nodded, wanting to know why, but she didn't push.

"She says I'm too friendly. Too trusting of strangers."

"Ah."

"I am, aren't I?" She laughed. "No need to answer. Your face says it all."

Hannah flushed again. "I'm not sure what to say."

"Say what to who?" Mickey asked, pulling out a chair to sit down. "You're early. What gives?"

Brandy laughed again.

"Nothing."

"Who's this?" Mickey asked.

"Brandy," she said and stuck out her hand again. "I was just having a conversation with your friend here."

"Really?" Mickey raised her eyebrow at Hannah, and Hannah wanted to smack her. "About what?"

"Oh, it's top secret. For us only."

"I see." Mickey was grinning.

"Why don't you go get the coffee?" Hannah asked Mickey. She couldn't bear to look at her.

"Good idea. I'll just go get the drinks." She stood and made her way to the counter. She knew what Hannah wanted. What Hannah always got. An iced chai latte.

"She's spunky," Brandy said. "But she's not yours."

"What? No."

"What a relief."

Hannah looked at her and found her eyes penetrating. "So, Hannah. When are you going to ask me out? Before your friend gets back or after?"

Hannah looked to Mickey who was giving her the thumbs up.

"Or are you going to tell me you are taken after all?"

"I'm—not taken."

"Good."

"I'm just—"

"Painfully shy?"

Hannah pushed out a held breath. "I'm just not sure I'm ready."

"I see. Well, how about I give you my number and you can take your time and decide?"

She rose from her chair and came to stand next to Hannah. She reached for her hand and tickled her palm with a pen. Then she gave it a squeeze and let go.

"I hope you call, Hannah. You seem to be something special."

She started to walk away.

"Aren't you going to wait for your friend?"

"Oh, I'm not waiting this morning. I'm just observing." She winked at her and walked out the door.

Mickey hurried back to the table and set down their drinks. "Who in the holy hell was that?"

"That was Brandy." Hannah stared off after her. What just happened? Did she just get hit on? She looked at her palm. Yes, she had.

"She wrote her number on your hand? Sexy. A little junior high but sexy nevertheless."

"She wants me to take my time and decide if I want to ask her out."

Mickey slapped the table. "That's what I'm talking about. Good people. I told you there were good women out there for you."

"You did not."

"Well, in a roundabout way I did. I found someone too that I'd like to introduce you to."

"No."

"You haven't even heard me out."

"Mick, I know you, and I know for a fact I will not like the woman you chose for me."

Her mouth fell open. "Take that back."

"I won't."

Mickey sipped her coffee and sighed. "You know, Hannah, sometimes you're a real pain in the ass."

"So I've heard. I'm still not meeting your woman."

She held up her hand. "Fine. Have it your way. But please tell me you're going to call Brandy and ask her out."

Hannah shrugged.

"Hannah."

"I'll think about it." She said it mainly so Mickey would get off her case, but deep down she did intend on thinking about it. Brandy was attractive and witty. She'd made her laugh as well as made her blush. Why shouldn't she give it a shot? She had nothing to lose at this point.

Could she really do it though? Ask out another woman? Could she fight off the fear and the guilt both?

She drank her chai tea latte and mulled it over. They say this was how these things happened. That you could literally just stumble into love when you least expected it. She'd never given credence to such beliefs, but then again she'd never had to.

"You're thinking too hard," Mickey said. "I can hear the old rusty cogs a turnin'."

"I'm just worried I'll ask her out and then not be able to follow through. Or that I'll clam up and be a dud. I haven't done this in a very long time, and my heart…is shattered. I don't even think it beats the same way it did before."

She spun her cup.

"If I do this, Mick. If I do this, will you swear to get off my case about dating? As in never say another word?"

Mickey leaned back and crossed her arms. "I don't know about never."

"Then I won't do it."

Mickey eyed her and chewed on her lower lip. "Okay. But only because I really do think this will be good for you."

"Shake on it." Hannah squeezed her hand.

"Great, now when are you going to call her? And where are you going to take her?"

Hannah stared at her drink. "That, I don't know."

"What about dinner?"

Hannah shook her head. Everything was making her think of Sasha.

"A movie?"

She shook her head again. Sasha.

"Okay, how about—"

"I'll know it when I see it," Hannah said. "For now, I've just got to work up enough guts to make the phone call."

Mickey nodded.

Hannah's knee bobbed up and down, and she couldn't seem to calm herself down. She tried to drink more of her latte, but the nerves only grew in size. She drummed her fingers on the table. Her mind spun. Sasha and Brandy swirling around together in a sick twister of sorts.

"I can't sit here any longer." She pushed away from the table and stood.

Mickey did as well, concern lining her face.

"What's wrong?"

"I just have too much on my mind. I need to take off."

"Okay, okay. I know the perfect place." She led her from the coffee house to their vehicles. "Follow me, my good friend. I'm about to make you feel a whole lot better."

Hannah collapsed onto her bed after spending nearly three hours with Mickey at the batting cages. Her arms felt like spaghetti, and the rest of her didn't feel all that much better. If she didn't have to move in the next few days, her life would be great.

"Mom?"

She didn't budge. "Yeah?"

"Did you work out without me?"

"No."

"Then why are you all sweaty? And you've been gone forever."

"Hit balls. With bats. Mickey."

"Oh. Mick, huh? I'm surprised you're not drunk."

"No. No drink. Not anymore."

She felt him sit on the bed. She desperately wanted to fall asleep, but she could tell by his tone that he wanted to talk.

"What's up?" she asked.

She felt him fidget.

"Case?"

He laughed but she heard the nerves. "I, uh, I've met someone."

She managed to lift her head. "Huh?"

"I've met someone, and I think it's time you meet her."

She pushed herself up. "Wait. When? Who?" Casey had dated off and on in high school, but he'd never come to talk to her about a girl before.

"We met at the community college. Her name is Abby."

"Oh."

But he wasn't finished. She could tell by the way his face was void of color. By the way he picked at the comforter. By the way he wouldn't look at her.

She waited.

He took a deep breath. "She thinks she might be pregnant."

Hannah choked on her own saliva. "Wha?"

Casey tried to smile. "It's not for sure yet, but I'm acting as if it is. Trying to prepare I guess. So I thought I'd better let you know about her before, you know, we find out."

Hannah coughed and slapped her own chest.

"Pregnant? Girlfriend? Casey, you didn't even tell me you were seeing someone."

He lifted a shoulder. "I know. I guess because at first it wasn't very serious. But then as time went on, we grew closer and saw each other more. I don't know, I guess I wanted my privacy?"

Hannah stared at him in disbelief. "Privacy? Are you kidding me? Casey I've never done anything to you to warrant you keeping things from me. Have I?"

"No. Not really. But you don't understand. This made me feel so grown up."

"Well, how grown up do you feel now?"

He hung his head and started to stand.

"Casey, I'm sorry. I'm just shocked. And I don't understand how it could happen. I taught you about protection, gave you condoms."

"We did use protection, Mom."

His concrete stare told her he was telling the truth. She wiped sweat from her face and stood.

"When will you know for sure?"

"When she tells me."

Hannah took a big breath and tried to calm her heart rate. To think, her baby boy, a father. It terrified her for him. "I need to take a shower. We'll talk about this later."

He stood as well. "There's nothing to talk about. It is what it is." He left her room and slammed the door behind him.

I did not handle that well.

She reached for her phone and began to dial. But then she stopped and tossed her phone on the bed. She was going on instinct. Wanting and needing to talk to the one person who would understand. She was about to call Sasha.

Chapter Eighteen

Sasha slowed and pulled along the sidewalk four houses down from Hannah's. She tugged down the bill of her ball cap and adjusted her shades. It was nearing six and most folks were returning from work. It really wasn't the best time to be incognito, but she had to know what Hannah was up to. Was she seeing anyone? Was anyone coming to the house?

It was a madness she could not explain. A madness she could not control. She had to know, and she'd been dying to know since her encounter with Charlie. She'd told no one about what happened up on that mountain, not even Bonnie. Nor was she planning to. It was something she'd keep to herself until she figured out exactly what she felt about it. And at the moment, no answers were forthcoming. She sank down lower in her seat as a car pulled into the driveway at Hannah's.

"Please don't be a woman, please don't be a woman."

Someone crawled from the sedan. A woman, average size with long dark hair. Sasha's breath hitched. She started her Jeep and crept up to the house slowly. She saw the woman ring the doorbell. Saw the door crack open and then she couldn't take it. She peeled out with tears in her eyes. She couldn't take seeing Hannah's face at the door. She couldn't take watching them hug or kiss.

She drove home so upset that she wasn't sure how she'd gotten there. She parked, bypassed Bonnie, and ran up to her room to collapse on the bed. Hannah had obviously moved on. Why was she surprised? She hadn't given Hannah any reason to stick around. She'd told her there was no hope, that she should get lost. But God, why did it hurt so badly? Why was she so confused?

Bonnie knocked on her door, but she shooed her away. She needed to be alone. She hugged her body pillow and cried into its softness. She cried until she fell asleep.

❖

Sasha awoke to someone gently sitting on her bed. A voice came, soft, persuasive.

"Sash?"

She blinked her eyes open. It was Bonnie.

"Hm?"

"There's someone here to see you."

She sat up. "Who?" Maybe Hannah had seen her Jeep. Maybe Hannah had come after her.

"Charlie."

"Charlie?"

Bonnie looked guilty and uncomfortable. "I tried to tell her you weren't up for being seen, but she insisted."

Sasha rubbed her face. She pushed out a breath in frustration. "Fine."

"Should I send her up?"

"No. I'll talk to her downstairs."

"Okay, I'll give you some privacy."

Sasha smoothed down her jean shorts and blouse, finger combed her hair, and headed downstairs. Charlie stood looking at photos in the living room, a huge bouquet of roses in her hands. When she heard Sasha approach, she turned and smiled.

"Hey, gorgeous." She crossed to her, kissed her cheek, and when Sasha turned away from her, she handed over the roses. "I thought you might like these."

Sasha took the massive bouquet. "Thank you." She had no idea where to put them. She hadn't received flowers from a woman in so long she was a little awkward with the whole process. Luckily, Bonnie came downstairs right behind her and swept them from her arms.

"I'll take care of these for you." She gave her a quick wink.

Sasha thanked her with her eyes.

"I hope you like them. A woman like you deserves roses every day of the week," Charlie said. She held Sasha's hands in hers. "Where have you been? I haven't heard from you since our bike ride to the mountain." She was speaking softly, obviously afraid of being overheard.

"I know. I just needed some time I think."

"Okay, you've had some time. How are you now? Will you please talk to me?"

Sasha hesitated. She wasn't sure what to say. She felt cornered. "I don't know, Charlie. This is all so new for me."

Charlie searched her eyes. "Will you let me take you out? I brought my Accord. We don't have to ride the bike. Let me take you out for some coffee or something."

But that was the last thing she wanted to do. She couldn't handle another waiter fiasco at the moment. "I don't think so."

"A movie then? We don't even have to talk. Just let me spend some time with you. Let me be there for you."

Sasha looked back toward the kitchen. She knew it wasn't going to be easy getting rid of Charlie, and the way she'd been feeling with Hannah and what she'd seen maybe it would be a good thing to get out and get her mind off of things.

She called out to Bonnie to let her know she was leaving. Then she allowed Charlie to lead her out the door.

She took one last look back and found Bonnie eyeing her with concern. She knew exactly how she felt for she was concerned about herself as well. She climbed into Charlie's Honda and tried to smile politely when Charlie wanted to hold her hand. She wasn't up for the contact, but she let it happen, hoping it would change her spirits.

To Charlie, it seemed to feed her ego, because she was all grins and bad humor the entire way to the theater. To her, it seemed funny to make fun of her coworkers or some poor man on the street corner holding a sign.

Sasha wanted to duck in her seat as Charlie began talking to the old man through closed windows.

"I'm not giving you anything. No, sir. I don't feel sorry for you, buddy. Get a job." She looked at Sasha for approval as if she'd actually agree with her. "Can you believe these people?" She hit the gas and sped through the green light, leaving the man far behind.

Sasha released her hand and pretended to cough. She broached the subject carefully, unable to hold her tongue.

"How do you know he doesn't really need help?"

Charlie raised her eyebrows at her. "Help? A handout is what he wants."

Sasha steeled her jaw. "He may really be sick and down on his luck."

"Oh, don't tell me you fall victim to those people? Sasha, come on. You're sick but you don't go begging for money from strangers."

"No, but that's because I'm lucky. I have friends. I have family. Bonnie for instance. She's allowing me to stay with her. And Hannah—"

Charlie burned a look at her. "Hannah. Of course she's probably an angel. Let me guess…she would give him money."

"No." But she would talk to him. Find out his story. Offer him a ride to somewhere he could get help. Or she'd go get him a meal. But Sasha didn't voice any of that. The realization just made her sad.

"At least some people have good sense," Charlie said.

"Some people don't have anyone," Sasha said softly.

Charlie shook her head. "Probably their own fault then. Addiction. Probably ran their family off."

Sasha turned on her. "How can you be so—"

But she closed her mouth. She did not want to get into it with Charlie. They were supposed to be having a good time.

"So what?"

"Nevermind."

They hit a red light and Charlie looked over at her. "No, I want to know."

"Listen, let's just drop it okay? I want to have a good time and forget my day."

Charlie tapped her hand on the steering wheel as if thinking it over. Then she reached over and grabbed her hand again.

"Okay." She squeezed her hand. "I'm sorry you had a bad day."

Sasha shook her head. "It wasn't awful. I just…realized some things I'd rather forget." Like the woman at Hannah's house. Who was she? How long had she been seeing her?

It was a whole new obsession now and she had to make it stop. She squeezed Charlie's hand in return.

"What are we seeing?"

Charlie grinned. "It's a surprise."

"Oh God, I hate surprises."

"Well, you'll learn to like them. Especially this one. It's a new action movie. Supposed to have kick-ass special effects."

Sasha tried to smile, but the confession disappointed her. She wasn't a big fan of action movies. But she swallowed her pride and decided to give it a chance. Maybe the explosions and craziness would take her mind off Hannah and the mysterious woman.

They parked what seemed like a mile away from the theater. Sasha almost asked to be dropped off because she was still somewhat weak, but she figured with Charlie being a nurse, she'd know her limits.

By the time they sat with their popcorn and drinks, Sasha was exhausted. She tried to control her heart rate and her breathing, but it took a few minutes before she felt any relief. Charlie, however, didn't seem to notice, and when Sasha went to sip her drink Charlie stopped her.

"You have to wait for the movie to start!"

Sasha stared, totally confused.

"It's the rule. Otherwise you'll be left with nothing by the time the movie begins." She laughed and nudged her, and it dawned on Sasha that she was being playful. But she was too tired to carry on. She sat and stared at the advertisements, wanting nothing more than a drink of her water. And when the lights dimmed, she nearly inhaled it and pushed her popcorn away. Suddenly, she wasn't hungry, and when Charlie finished her own popcorn she happily took hers. Soon Sasha was leaning into her falling asleep, and Charlie seemed to enjoy it, wrapping her arm around her and allowing her to settle.

Somehow Sasha slept through the movie, even between body shaking laughter and brief squeezes of, "Hey, did you see that?"

When it was over Sasha walked zombie like back out to the car and rode home listening to Charlie go on about the film. She struggled to keep her eyes open to pay attention. She kept leaning into the door and jerking awake. Her senses were dead and her mind mush. And she realized that even though the night hadn't been one to write home about, it had served its purpose. She was now too tired to think much about anything.

CHAPTER NINETEEN

Hannah stood at the kitchen counter and stared in disbelief. The note in her hand shook as she read it over and over again.

"Dear Mom, the test is positive. She's pregnant," Hannah read aloud. She thought about crumpling the paper up in a fury, but she knew it wouldn't change anything. So she left it sitting where she'd found it and walked over to collapse on the couch. The Diamondbacks were playing, but she didn't bother to turn on the television. Her mind was afire with the thought of Casey being a father and her being a grandmother. It seemed impossible. Unfathomable. And yet here it was, smacking her in the face, forcing her to accept it.

No tears came, and she didn't curse and carry on. The shock was too great. Too overwhelming. She had to think. She and Casey had to think. To plan. To somehow figure this out. The young woman too. They all needed to sit and figure things out.

She eyed her watch. Casey wasn't due home until after nine. That left her five hours of doing nothing but stewing in the news. She'd drive herself crazy. Mickey. Where was Mickey? She called her and waited. She picked up just before the voice mail.

"Hannah, what's up?"

Hannah palmed her forehead. "Um, Casey is going to be a father that's what's up."

Mickey was quiet for a long moment. "Congratulations? I don't know what to say."

"Neither do I. Something in me was hoping you would."

"Sorry, pal. I got nothing. Are they sure?"

"The note sounded like they are sure."

"What's she like? Your soon to be daughter-in-law?"

"Shut up." Casey hadn't mentioned marriage, but she now knew he didn't always mention what was going on in his life.

"Seriously, what's she like?"

"Abby? She seems okay. She's sweet. Levelheaded. Quieter than Casey, but then again most people are." She'd liked Abby well enough. Just not enough for her to be pregnant and having her son's child. Ten years from now, sure. But now?

"I'm going nuts over here, Mick, and if I lift one more weight today or go for one more run I think my body is going to protest by crumpling up and evaporating. You'll never see me again. I'll be gone with the wind."

Mickey laughed. "Sounds serious. I'll tell you what. Why don't you call that Brandy girl of yours and ask her out tonight? We can double. I can hold your hand so to speak."

"Double-date?"

"Sure, why not? Couples still do that."

"Who are you bringing?"

"Someone from softball. Her name's Faith. She's a riot. I've been wanting to ask her out for a while, but she'd been seeing someone else. Now it's all me, baby."

Hannah wanted to roll her eyes, but she was too tired. She needed to expend as little energy as possible this evening or she'd crash and no doubt have nightmares about a baby and bills and Casey being consumed by it all.

"Yeah, sure. I'll do it. Why not?" Why the hell not? It beat sitting there.

"Meet us at Barro's at six. She wants to watch the D-backs game. Can I pick them or what?"

"That doesn't give me much time."

"It'll be enough. Besides I think Brandy will be game for anything with you. See you soon."

She ended the call and Hannah was left sitting there staring down at her phone. She had to call Brandy now. Luckily, she'd put her number in her phone as soon as she'd arrived home from the coffee shop at the behest of Mickey. Now she was glad she had.

She pressed call and waited with bated breath. Would she answer? If so would she remember her? Oh God, what if she didn't? Or what if she said no?

"Hello," a friendly voice answered.

"Hi, is this Brandy?"

"Well, now that depends. Are you selling something? Or taking a survey? Or wanting money of any sort?"

"No, I—"

"Then yes, this is Brandy. Who is this?"

"This is Hannah. We met the other day at the—"

"Hannah from the coffee shop. Of course. I was hoping I'd hear from you."

Hannah could hear the smile in her voice. It caused her to smile.

"You were? I mean that's great. I, uh, was wondering if you would like to go out tonight?"

"Tonight?"

"Yeah as in like an hour?" She winced as she said it. "It would be a double date. We're going to watch the Diamondback game over pizza."

"I don't really do sports," she said. "But I'll do anything to see you again."

Hannah fought off a flush, and she pushed away the part about not caring for sports. She'd said yes and that was all that mattered.

"Okay. Good. Should I pick you up or meet you there?"

"I can meet you there."

Hannah relayed the address and ended the call with Brandy mentioning that she couldn't wait to see her. The words left Hannah smiling, and she hurried into the bedroom for a quick shower and spray of cologne. But she immediately wiped it off because it was what she'd always worn and it reminded her of Sasha, who loved it.

Instead, she found a small bottle that had been a Christmas gift from Casey a couple of years before. She sprayed that on, then dressed in jeans, a button-down, and ankle boots and hurried out to her truck. She tried to calm down, to slow her breathing, but she was keyed up. She drummed the steering wheel, and the slow song on the radio drove her nuts. After the first stoplight she realized she was going to arrive too early so she slowed and forced herself to drive along nicely, calmly. The whole time she was gritting her teeth and humming a tune she didn't even recognize. When she finally arrived she pulled in a parking space and saw Brandy walking in wearing shorts and a flowy peasant blouse. Her long hair was pulled back in a ponytail, and she had a long leather purse swung over her shoulder.

She looked amazing.

Hannah turned up the radio, hoping to drown out her anxiety. If she went in now it would be just the two of them. Should she go? Should she wait?

Her thoughts went back to Mickey and how she'd said she would hold her hand.

She didn't like that.

"Ah, fuck it." She killed her engine and climbed from the truck to go inside.

CHAPTER TWENTY

Hannah entered quietly and found Brandy filling a drink at the soda fountain. She seemed calm and casual, and Hannah was at once envious. Hannah took a deep breath, sank her hands in her pockets, and approached.

"Hi."

Brandy looked over and smiled. "Hey, you. Long time no see." She stepped into Hannah and kissed her on the cheek. Hannah smelled her musky perfume and her heart flipped.

"Do you want to get a drink? I didn't know if you guys were having beer or not. I assumed you were, so I got myself a soda."

Hannah looked out the floor-to-ceiling windows. No sign of Mickey.

"I'll just sit with you for now."

Hannah gestured for Brandy to lead the way, and she chose a table near the large flat-screen hanging in the corner.

"This good?"

"Yes."

Brandy waited for Hannah to sit and she slid in across from her.

"Hope you don't mind, but I want to see your face." She sipped her Diet Coke with mauve lips. She winked.

"It's fine," Hannah said. She rubbed her palms on her jeans. "I—I'm a bit nervous," she confessed, unable to think of anything else to say. "I haven't done this in about sixteen years."

"Really?" But then her eyes clouded. "You've been in a relationship haven't you?"

"Yes."

"Can I ask how long it's been since you broke up?"

"We've been separated for about three months now."

Brandy played with her straw. "That's not too bad I guess." She looked at her. "I just don't want to get hurt, you know. I've been there, done that with the whole rebound thing. It's not for me."

Hannah looked down at her hands. "I don't plan on hurting anyone. But I can't honestly tell you that I'm okay inside. I've got a lot going on as far as healing myself, and I don't think that will end anytime soon."

Brandy took another short sip of her drink. "At least you're being honest."

"Yes. Which is why you might want to remain friends. Because honestly, I can't promise you anything. I don't know where I'm headed as far as love goes. Does that make sense?"

"Sure. It sounds like we all do after a breakup. But most of us don't voice it. We just jump back into another relationship hoping it will solve everything."

"Yeah, that's not me. I'm old-fashioned, I guess you'd say. I hope you don't think I've wasted your time."

"Oh no, definitely not. I kind of like you, Hannah. You're honest and adorable. I'd love to get to know you."

Hannah smiled and then nearly jumped out of her skin as a firm hand clamped down on her shoulder.

"Hannah, you beat me here. What's up with you suddenly arriving early to things?" Mickey rounded the table and sat next to Brandy. "M'lady." She gently took her hand and then stood as her own date arrived. "There she is. Ms. Faith. My very lovely date." She stepped over to kiss her softly on the mouth.

It was intimate and something Hannah wasn't ready to see, so she looked away. Brandy, however, was watching intently and grinning. When she looked at Hannah she winked slowly and reached across to pat her hand.

Hannah registered the heat from her touch, but she didn't draw her hand back. She left it there, and Brandy gave her a squeeze and retrieved her hand, letting Hannah off the hook. Hannah was grateful she did so because she felt like she was about to burst into flames, she was blushing so badly.

Mickey took one look at her and mouthed something to her. Hannah didn't understand, and Mickey waved her off and took care of the introductions. Faith was friendly and all giggles and petite muscles. Hannah pegged her for a catcher and found out she was right. Brandy greeted everyone with polite smiles and handshakes. She made a crack about already having drunk all the beer. Mickey laughed, asked everyone what kind of pizza they wanted, and then motioned for Hannah to follow her so they could order.

When they were out of earshot, Mickey started in. "So? How's it going? You were so red back there I thought I'd have to put you out with a fire extinguisher."

Hannah felt her face. It was still hot.

"It's going…well. I was honest with her about my situation and we agreed to just get to know each other."

"Wait, what situation?"

"My relationship situation. You know, my breakup and what the future may or may not hold?"

Mickey slapped her head and turned her ball cap backward. "No, no, no, say you didn't."

"I did."

"Hannah, what the hell? You trying to scare her off? Don't ever talk about your ex unless you're sure you know you're over her."

"I need her to know the truth, Mick. I'm not going to play games with her just because I'm still healing."

Mickey shook her head and then ordered a large pepperoni and two salads for their dates. Then she ordered two pitchers of Miller Lite.

"You want wings?" she asked.

Hannah shook her head and dug out her wallet. She and Mick split the bill, took their order number, and returned to their seats.

Their dates were happily conversing.

Brandy spoke up. "So it seems that we are all on first dates here."

"That would be right," Mickey said. "I met Faith on the softball field. Her team clobbered us, but I really didn't seem to mind. My eyes and thoughts were always on her."

Faith nudged her and they kissed again. Mickey wasted no time in putting on the moves. She'd always done so. But it made Hannah feel uncomfortable, like she was supposed to do something with Brandy. It made for an awkward silence.

Brandy leaned across the table. "Don't worry. I don't kiss on the first date."

Hannah laughed.

"You were worried," Brandy said.

"Maybe a little."

"More than a little. I thought you were going to pass out."

"Hannah tends to be a little anxious about some things," Mickey said. "So, be gentle."

The three of them laughed, and Hannah buried her hands in her hair. So far so good. She'd been thoroughly embarrassed within the first half hour. Good times.

"Come on, Hannah. I'm just messing with you. I promise nothing more will be said at your expense. Now, how about a beer? The game's gonna start."

Hannah took her full cup and sipped lightly. It felt like heaven against her parched throat. The flavor wasn't bad either. She smiled at Brandy who was watching her closely.

"So are you a D-backs fan?"

"Absolutely."

Brandy politely declined the beer Mickey tried to offer her. Meanwhile Faith downed half her cup and clapped as the game began. A few other patrons looked their way but then returned to the game and their pizza. Hannah was surprised it wasn't more crowded. But then again the D-backs were down in the series and it was a Tuesday night. Most folks were home with their families.

Her stomach tightened at the thought, and she forced a smile and pushed it away. She sipped her beer which was her first in a while. She'd promised herself she wouldn't use it to escape anymore, and she planned on keeping that promise. So she finished her cup and then rose to buy herself a soda cup. Mickey watched her curiously from across the restaurant.

Hannah hoped she wouldn't bring it up, but Mickey didn't know the meaning of manners or keeping things private. So Hannah steeled herself as she sat down with her Dr Pepper.

"You're not going to help us drink the beer?" Mickey asked.

Hannah fought cringing. "Not tonight. I've got a long day tomorrow."

Mickey raised an eyebrow. "You're really serious about this no drinking kick aren't you?"

Hannah wanted to kick her under the table, but she was afraid Brandy would notice.

"For the time being, yes." Hannah met Brandy's gaze and found unasked questions. Hannah changed the subject.

"So, you said you aren't into sports very much. What do you do for fun?"

"I'm not so much into mainstream sports, no. But I do lots of other things."

"Such as?" Mickey asked.

"I rock climb almost every weekend. I have a large group of friends who climb, and we travel to all kinds of places."

"Wow," Faith said. "Sounds like fun."

"Oh, it is. It's such a rush when you conquer that rock. You should try it sometime." She looked at Hannah. "What about you, Hannah? You think you would ever give it a shot?"

Hannah squirmed a little. "I don't know. I'm not very good with heights."

"I promise I'll take good care of you," Brandy said. "We could start slow. I'm a great teacher."

Hannah wasn't sure how to respond. She wanted to be polite and adventurous, but she was uncomfortable with even the mere thought of climbing something.

"We'll see," she said.

"That means good luck getting my ass to do it," Mickey said.

Hannah gave her a look, and Mickey held up her hands. "I'm just telling her the truth."

But Brandy didn't seem to be fazed. "I don't know. Something tells me I might be able to persuade her."

"Good luck," Mickey said.

"Well, I want to do it," Faith said.

Brandy lit up. "Wonderful. Maybe we should all make a date of it sometime."

"Yeah," Faith said, looking to Mickey. "You'll do it, won't you, Mick?"

"Hey, I'm game for just about anything." They kissed quickly and grinned at each other.

Hannah still wanted to kick her. Instead she tried to focus on the game, but not much was happening. Brandy watched as well, but she seemed bored, leaning on her hand.

Hannah didn't like how the evening was panning out. Thanks to Mick she came off as a chickenshit who wasn't willing to try things, and Brandy seemed to be bored with the game. Hannah knew she should do something; after all, she was all about change and bettering herself. So she did the only thing she could think of.

"I'll do it," she said, causing everyone to look at her. "I'll go rock climbing."

Brandy lit up and Faith clapped and cheered. Mickey grinned at her in a devilish way, and a waiter brought their food. Hannah felt fluttering in her chest at what she'd just agreed to, but no one seemed to notice her nerves. So she spent the evening eating and talking and making plans with Brandy.

She considered everything that had been bothering her lately. Sasha, Charlie, and now Casey and his pregnant girlfriend. She let them go and concentrated on rock climbing. It was nice to have something else to worry about for a change.

Chapter Twenty-one

Sasha sat behind her desk with her office door closed. Her knee was shaking with nerves, but she smiled into the phone as if her client could see her. She promised she'd have details for them soon and even threw in the promise of lunch just to get them off the phone. The move was very much unlike her. She usually poured the sugar on thick with potential sponsors, but today was different.

Today she felt like hell. Very near to what she'd felt the night she'd been rushed to the hospital. She'd been feeling a little low on energy the past few days, more so than usual. But she blamed her crazy hours and her stress over Charlie. But now, now it was not good and it could not be ignored.

She slipped off her heels and eyed her swollen feet and ankles. Her muscles were so stiff and achy she didn't want to stand.

"Shit."

She was due to see her nephrologist in mere days. She just had to get her labs done first.

Sighing, she called Bonnie. She was going to need help getting out of there without causing anyone alarm. Her knee continued to shake as Bonnie's line went to voice mail. She left a message but wasn't hopeful. If Bonnie didn't answer, it meant she was truly busy. She stared at her phone and considered her options. She didn't have many. Not everyone could just up and leave work. Like Charlie for instance. It would be a miracle if she was available. And truthfully, she really didn't want her coming to her office. The last thing she needed was Charlie saying something rude to her colleagues, or worse, her boss. But she felt she had little choice. She pressed the button on her cell phone and called her. It, too, went to voice mail. She left no message.

"Shit," she said again. She rubbed her face and considered Casey, but she knew he was at school. And did she really want to get him involved? She knew he'd do anything for her, but it would only cause him to ask questions he shouldn't be asking. She didn't want to put him in that position.

"Come on, come on, think, damn it." She scanned her contacts and stopped when she came to Hannah. There was a chance she'd be home. She sat back in her chair. Should she? Hannah would help, yes. But how would that go? Sasha considered the possibility of a new woman in Hannah's life, and she made up her mind.

She called.

Hannah answered on the third ring.

"Sash? What is it? What's wrong?"

Sasha fought for words, the concern overwhelming her. "I'm fine. I'm okay."

"Oh, thank God."

Sasha bit her lower lip. "Actually, that's not totally true. I need your help."

"What's going on? Are you sick?"

"Yes."

Hannah started rambling, and Sasha had to calm her down. "I'm still at work. I'm not throwing up or running a fever that I know of. But something is definitely wrong."

"Okay. What can I do?"

"I need you to come and get me. And take me to get my labs done."

"Okay, I can do that."

"I need to keep it a low profile though. I don't want to freak out anyone here."

"Got it. I'll just say I'm swinging by to take you to lunch."

Sasha hesitated. "They know we broke up."

"So? We can't have lunch?"

"You're right. I'm being ridiculous. How soon can you get here?"

"I'll be there in ten. I'm not far away."

"Great. And, Hannah? Thanks."

Sasha ended the call and gathered her things. Then she called her colleagues and told them she was going to lunch and then going to the doctor for some routine lab work. She was relieved when no one protested or asked anything further. She stood to open her door, but Dennis beat her to it, knocking as he opened it.

"Hey," he said.

"Dennis, hello."

"I hear you're taking off."

"Mm-hm."

"Are you okay?" His baby blue eyes seemed to penetrate her. She looked away.

"Yes, I'm fine."

He rubbed the back of his neck. "It's just that, I noticed your ankles are swollen today. I was afraid something might be wrong.

Sasha collapsed into her chair. "I see."

"I'm sorry. I shouldn't have said that. I respect your privacy, I do, but I'm a little worried. Are you sure you're okay?"

Sasha thought briefly about telling him, about spilling the beans and letting it all out. But she was his superior and he was very young. He also probably had a serious crush. Three things that kept her mouth shut.

"I appreciate your concern, I do. It's very kind. But I'm fine. I'm just waiting for Hannah to pick me up. We're on our way to lunch."

His face clouded and he tried to cover quickly with a smile. But she saw right through it.

"Oh, Hannah. How—nice."

"It is nice." She continued to straighten her desk.

"I didn't know you two were—"

"We're friends, Dennis."

"Oh. Well, good. It's good to have friends." He turned to leave, and she held her breath, hoping he would indeed do so. But he turned at the door.

"If you need anything, you know where to find me." He gave a half smile and tapped the doorframe. Then he left.

Sasha exhaled and tried to relax in her chair. She closed her eyes for what felt like mere minutes, but when she opened them she saw Hannah knocking at her open door.

"You ready?"

"Hannah, thank God—" She stared, unable not to. Hannah had on a black tee and white jeans. Tight, white jeans. It seemed as if every muscle on her body was accentuated. Every single muscle. Sasha glanced away, hoping Hannah didn't notice the lingering look. "We have to go. Dennis is lurking and he's suspicious."

"Suspicious of what?"

"Of my being ill."

"Isn't that nice that he cares?"

"No. He smothers me. And he'll tell everyone and make it more dramatic than it is."

"Oh." Hannah looked behind her. "Coast is clear."

Sasha grabbed her purse and leather satchel. Hannah took them from her immediately.

"Don't even think about arguing," Hannah said. She crossed to the doorway, checked both ways, and then motioned for Sasha to move.

Sasha followed her carefully with her high heels dangling from her fingers They passed a few colleagues who seemed surprised to see Hannah. Thankfully, that distraction kept them from focusing on Sasha. Hannah was polite, giving nods and a couple of handshakes.

Sasha had to explain they were just going to lunch. But a few had raised eyebrows and one even commented on it being a first step. Sasha laughed it off, but on the inside she was a wreck already with not feeling well and her physical reaction to seeing Hannah once again.

Somehow they made it to the elevator without too much interference. They were alone and Sasha could smell Hannah's cologne and her heart fell. It was a scent she did not recognize. She wondered if Hannah bought it for the woman she was seeing.

"You doing all right?" Hannah asked softly.

Sasha nodded. She was short of breath.

"You really don't look well. I'm worried." Hannah motioned for her to exit the elevator first. Then she walked next to her nice and slowly to the parking lot.

"Wait here," Hannah said. "I'll get the car." She jogged off and Sasha thought about Charlie and how she'd probably make her walk to the car. She wondered if she would've even tried to help carry her belongings. Surely she would've. Especially if she knew she wasn't feeling well.

Sasha didn't want to think about it. Thanks to Hannah moving quickly, she didn't have to. Hannah pulled her truck up, slammed it in park, and rushed out to open the door for Sasha. Then she took her hand and helped her to the car.

"Do you want to rest in the back?"

"No, front is fine."

Hannah eased her in the truck and gently closed the door. Then she rounded the hood and crawled behind the wheel.

"Where to?"

"My nephrologist."

"Got it."

Sasha rested her head on the seat and tried to close her eyes. But the motion of the truck moving made her feel nauseous.

"I really appreciate you doing this," Sasha said.

"I'm glad I could help."

"How have you been?" Sasha asked.

"I've been okay. Trying to stay busy. Casey and I have been on a pretty hardcore workout regimen."

"I can tell." Sasha clamped her mouth shut. "I mean you look good. You look healthy." She rolled her eyes at herself.

Hannah didn't seem to notice her struggle to say the right thing. "Thanks. It's been hard work, but I feel so damn good I don't want to stop."

Sasha studied her. Who was this Hannah? This happy, healthy Hannah who enjoyed intense exercise? What the hell was happening?

"That's great. I'm happy for you."

"Well, you know how down I was after my surgery. I just kind of turned into a slug. I decided that needed changing or I wasn't going to make it."

Sasha didn't ask what she meant by that. Though she was concerned, she didn't think it was her right anymore to ask such personal questions. So she let it go.

"I would ask how you are, but it seems pretty obvious."

"Actually, I was doing pretty good. I mean I was still struggling with my energy and stamina, but I wasn't like this. I wasn't sick."

Hannah looked over at her. "What happened? Anything change?"

"No, nothing. I don't know what the hell is wrong."

"We'll find out. Hang in there." Hannah turned on her signal and pulled into the doctor's office.

"You don't have to come in," Sasha said.

"I want to help you in, if that's okay?" Sasha saw the sincerity in her eyes. She was genuinely worried.

"Okay."

Hannah rounded the truck and helped her inside the doctor's office. Sasha checked in for her labs and then turned to sit. But Hannah came to stand next to her, and she spoke to the woman behind the counter.

"Did she tell you how sick she is right now? Is there any way she can go right back or at least go back in a room and lie down while she waits?"

The woman looked to Sasha and Sasha explained her symptoms.

"I'll be right back," the woman said.

Sasha leaned on the counter and grabbed her head. She felt like complete shit. She prayed she wouldn't end up in the hospital. "You didn't have to do that, Hannah, but I appreciate it."

"Yeah, well, I didn't do it enough while we were together. And there's no time like the present."

"You've changed," Sasha whispered, mostly to herself. But Hannah heard her.

"I'm bettering myself. At least I'm trying to anyway."

"You are."

Sasha's name was called from the patient entryway. Hannah made sure she made it back to the lab room, then she left her. Sasha sat in the elevated seat and rested her arm on the swinging edge. She closed her eyes as a young man took her blood and then showed her where the restroom was to leave a urine sample. On the way out, she double-checked her appointment for the following week and returned to Hannah. She didn't feel any better physically, but she was relieved she'd given labs. At least now her doctor could see what was going on.

Hannah helped her back into the truck. She'd brought it around to the front and had the air on. It was pushing one hundred thirteen degrees, and Sasha was more than grateful.

"Thanks so much for bringing the truck around and starting it."

Hannah pulled out of the parking lot. "No problem."

Sasha tried to relax into the seat. But she was uncomfortable any way she moved.

"What can I do for you?" Hannah asked. "Are you hungry?"

"God no."

"Thirsty?"

"Yes."

"Say no more." Hannah pulled into a drive-through and ordered two large ice waters. Sasha had barely thanked her before she took her first miraculous sip. It was difficult not to drink it quickly, but she didn't want to shock her system.

"What are you going to do about work?" Hannah asked.

"I don't know. I guess I'll see how I feel tomorrow."

"You always do better after you sleep. Early mornings are your best time. Maybe you should just go in for a half day."

Sasha looked at her. "You remember all that?"

Hannah met her gaze. "Of course I do. We may be apart, Sasha but I haven't forgotten you or our lengthy past. I couldn't even if I wanted to."

Sasha's throat tightened. "Yeah, I know what you mean."

They rode in silence the rest of the way to Bonnie's. Hannah pulled in the drive and helped her in the house by carrying her things. She even helped her upstairs and into bed. Sasha's eyes threatened to close so she spoke as quickly as she could.

"It was good seeing you, Hannah."

Hannah sat beside her and held her hand. "You too, Sash."

Sasha focused on her face and then let her eyes remain closed. "I miss you."

She wasn't aware of any response.

CHAPTER TWENTY-TWO

Hannah tossed and turned in bed. Each time she finally settled, Sasha's words replayed in her mind.

I miss you.

She couldn't escape the words. Had Sasha really meant them so sincerely? Or was she so tired she probably wouldn't even remember having said them? Either way, they'd been said, and the way they had been together had been good. So good. Like a baseball in a well oiled glove, they fit. An analogy Brandy would not understand.

Hannah grew frustrated and sat up. Brandy. She had been calling, and Hannah had been avoiding her since she'd seen Sasha. It was so clear to her that Brandy wasn't who she wanted, and she knew she'd tried to make sure they were only friends, but people were human and they had wants and desires, despite being told no.

She could remember being younger and falling for a woman who only wanted to be friends. She'd agreed only to get a chance to be around her, hoping that something would somehow change. But when it didn't, she was completely heartbroken. It had been the first time she'd cried over a woman.

She crawled from bed and headed for the shower. She should probably end things with Brandy before it got bad. Because she knew Brandy liked her and it could never end well. But Mickey was so excited she'd made a new friend so they could have double dates and do things together. And she had promised to try rock climbing.

She sighed as she stepped into the shower and allowed the lukewarm water to slosh down her skin. She soaped herself and admired the work she'd done so far on her body. She was not only firm and tight, she was pushing built. She felt stronger than she ever had, yet she was still so confused inside.

She wished Sasha was the worst of her worries, but she no longer was. Now it was Casey and his girlfriend. She'd thought about telling Sasha about the situation, but she figured she had enough to worry about. Besides, they weren't exactly close anymore or discussing anything very personal. She didn't even know if she'd see her again.

Frowning, Hannah exited the shower and dressed. It was early morning and she knew Casey would be up soon to work out. She was proud of him for sticking with it, but this morning they needed to work their minds, not their bodies.

She walked to the kitchen and started the coffee. Then she took a mug down the hall to his room. The door was slightly askew, and she entered quietly. It still smelled the same as it had since his high school days. Like cologne and shoes. She sat at his bedside and shook him awake. He rolled over with his arm over his head.

"What? What is it?"

"Get up, cowboy. We need to talk."

He pushed himself up on his elbows. His hair was sticking up on one side and his cheeks were ruddy from sleep.

"Huh?"

"Here, have a few sips and get dressed. Join me in the living room."

She left him to return to the kitchen where she poured her own cup of coffee and sat on the couch. She crossed her legs and looked out the window. The family of jackrabbits that often visited their yard was moving about near their large palo verde. She watched them for a little while and recalled how one spring Sasha and Casey had nursed three abandoned babies back to health.

Casey had been so excited to help and Sasha had been so kind and patient. The babies had thrived and moved on to live their lives. Casey had cried and Sasha had explained to him that they had to go make their own families now.

Casey entered the room and sat on the cushioned chair across from her. He groaned, put his feet up on the ottoman, and slurped his coffee. His bony feet looked huge sticking out from his flannel sleep pants. He hadn't bothered with a shirt.

"So what's going on, Mom?" he asked.

She looked out the window again. The rabbits were gone.

"I wanted to talk to you about your girlfriend. And the baby."

He pushed out a breath. "Yeah, well, there's nothing to say. She broke up with me."

Hannah reared back. "She broke up with you? When? Why?"

"She said she wanted to handle things on her own. That she didn't need a man. Specifically, me."

"Well, what about the baby?"

"She says she may not have it."

Hannah's stomach lurched. "How do you feel about that?"

He pinched the bridge of his nose. "How do you think I feel? I'm fucked up over it. I tried to talk her into keeping it. I tried to tell her she wasn't alone, that I would be there. But she doesn't believe me." He breathed heavily and then wiped a tear. "I have to convince her, Mom. I have to."

"You want the baby?" she asked softly.

His breath hitched. "Yes."

She nodded.

"I thought everything was okay. I thought we all connected, wanting and planning for the same thing."

"I thought so too. She seemed to like you. She said she loved me. She said she wanted us to be a family. Hell, I wasn't even pushing for marriage, Mom. I was willing to let her breathe and not be so overwhelmed so soon. She just freaked out. Went off on me."

"She's scared, Case. Really scared. Maybe you not offering to marry her frightened her. Maybe that's why she thinks you will leave her."

He sat forward. "But I would marry her. I really would."

"Are you sure? It's an awful big step to take so young."

"She's having a baby," he said. "We're a little late on being too young for things. That ship's kind of sailed."

She looked back out the window again. "Remember when you found those baby bunnies in the flower pot when you were little?"

He closed his eyes and took a breath. "Yeah. Sasha showed me how to bottle feed them. How to care for them. I did a pretty good job."

"You did. You took care of them right up until they were ready to go."

"I cried," he said. "Cried like a baby."

"But you did it. You did the right thing. You were strong even though you didn't feel like it."

"Yeah."

"Casey, you've always been strong. Often times even stronger than me. And you've always done the right thing. That's why I know this will work out. You'll follow your heart and do what needs to be done and it will work out the way it's meant to be."

"Think so?"

"I know so, son. I just think you need to go have a heart to heart with her. Do whatever it takes. If you love her."

He studied her for a long moment. "That's good advice, Mom."

"It is. I've learned a lot these last few months. Hopefully, you'll be able to profit from it. I think it's a little too late for me."

They both sipped their coffee and looked out the window. A hummingbird was at the back patio feeder.

"I love her, Mom. Like you love Sasha."

"Then give it all you got, Case. Give it all you got."

He rose and leaned down to kiss her cheek. Then he disappeared back into his bedroom. Soon she heard the shower start, and she saw the family of rabbits return. She left her coffee mug and stepped out onto the back patio where she filled the low sitting birdbath with cold water. Then she sat and watched as the rabbits drank and disappeared once again.

And she wished with all her might that she could take her own advice. And they could be a happy trio once again, just like the rabbits.

Chapter Twenty-three

Sasha had barely made it into her office before her phone started to ring. She collapsed into her desk chair completely out of breath and scrambled through her purse to find it.

"Damn it, where are you?"

Frantic, she dumped the contents of her bag onto her desk and sifted.

"Bingo." She fumbled with the phone and answered only to find the call had already gone to voice mail. "Double damn."

"Good morning." She looked up to find Dennis hovering in her doorway.

"Dennis, hi." She concentrated on the phone. The call was from her nephrologist.

"How are you this fine morning?"

"Crazy." She finally met his gaze. "I really need to return a private phone call."

He held up a hand. "Say no more. I just wondered if you had a chance to look at my latest graphics?"

She was supposed to look at them last night, but she'd fallen asleep soon after she'd forced something down for dinner.

"I'll get back to you as soon as I can."

He nodded and smiled. "Got it." He turned to leave and she called out for him to close the door. He did so with a curious look.

She knew he wanted to ask her if everything was okay. But he held back and she thanked the stars above.

She dialed into her voice mail and her heart fell to her feet when she heard his nurse explain that he wanted to see her that day. She deleted the message and turned on her computer to check her schedule. She would have to go at lunch and hope that she could make it back in time. It was getting more and more difficult to hide things from her colleagues. Everyone had noticed a change in her, but they all commented on how it must be because of her illness and recent hospital stay. They checked in on her and offered help, and sometimes she had no choice but to accept it. She gave little in the way of a reason though. She wanted to keep her physical problems to herself. At least until she knew what the hell was going on.

Another knock on the door. This one from a young intern who popped her head in. "Meeting in five."

"Thanks."

She scrambled again, looking for her folder. When she found it, she rose and headed for the conference room. She wanted to arrive early so that all eyes wouldn't be on her as she entered. But she was too late. Half her colleagues were already there, munching on bagels and donuts. Dennis came at her like a ninja, moving swiftly to sit beside her. He slid a bagel and cream cheese along the table in front of her and pulled out her chair.

She thanked him quietly and sat, blushing from embarrassment. A few of her colleagues noticed his attention, and they wiggled their eyebrows at her. She narrowed her eyes at them playfully. Dennis sat beside her and started talking a mile a minute.

Even if she had wanted to, she couldn't pay attention to all he was saying. Her mind was on her doctor and her lab results and what all he was going to say. She was due for her regular appointment in two days, but whatever it was it seemed he didn't want to wait. Knowing that, unnerved her, more so than Dennis leaning into her, talking excitedly next to her.

She nodded politely and said a few words in return to him while playing with her bagel. She took two small bites and tore up the rest to make it look like she was eating it. He didn't seem to notice. He just kept talking.

He paused however and took a turn for the personal. Asking her about Hannah.

She gave him a look, and his mouth clamped shut. The meeting started, and she was glad she didn't have to deal with him any longer. Instead she did her best to concentrate on the meeting, and when it came to her turn she and her team gave an excellent report. Dennis was all smiles, and she knew he had worked really hard. She'd have to thank him later, and she was dreading it. The meeting droned on, and she grew weak and tired in her chair. She rested her chin on her hand and drifted, thinking of all things soft and warm and snuggly. She was just about there completely when she felt a kick to her ankle and she jerked to attention.

A hand gripped her forearm tightly and Dennis was in her ear.

"You fell asleep."

She blinked wildly and searched her coworkers' faces. All eyes were on the graphics on the big screen. No one had noticed.

"Thanks," she whispered back to him.

"You're not okay, are you?"

She ignored him, and at last the lights came on. Everyone walked out like zombies just having their brains sucked out. Everyone except her boss and Dennis.

"Sasha, would you mind staying a moment?" Gavin, her boss of ten years, asked.

Dennis gave her a wide-eyed look and left them. Gavin came to her and sat on the windowsill across from her. It was a casual position so she tried to relax a little. Gavin had always been more than kind to her, and he'd been more like a father figure to her than anything.

He cleared his throat and clenched his hands.

"I need to know how you're feeling, Sasha."

Sasha watched as he stared out over the sunny valley. She blinked against the brightness.

"I'm okay, sir."

He turned to pin her with a look. "I need honesty, Sasha. Not the usual bullshit we all give as an answer."

Her breath quickened and her throat tightened. "I'm…something's going on. I don't know yet what it is, but I'm hopefully finding out today at lunch. I see my doctor then."

He nodded and stroked his chin. "I want you to take the afternoon. Find out what's going on. Got it?"

"Yes, sir."

"I'm worried about you. I think everyone here is." He stood and began to pace. "You know my aunt had kidney disease. She seemed fine for a long time. And then one day she wasn't. She had reached the last stage and it finally took its toll on her. She was exhausted, slept twelve hours or more a day, she was weak. Couldn't even open a jar of pickles. And she looked, well, she looked like you do, Sasha."

She swallowed hard.

"I'm telling you this because I want you to know I understand. And that I'm here for you."

She wiped a tear and forced herself to calm down. "I'm worried about my job," she confessed.

"I figured as much." He stopped and stared out the window with his hands behind his back. "I don't want you to worry about that right now. I've spoken to your team, the ones you hired and trained, and they are ready to do what's necessary. You've done a damn good job in showing them the ropes, and I have every confidence they can cover for you if needed. I'll oversee them of course, and you…you do what you need to do."

She closed her eyes. "Thank you."

He looked at her. "You'll call me this afternoon?"

"Yes, sir."

"Very good."

He reached out and helped her stand. And then he hugged her. Sasha once again fought tears, but she managed to hold them back. He seemed a bit emotional as well and patted her shoulder as they parted. Sasha walked back to her desk in a daze. Somehow she managed to go over figures and converse with a few more promising sponsors before lunch. Dennis passed her office often, and he'd always look inside with searching eyes, but he never stopped to speak. She knew he must've known somewhat as to what Gavin was going to tell her since he was part of the team working for her. Maybe he felt guilty in knowing and not telling her. Maybe that was why he was suddenly so quiet. Either way, she was glad to be left alone. The news station carried on per usual, and she got lost in the sounds of the hustle and bustle outside her office door.

By the time lunch came, she was already fatigued and starting to feel weak. But to her surprise, someone knocked on the frame of her door. She glanced up, gathering her purse and satchel, expecting it to be Dennis. She was shocked when she saw Charlie.

"Hey, gorgeous. How about lunch?" Charlie had on her dark blue scrubs that showed off her stormy blue eyes. Sasha's breath caught at the sight of her, but not out of sheer attraction.

"Charlie."

"What do you say? Hawaiian burgers?"

She rounded her desk. "I can't. I have something to do."

Charlie took her closeness as her wanting to embrace and kiss. Sasha pulled away.

"I'm sorry. I have to go. I'm going to be late."

Charlie stood in front of her, blocking her. She appeared lost and a little panicked.

"What's going on? Where are you going?"

"I don't have time to get into it."

"Sasha. Talk to me."

Sasha gave up trying to bypass her. "I have to go see my doctor."

Charlie stepped back. "Oh."

"Now, if you'll let me go—"

"I'll take you."

"No—"

"I insist." She led the way out of the office, guiding Sasha by the elbow. Sasha was too worried about being late to fight it. As long as she got there and got her information, it didn't matter who took her.

She did wish, however, that it was Hannah, because she was struggling to make it to Charlie's Honda carrying her purse and satchel. When she did reach her car she had to lean against it to catch her breath, and she noticed that her feet were swelling in her flats. At least she'd been smart enough not to wear heels.

"So is this a checkup?" Charlie asked as she drove.

Sasha gave her directions and hesitated in telling her that she hadn't been feeling well. She decided to tell her as much as she knew, being too tired to be shady.

"Not exactly. He wants to see me to go over my labs. I haven't been feeling well so I'm afraid something may be wrong. I'll know more after I see him."

Charlie turned down the radio. "You're not feeling well? Since when?"

"For a while now."

"Why didn't you tell me?"

"It never came up. That and I haven't seen you much lately."

Charlie frowned. "Whose fault is that?"

"No one's. I've been super busy with work."

Charlie shook her head. "You don't tell me things, Sasha. Not like a normal couple does."

Sasha looked at her incredulously. "I'm sorry. Are we a couple?"

Charlie glared at her. "Are you kidding me? Of course we're a couple. What have we been doing the past two months?"

"Dating."

"Dating? Is that all?"

Sasha rolled her eyes and prayed for the doctor's office to come into view.

"I don't want to do this now. We can have this discussion later."

"I don't want to have it later."

"Well, too bad."

Charlie sped ahead and Sasha gripped the armrest. Charlie turned hard into the doctor's parking lot and screeched to a stop in front of the main entrance. A few patients jumped, scared to death. Sasha covered her forehead and sank lower in her seat.

"You know what?" Charlie said. "There isn't going to be a later. I'm done."

Sasha was beyond confused. "What?"

"You heard me." Charlie was gripping the steering wheel so tight her knuckles were white. She was looking straight ahead. "Now get out."

Sasha felt her mouth fall open. The words finally registered and she laughed, grabbing her things. No more Charlie. She was free! She exited the car and didn't bother to look back. She left the door open and heard Charlie peel out regardless. Sasha closed her eyes and breathed easy.

No more drama.

Chapter Twenty-four

Hannah had just hung up from speaking with the third coach when her cell phone rang in her palm. She jumped and almost sent it to voice mail, but then stopped cold. She leaned against her truck and answered.

"Sasha?"

"Hi."

She could tell something was wrong right away. "Are you all right?"

"You're not going to believe this…could you give me another ride home?"

Hannah eased into her hot vehicle and started the engine, blasting the AC. She had a million things to do. Like find a hotel for the dozens of softball players coming in next month for a big tournament. Then she had to find coaches and umpires. Not to mention going over paperwork from last weekend's tournament. She couldn't have called at a worse time.

But worrying about work was what the old Hannah would do. She knew if Sasha was calling and asking, there was a good reason why. She headed out of her office to the parking lot.

"Are you at work?"

"No, I'm at my nephrologist. Do you mind?"

"I'm on my way."

Sasha sounded completely relieved. "Thank you so much, Hannah. I owe you."

She ended the call, and Hannah thought of all the ways she'd like her to pay her. Times past came to mind and she remembered many an intimate moment. But she shook them from her mind and wondered instead why Sasha was there. She recalled that her appointment wasn't for a few days yet. She hoped all was well, but she didn't count on it. Why else would Sasha need a ride home? She must be sick.

Hannah sped up, too worried about her not to. She reached the doctor's office in record time and pulled up to the front quickly. She got out to run inside, but Sasha was already on her way out. To Hannah's dismay, she looked worse than she had the last time she'd seen her. Hannah tried to hide the shock that she knew was on her face.

"Hi." She took her things, tossed them in the back, and then opened the door for her. Sasha slipped on her designer shades but not before Hannah saw the red around her eyes and the smudged eyeliner and mascara.

Sasha crawled in the truck. Hannah pushed the door closed and hurried to her side. She climbed in, closed her door, and looked at her.

"What's wrong?"

Sasha shook her head.

Hannah didn't press. They were no longer together and she had no right to. If Sasha didn't want to share the details of her health, she didn't have to. Hannah reached for her hand and squeezed. To her surprise, Sasha gripped her hard and held on to her. She began to softly cry.

Hannah drove on, slowly and carefully, toward Bonnie's. Sasha had settled a bit by the time they arrived. Hannah killed the engine. Sasha stopped her from getting out by pulling on her hand.

"I don't want you to leave," she said.

Hannah nodded. "Okay."

Sasha released her, and Hannah helped her from the truck. Hannah carried her things and they went inside. Sasha sat on the couch and blew her nose. Hannah sat with her. She brushed her hair back from her face, and Sasha leaned into her and held her tight.

Hannah held her in return and allowed her to cry. She stroked her back and told her all would be well. That everything would be okay.

But Sasha shook her head and sat up. "It's not, Hannah. It's not going to be okay."

"Why?" Hannah asked softly. "Can you tell me?"

Sasha held her forehead. "My kidneys. They are spilling too much protein and he doesn't know why. It's a condition called nephrotic syndrome."

"So what does this mean?"

"It explains why I feel like shit. I'm retaining fluid; I'm weak and short of breath."

"Is it something he can fix?"

"He's not sure because he doesn't know what's causing it. He wants me to have a biopsy."

Hannah sat back and stared at the painting on the wall. "Okay."

"I knew something was wrong. I knew it."

Hannah tried to calm her. "I'm sure the biopsy will help him and we'll get a handle on it."

Sasha wiped her eyes. "Thing is…my kidney function has lowered. He's worried it's damaging my kidneys." Sasha looked at her. "My function can't go much lower, Hannah. I'll need dialysis."

Hannah patted her hand. Touched her face. She wanted so badly to kiss her. So gently. So carefully. But instead she said the only thing she could think to say.

"It'll be okay, Sash. You'll see. Please try not to worry before you have definitive answers. You will only hurt yourself if you do."

Sasha eventually nodded. Sniffed. "I know, I'm being ridiculous. I'm just so damn scared. I wasn't planning on dealing with this shit until I was older. I was hoping my kidneys would last that long."

"I know. And they still might. We just don't know anything really right now."

"No, we don't."

Sasha leaned into her once again. "I'm tired now. Will you walk me up to bed?"

"Of course."

Sasha sat up. "Thank you, Hannah, for being there for me." She smiled and then looked at her hands as if nervous. "It's funny, but I feel closer to you now than I did when we were together these last couple of years."

"I'm glad I can be here for you. Whenever you need me. I should've always been."

They rose without another word, and Hannah walked her up to her room. She helped her into bed and then sat beside her.

"Do you need me to stay?"

Sasha blinked her eyes closed. "No, I'll be fine. I just needed someone who cared. And that happened to be you."

Hannah kissed her cheek, careful not to linger. She didn't want to inhale the scent of her soft skin or the fragrance of her shampoo. She wouldn't be able to handle it.

She left her quietly and pulled the door closed partway. Sasha was already softly snoring. Hannah's heart warmed at the sound, and she hurried down the stairs and back out the door before her heart got the better of her and she ran back upstairs to crawl in bed with her, holding her and this time never letting her go.

The thought was wistful and magical, and she was lost in it as she walked to her truck. The intense heat saturated her skin, lulling her along in her dreamlike state. She was blissful and content when someone put their hand on her truck door preventing her from opening it.

Charlie.

Hannah stepped back in shock. "What the hell?"

Charlie whipped off her mirrored sunglasses. "Well, at least now I know why Sasha's happy to be rid of me."

Hannah knotted her eyebrows and heated with anger. "What are you talking about?" She yanked open her door, causing Charlie to move back.

"You. You're back in the picture. I should've known. I should've known."

Hannah steeled herself behind her door. "I don't know what the fuck is going on with you. But if Sasha got rid of you it was for a damn good reason. Now get the hell out of here or I'll be the last face you ever see."

"Are you threatening me?"

"Damn right. If she doesn't want you around then you better not be around. Got it?"

Charlie laughed and held up her hands. "Yeah, whatever, Grandma." She grinned.

The comment stung, but Hannah didn't react by showing it. Instead she waited and watched as Charlie climbed back into her car and drove off.

"Asshole." She got behind the wheel and started the engine. She sat for ten minutes making sure Charlie didn't come back, all the while wondering what had happened between Sasha and Charlie. But most of all she wondered yet again what had happened between Sasha and herself.

CHAPTER TWENTY-FIVE

Sasha sat at the kitchen table in Bonnie's house and stared at her phone. Hannah's name and number were staring back at her, but she just couldn't bring herself to dial. She knew Hannah wouldn't mind the call or even the request, but really, what was going on? Why didn't she mind? Wasn't she seeing someone?

Sasha groaned. What was she doing in asking and depending on her? Was it fair? It was obvious there was still love between them, but hadn't she told Hannah it was too little too late? She couldn't keep playing with their emotions like this. It wasn't right. Even if being with her felt so right it hurt.

She rested her chin in her hand and tried to come up with a plan. She had friends, sure, but they all worked. And this was a last-minute thing. Her doctor wanted the biopsy pronto. Who could take a Monday off to help her? There was no one except Hannah. And who's to say Hannah wasn't busy? It might be easier for her to take time off, but clearly, she worked very hard and Sasha knew the long days she put in. She'd have to make up the work sometime.

"No, I'll just take an Uber there and back," she said aloud, turning her phone over.

Bonnie breezed into the room. "What's that, sugar?" She stopped at the sink and began rinsing dishes and putting them in the dishwasher.

"Nothing." But then Sasha groaned again with frustration. "I can't find anyone to go to the biopsy with me tomorrow."

"Oh." Bonnie continued to rinse. "Well, I can drop you off. Can someone pick you up?"

Sasha shook her head. "I'll just take an Uber."

"Um, no. You won't." She turned off the water and dried her hands. Then she sat across from her. "What about Charlie? I know you know I don't care for her, but—"

"That's over," Sasha said.

Bonnie slapped her hand on the table. "What? When? Fill me in."

"Last week."

"Thank God. She was a little too pushy and cocky."

"She ended it."

"No."

"Said I didn't tell her things. Guess she wanted to know every detail of my life all the time. And she thought we had moved beyond dating to couplehood."

"Oh. Yeah. That line can be so fine between people. Sounds like she wanted a lot more than you did."

"I think so."

"Then who's been driving you to the doctor and home? I know someone has because I've been taking you to get your car at work." She raised an eyebrow. "Sash?"

"I'm not telling you. You'll yell at me."

"Oh, Jesus, no. Not Hannah." She grabbed her forehead. "Oh, Sasha."

"You don't understand. She's really been there for me lately."

"Yes, because she wants you back."

"No, it's more than that. And she hasn't even said anything about it. Hasn't made a move, nothing. She's been very kind and caring. A side I haven't seen of her in years."

Bonnie studied her and pushed out a breath. "I don't buy it. I still say it's a show."

"She's dating," Sasha said, mainly to shock her. "At least I think she is." She told her about the night she saw the woman at her house.

Bonnie pursed her lips in thought. "Could be anyone."

"Could be. But I saw something curious in her truck."

"What?"

"There were books and magazines on rock climbing."

"So?"

"Hannah is deathly afraid of heights. She won't even climb a ladder."

Bonnie laughed. "So maybe she's facing her fears. Changing."

"She is changing. She said she's bettering herself. You should see her body."

Bonnie gave her a sheepish grin. "Yeah?"

"Yeah."

"You noticed?"

"Hard not to."

"Are you falling for her, Sash?"

Sasha looked away. "I don't know what's going on. I'm so confused. That's why I don't want to ask her about the biopsy tomorrow. I don't want to confuse her or make our situation all the more messy."

"I understand."

They sat in silence and both jerked when Sasha's phone rang. She turned it over and felt her eyes widen. It was Hannah. She showed Bonnie.

"Answer it!"

"I am, I am."

Bonnie hurriedly excused herself as Sasha answered. "Hello."

"Sasha. It's Hannah. How are you?"

"I'm about the same, but I'm in much better spirits."

"Good, that's great."

Silence.

"I was calling to see if you needed help tomorrow with your biopsy. I can take most of the day if you need me."

Sasha sat back in her chair, relieved but overwhelmed all at once.

"I don't know, Hannah. I'm afraid I've been taking advantage."

"How so?"

"By asking you for help all the time under our circumstances."

"Sasha, I love you for life. And I think you feel the same about me. I'm always here for you whether you want to be with me or not."

Sasha fought the burning rising in her throat. "That's very kind of you to say."

"It's the truth. And I'm not trying to get under your skin or anything like that. I'm just genuinely worried about you and I know you need help right now. So what do you say? Will you let me help?"

Sasha fought for breath, battling her stirred emotions. "Yes."

"Good."

Silence.

"What time tomorrow?"

"I have to be there at seven."

"Okay, I'll pick you up at six."

"Okay."

"See you tomorrow."

"Bye."

Sasha ended the call and sat in the quiet. Eventually, Bonnie called out from the living room. "Is she taking you?"

"Yes."

Bonnie came in the kitchen and leaned on the wall with her arms crossed.

"What did she say?"

"All the right things."

"That's Hannah for you."

Sasha looked down at her hands. "Yeah, only now…she truly backs them up."

CHAPTER TWENTY-SIX

Hannah watched as Sasha switched off the radio and sat back in her seat with yet another long sigh.

"Nervous?"

"As hell."

"It won't be too bad." Her biopsy on her breast had been no fun at all afterward, but she hoped Sasha didn't remember.

"Oh? And you've had a renal biopsy when?"

Hannah laughed. "I know, I know. I don't know what I'm talking about."

"Thank you."

She crossed her arms. "I know it's nothing that serious. I'm just more nervous about what they're gonna find."

"That I do understand."

Sasha seemed like she was about to say something but then changed her mind. They rode in silence to the parking lot of the hospital where Hannah let her out. She then parked quickly and joined her at outpatient check-in. They registered Sasha and gave her a hospital band and then encouraged her to sit. They both did so in the waiting area where there was a man with a golden retriever wearing a vest. Sasha gripped her knee.

"Oh look, a therapy dog." The man heard her and approached.

"Would you like to pet her? She's here for the patients."

"I would love to. I'm about to be a patient." Sasha knelt with her and they had a quiet conversation, one that Hannah couldn't hear. Sasha was in heaven though, hugging and loving on the dog. Hannah smiled, knowing no one could love an animal like Sasha. It was as if she were born to do so. The animals seemed to feel it too, because they flocked to her and then hesitated to leave her side. Hannah had never seen anything like it.

Sasha eventually said good-bye to the man and the dog. She was smiling and she seemed way more at ease.

"That was Sunny," she said. "Beautiful, sweet dog."

Hannah smiled in return. "Do you feel a little better?"

"Yes."

Just then her name was called and she tugged on Hannah's hand to go with her. Surprised, Hannah followed. She had no idea Sasha wanted her right next to her. She had been planning on waiting in the waiting room. She'd even brought her Kindle.

"Sasha, are you sure?"

Sasha turned and whispered, "Yes."

They were led to a large room with curtains that sectioned off beds. Sasha was shown to hers and told to undress completely. Hannah hesitated to follow her in. Sasha slipped off her shoes and looked at her.

"Will you get in here?"

Hannah hurried inside, and Sasha yanked the curtains closed. She began to undress and Hannah averted her gaze. She heard Sasha laugh.

"You've seen me naked more than anyone else in the world and you're worried about it now?"

"I'm being respectful." Seeing Sasha nude wouldn't be good for either one of them. Because Hannah would no doubt like what she saw, and Sasha would no doubt see it on her face.

She heard Sasha ruffle clothing and move the bedsheets.

"It's safe now," she said.

Hannah turned and found her sitting in the hospital bed with the sheets pulled to the upper part of her gown. She looked almost like a little girl, lost in the white of the bed. Her face was slightly swollen, giving her a cherubic look. And with her golden hair resting on her shoulders, Hannah thought of a doll. A fragile little doll. The only thing that got in the way of that were the dark circles under her eyes and the unusual pallor to her skin.

"I look awful," Sasha said.

"Never," Hannah replied. "You look like a doll. Like a porcelain doll."

"Oh God, I've always been afraid of those. Thanks a lot."

Hannah laughed softly remembering. "Oh yeah, I had forgotten."

"Please tell me you didn't. After all the fuss I made up at your father's cabin in Prescott? That room full of damn dolls your mother had made? I wouldn't even sleep downstairs next to that room, remember?"

Hannah tried not to laugh, the area was so quiet, but she couldn't help it. It hurt to hold it in. Sasha joined her and they fed off each other.

"You were so scared, you sent me down for drinks in the middle of the night."

"You're darn right I did. I just knew those little monsters were up walking around, waiting for me. God, it even makes me cringe now. Why did your father keep that room like that?"

Hannah shrugged. "It was my mother's. She used to sit in there for hours making those dolls. I guess when she went he just couldn't bring himself to do anything with them."

"He loved her," Sasha said.

"Yes."

They grew quiet and a nurse came in, all smiles and sunshine. She went over Sasha's personal information and started an IV. Then she asked her if she was feeling anxious. Sasha nodded and she gave her something to help relax her. When she left, Sasha grinned.

"I feel good."

"I bet so."

"No, I mean really good." She looked around the room and then focused back on Hannah. "I'm so glad you're here. Charlie's got nothing on you, Hannah. Not a damn thing." She scoffed and threw up her hands. "I was so stupid. I'm always so stupid. I always think I'm doing the right thing, and then WHAM, I realize I'm not."

"You're not stupid, Sasha. You just follow your heart."

"A lot of good that does me."

"I think you're pretty special."

Sasha's face clouded. "Then why didn't you love me? What did I do?"

Hannah rushed to her bedside and held her hand. "Nothing, you didn't do anything wrong. I was the one who was stupid. I got so depressed I just let life slip through my fingers."

The curtains opened again and the nurse entered. She paused when she saw them.

"Oh no, honey, the medicine was supposed to relax you, not make you sad."

Hannah returned to her seat, and Sasha laughed as she wiped tears. "I'm fine. I just feel so open."

"Do you want a little bit more?"

"No, I'm really okay."

"All right, we're coming to get you in about five minutes."

Sasha nodded.

The nurse knelt and spoke to Hannah. "Let me know if she gets upset again."

"Will do."

Hannah stood and took her hand once more. "I'll be right here when you get back."

Sasha blinked slowly. "I know. That's what I'm counting on."

"I love you, Sash," Hannah said, unable not to.

Sasha squeezed her hand. "I know, Hannah. For the first time in a long time…I feel like I really know."

Three nurses came then and wheeled her away. Hannah watched her go with Sasha's words replaying in her mind.

She finally knows.

I'll never be more grateful.

Chapter Twenty-seven

"I don't understand," Sasha said. "How can they not know?" It had been a week since her biopsy, and she'd just seen her doctor for the results. Only, he had no definitive answers. His best guess was to treat her as if she were pre-diabetic and that the diabetes might be causing the spillage of protein. She hadn't been happy with the news and his lack of answers.

Bonnie served her a hot mug of tea and then sat across from her at the table. "I don't understand either. It doesn't make sense."

Sasha stirred the tea, blew on it, and then took a sip. "I have to limit my fluid, for a while, see if it helps." She shook her head. "I have to take diuretics when I get too swollen and something for the diabetes that I don't really have. It's crazy."

Bonnie sipped her tea and then added a sugar substitute. "So what now? When do you start?"

"I just picked up the medicine at the pharmacy. He told me I might want to stay home to see how I feel. Apparently, I will be peeing a lot."

"Oh, fun."

"I just hope it helps with this damn swelling. Do you know I've actually gained weight, despite my limited appetite? It's all the fluid retention."

"No way. You hardly eat."

Sasha stared down at her tea. "I just hope all this helps. I just want things to be back like they were before the hospital."

"I know, sweets. I'm sure it will get better. Just give it some time and don't overdo. Rest, for God's sake."

"I plan on it. I'm so fatigued it's not even funny."

Bonnie met her gaze. "Have you told Hannah?"

"Not yet. She called, left a message."

"She remembered the date of the doctor visit for results? Wow, I'm impressed."

"She did. I'm telling you she's changed."

Bonnie didn't respond. She just drank her tea in silence. And then, with a whisper, "Do you want her back?"

Sasha whipped her head up and met her curious eyes. She almost looked afraid, as if asking were somehow taboo. Sasha supposed it was in some ways. She fidgeted in her seat and tried to put into words what she'd been thinking.

"I honestly don't know how to answer that."

"But you do think about it."

"Yes. A lot lately in fact."

"Maybe you two should talk about it."

"Maybe."

"You hesitated. Why?"

"What if she's moved on? Or what if my health gets worse? I feel like I don't have anything to offer her. She's got it so together now, I don't want to ruin that."

"Okay, first of all, I doubt she's got anyone else. Second of all, you have everything to offer. You always have. She loves you."

Sasha pushed her tea away. "I think…I think I'm going to go for a drive. I need to get out of here. I've been cooped up in here most of the week."

"Want a sidekick?"

"No, maybe some other time. Tonight I need to think."

Sasha bent and kissed her cheek, and then grabbed her purse and keys and walked out the door. The night was warm with the hint of a breeze. It teased her hair and then her nose, promising dust and possibly rain. She crawled in her Jeep and started it, then backed out onto the road. At first, she didn't know where she was going. She was just intent on driving around, lost in her thoughts. But eventually the conversation with Bonnie got to her, and she soon found herself at Hannah's. The garage was closed, and Casey's truck was in the driveway. The lights were on in the house.

Sasha eased up along the sidewalk and was just about to kill the engine to get out when a familiar sedan pulled into the driveway. Sasha felt her stomach churn as the same woman as before got out.

"No. Please, no."

She watched helplessly as the woman walked to the door and rang the bell. The door opened, and Hannah enveloped her in a hug. Sasha had never considered what it might be like to see Hannah with another woman. But now she knew. It was god-awful. Like someone had just gutted her and stomped on the entrails. She felt sick. Worse than any kind of sick she'd ever felt before.

She put the Jeep in drive and peeled out, trying to get away as fast as she could before being seen. Tears nipped her throat, but she was too hurt to cry. Too shocked to give in to the sobbing. She drove around the corner and slammed on her brakes. She gripped the steering wheel so hard it hurt. She closed her eyes and tried to get control of her breathing.

"You let her go, so what did you expect?"

She said the mantra again and again.

She opened her eyes, and the sky cried for her with big fat droplets of rain. They smattered her windshield, and she sat back and stared into the oblivion they created.

She screamed when a knock came from the passenger door.

"Sasha? Sasha, it's me. Let me in."

It was Hannah and she sounded frantic. Sasha thought about driving away, but she changed her mind at the sound of Hannah's voice. She unlocked the doors, and Hannah hopped inside, hair and clothes dripping with rain. She was breathless.

"Why did you take off? I had to chase you down on foot."

Hannah's eyes were wide and seeking.

"Sash?"

"I changed my mind. I thought I wanted to stop by, but then I changed my mind."

"Why?""

"I saw that you had company."

Hannah looked confused for a moment. "Oh, Casey's girlfriend."

Sasha blinked. "Casey's girlfriend?"

"She came by to talk."

Sasha laughed.

"What's so funny?" Hannah was smiling at her, but obviously confused.

"I thought—oh, nothing. I'm just being an ass. As always." She rolled her eyes at herself.

Hannah studied her. "Ohhhh, you thought. No, she's not with me. She's a little young for me."

"That's what you used to say about me."

Hannah leaned back in the seat. "I did, didn't I?"

"Yes."

Hannah brushed her hair back from her face. "You didn't tell me about the biopsy results."

Sasha looked away in frustration. "There's nothing really to tell. They don't quite know what's causing the protein loss." She sighed, getting all upset all over again. "Can we talk about it later? I just want to get home, go to bed, and pretend this day never happened."

"That bad of a day, huh?"

Hannah grabbed her hand, and all Sasha could register was the heat of her hand and the pulse of her breath. They were both breathing hard with the rain beaming down around them. Sasha could hear the droplets of rain fall from Hannah's hair to the leather seat below. She could feel her heartbeat in her hand.

"Hannah, I really should go."

But Sasha didn't move. She didn't dare.

"Okay," Hannah said.

Sasha jumped when Hannah brushed her hair back from her face. She took her hand in both of hers. "Hannah. I have to go. I can't—"

"Can't what?"

But Sasha was leaning toward her, all inhibitions dripping off her just like the rain from the car. Flowing down the gutter they went, almost as if they were never there.

She looked into Hannah's eyes and found everything she'd ever been searching for, right there in Hannah, right in front of her. She closed her eyes, wrapped her hand in Hannah's hair, and pulled her so close she could feel her hot breath on her lips.

"Hannah," she said. "Oh God, Hannah." She pressed her lips to hers hard and heavy, and when Hannah answered by clinging to her, their lips parted and their tongues darted. Hungry, she and Hannah fed, like they'd never touched before. Exploring and seeking, finding and taking. Sasha moved her hand up Hannah's shirt and like a strike from a snake, Hannah jerked and pulled away. Sasha touched her lips, where Hannah's had just been, missing them instantly.

"Hannah—"

But Hannah fumbled with the door. "I'm sorry, Sasha. I'm so sorry." She opened the door and nearly fell out of the Jeep. She slammed the door and took off running. Sasha breathed deeply and this time allowed the tears to come.

How could she have been so stupid?

Chapter Twenty-eight

Hannah stood inside the rock climbing center staring at her friends wondering what the hell she'd gotten herself into. Mickey and her girlfriend were already almost to the top, while Hannah hung toward the back, all geared up but still scared shitless.

Brandy, who come to find out was actually an instructor part-time, had gotten her outfitted and ready to go.

"Here's some chalk for your hands," she said, showing Hannah how to apply it. Hannah did so and then shook her arms out as if that would help her nerves somehow. Then she marched in place and Brandy laughed.

"You don't have to do this, you know."

Hannah stopped her movement. "No, no, I'm going to do it. I said I would and I will."

She'd thought about it so much that she had to do it now. She wouldn't let her mind rest otherwise.

"Are you trying to impress me?" Brandy asked. "Because it's not needed. I already like you." She tugged on her shirt at her hips. Hannah could see the desire in her eyes and on her cheeks. Her lips were full and parted. She wanted to kiss her. Hannah knew it. She backed away.

Brandy looked perplexed. "Too close too soon?"

Hannah laughed nervously. "Something like that." She recalled the same look in Sasha that night in the Jeep. The way she'd looked at her so hungrily like she'd never wanted anything more. She recalled the feel of her moist lips, the heat of her pressing tongue. It had been enough to send her over in climax that night alone in bed and every night since. If only she wouldn't have reacted so strongly to her touch. She'd cursed herself relentlessly over it, trying to understand it. It had just been such a shock that she'd panicked and fled, more than embarrassed. Of course who knew where that left Sasha. She probably felt worse, as if she'd done something wrong or hurt her. Hannah had tried calling her again and again, but Sasha wouldn't return her calls. She'd even driven by Bonnie's house only to find the Jeep gone.

What was there left to do? She had to talk to her somehow. To explain and apologize. If only Sasha would let her.

Mickey whooped as she came down from the top of the wall. Hannah smiled but only for show. Inside she was reeling with fear. But if she bowed out now, Mickey would never let her hear the end of it. In fact, Mickey was the only reason she was there. She wouldn't be able to stand her showboating and gloating if she didn't climb the wall too.

Brandy, on the other hand, had been a good reason to come. Hannah had thought she'd made a new friend. But the way Brandy was behaving today, it was obvious she was looking for more.

"Okay, tough stuff," Brandy said, pulling on Hannah. "It's your turn." She walked Hannah to the face of the rock wall and rechecked her gear. Mickey had just stepped out of hers and she was already starting.

"If you get stuck, don't cry." She slapped Hannah on the shoulder.

"If I get stuck, I will never forgive you," Hannah said.

Brandy frowned playfully. "You'll forgive me, right?"

Hannah didn't answer, just knelt to double-check her shoes. As she did, her cell phone fell out of her pocket. Brandy scooped it up.

"Won't be needing this," she said and slipped it into her own pocket.

Hannah wanted to protest, but Brandy was right. There was no room for it, and if it fell while she was near the top it would most likely break.

"Ready?" Brandy asked

"Come on, Hannah, you got this," Mickey said.

Hannah didn't look back and she didn't look up. She stared straight ahead.

I got this, I got this.

She took a deep breath, and with Brandy letting her know she had her, Hannah began to climb. The first thing she thought of as she moved up the wall, was that she needed way more hand and finger strength and her feet needed to be two sizes smaller. She struggled as she got close to halfway. Her hands were on fire and her right foot was supporting all her weight. She tried to calm her breathing, but she was millimeters from the wall. Her hot breath merely blew right back in her face.

"Shit." She tried lifting her left foot, but the next grip was too far away. It would have to be her right. She closed her eyes to concentrate and she heard voices below, calling up encouragement. Her arms began to shake. She had to do something. Gritting her teeth, she pulled herself up with all her might and landed her right foot on the peg just before her left one gave out and slipped off. She struggled and somehow managed to find another peg for her left foot. She pressed against the wall and took in a long, shaky breath. She then moved up some more, wanting the whole thing to be over with. Her legs began to ache and shake. She didn't look down, but she didn't have to. Her body knew. Her mind knew. She grew dizzy with fear, as if she were on a shaky old ladder.

She wanted to turn her head, to call down that she was finished, but she didn't dare. She still had her pride. Mickey's voice trailed off and so did Brandy's. They sounded like they were talking to each other. She no longer paid attention. Instead, she gathered her strength once again and pulled herself upward. She wanted to laugh, to smile, to shout with victory, but her breath was hitched with cold fear. One more step and she'd made it.

Sweat beaded down from her helmet. She blinked it away from her eyes and tried with all her might to move. But her right foot slipped, and she cried out and clung to the wall.

"Oh, God."

She had slipped. Now she was struggling to find the peg again. Her heart raced and she cried out again.

"I'm done. Get me down." She made the mistake of looking down at her friends. She yanked her head back up and slammed it against the wall. And with the air pushed from her lungs, she was falling. Her whole body tightened, and she gripped her safety rope just before it caught her fall. She cursed and called down to Brandy. She wasn't aware of her words, she just wanted down.

Slowly, Brandy eased her down, and as soon as her feet hit the floor, she tore off her gear.

"You did an awesome job," Brandy said. "Especially for your first time." She tried to help her, but Hannah pushed her hands away. Then she took off her helmet and flung it behind her.

She crossed to the bench where Mickey and her girlfriend sat. Hannah sat and ripped off her shoes.

"What's wrong with you?"

Hannah clenched her jaw. She didn't want to complain or sound like a baby. She just wanted to go home. She'd done it. She'd climbed the damn rock wall. She'd faced her fear. Enough said.

"Nothing."

"You made it to the top. I'm impressed."

"Well, then all is good isn't it? Mick is impressed."

Hannah shoved her feet into her Nike trainers and stood.

Brandy came to her. "Something wrong?"

"No, nothing."

"I'm really proud of you," she said. "Let's go out to celebrate."

Hannah was about to decline when Mickey handed over her cell phone. There had been a call.

"Sasha called while you were up there."

Hannah stared at her. "And you answered?"

"She kept calling and Brandy had to concentrate on you so she tossed it to me."

"And you answered?"

"Yeah. I thought it might be an emergency or something. But it wasn't. I told her you were busy climbing a rock at the moment."

"And I told her what a good job you were doing," Faith said.

Hannah couldn't believe her ears. "You did what?" She started pressing buttons on her phone, desperate to call her back. She didn't answer.

"What did she say?" Hannah pointed the question at Mickey.

She shrugged. "She said not to bother you. And she hung up."

Hannah gathered her things and grabbed her keys.

"You're leaving?" Brandy asked. She looked confused and a little hurt.

Hannah didn't have time to explain or to feel guilty. All she could think about was Sasha. Did she need her? Was something wrong?

"I've got to go." She turned and hurried out the door, leaving Brandy with a truly perplexed look on her face and Mickey calling after her.

CHAPTER TWENTY-NINE

Sasha lay on her bed looking up at her phone. Had she really just heard what she'd thought she'd heard? Was it possible? Even after what they'd shared the other night in her Jeep?

Maybe she was losing her mind. She'd been so fatigued and absentminded it was possible. Or maybe Hannah really didn't feel the same way. Sasha didn't want to believe it. Hannah had changed, hadn't she? Even if she hadn't totally changed, Hannah had never been a player. This just so wasn't like her.

Sasha's stomach hurt, and she began to feel like she had when she'd seen the mysterious woman hug Hannah. She rolled over and sat up, waiting for her stomach to decide if it wanted to empty itself. The doorbell rang before she could make a move. She heard Bonnie answer it and call her name.

It was Hannah and she was breathless, asking if she was okay.

Oh God. Not now. She was too confused, too upset.

But soon Hannah was at her door, softly knocking, pushing it open carefully, as if not to frighten her.

"Hi." She entered slowly. "Is it okay if I come in? Sit next to you?"

Sasha shrugged. "If you want to."

"How are you feeling?" Hannah settled in next to her, and Sasha shivered with desire as she caught the scent of her sweat mixed with pheromones.

Sasha hugged herself and rubbed her arms. Hannah took it as her being cold. She offered her a blanket, which Sasha declined.

"Not feeling well I take it?" Hannah asked. "Do you need me to take you to the emergency room?"

"No, nothing like that. I'm okay. No worse than usual."

Hannah reached out to brush her hair away from her face, but Sasha moved away. Hannah hesitated and then dropped her hand.

"Sasha, what is it? Why didn't you answer when I called? Did Mickey upset you?"

Sasha laughed. "Honestly, I think it's me who should apologize. I interrupted your date."

Hannah started to speak but stopped.

"So Mickey told the truth. You were on a date."

"Mickey said what?" Hannah stood and began to pace. Her face was red with what could only be anger.

"It's okay. You don't need to get upset. Of course you're going to date. You can't sit around waiting for me to make up my mind."

Hannah ran a hand through her hair. "Sasha, she's a friend. I met her and Mickey's girlfriend to rock climb."

"Rock climb?" Sasha laughed again. "Come on now, Hannah. You would only do something like that to impress a woman."

"I did it because I wanted to face my fear. To prove to myself and Mickey that I could do it."

Sasha shook her head. "You don't have to explain any of it to me, Hannah. I have no right to you. I gave it away. Said I didn't want it. That's my fault."

"Sasha, don't."

But Sasha stood. "You can go now, Hannah. Go and better yourself and be free. Be happier without me."

Hannah grabbed her shoulders, but her phone rang.

Sasha glanced at her pocket. "Better get that. It may be her."

"It's not."

"So answer it."

"No. I'm talking to you."

"Answer it."

Sasha took a step back, staring into her, daring her.

Hannah sighed and pulled the phone from her pocket. Her face fell and Sasha knew. She grabbed the phone and saw the screen before Hannah could snatch it back.

"Brandy." Sasha felt her lip tug in a smirk. "That's her isn't it? Your rock climber?"

"Sasha, don't do this. She doesn't mean anything to me. She's just a friend."

But it was too late. She remembered Mickey's words and now the woman was calling her. Probably wondering why she'd run off.

"A friend on a double date. Tell me," Sasha said. "Does she know you're just friends?"

Hannah's jaw flexed. "I've told her so, yes."

"But she wants more."

"Don't do this, Sasha. It's pointless."

"Oh, but I have to. I have to see the whole picture. What I'm doing isn't fair to you."

"Sasha, don't—"

"You should go now, Hannah." Sasha looked away from her. "Just please go."

Hannah stood very still and her phone rang again, startling her. She cursed it and silenced it before shoving it back into her pocket.

"Sasha…I love you."

Sasha hugged herself once again. "I love you too. Which is why I need you to go." She lay down once more and curled into a ball. She heard Hannah walk out and close the door behind her. Then, in the distance, she heard Hannah peel out and drive away, leaving Sasha all alone with her heart beating, but her life gone.

Chapter Thirty

Hannah fed her fury through her arms and hands and down through the baseball bat.

Ping!

She swung so hard she nearly hit her back with the bat on the follow-through. She grunted and readied herself for the next pitch. She swung and missed the curve. Furious, she pounded the ground with the bat.

"Jesus, take it easy."

Hannah set up again and waited for the next ball.

"Don't tell me to take it easy. Not after what you did."

"I said I was sorry. I meant no harm."

"Bullshit." She swung and lined it to the left. "Complete and utter bullshit." She pointed the bat at Mickey, who stood behind the fence. "In fact, you're lucky I'm speaking to you."

"Oh, come on. I didn't make you go on the date or to rock climbing. You did that on your own."

"True. But you did hound me. And not only that, I had explained to Brandy that I wasn't ready yet. That friendship would have to suffice."

"Yet, you showed up to the date."

Hannah swung hard and hit a high fast ball back over the center. It hit the net and dropped. She tore off her helmet and exited the gate. Mickey's turn.

"Fuck you and your date, Mickey. Most sincerely."

Mickey got set in the batter's box and swung calmly, waiting for the pitch. "I'll take that," she said. "As long as that's the end of it."

"Oh, hell no. That's not the end. Not the end at all."

"No? Then what will be?" She swung and missed, then cursed as Hannah laughed.

"You're going to support me when we get back together."

Mickey turned to look at her with shock on her face, and the next pitch whizzed by her and thumped into the backstop padding.

"I thought she told you to get lost?"

"She did. But she didn't want to. She thinks she's doing it for my benefit."

"Maybe she is."

"Don't even start, Mick. We are meant to be together. I'm more convinced now than ever."

She packed her things into her bat bag and took a long swig of water. Then she doused her head and face. Though it was evening, it was still warm.

"I'm out," she said, walking away.

"Aren't you going to wait for me?" Mickey called, but Hannah kept moving.

She was in no mood to wait for Mickey, no mood at all. What she had done was almost unforgivable. Telling Sasha she was on a date when she knew how she felt about her. It was a betrayal. She shouldn't have even answered the damn phone. But that's the way things went with Mickey. Very little boundaries. That had to change or their friendship would. She couldn't have a friend who didn't support her relationship. It just didn't work that way.

Mickey, however, always thought she knew best and she would listen to little else. She'd been trying to push Hannah into doing things her way for years, and Hannah had always fought it. Now, when Mickey had the chance to actually dig her hands in Hannah's pie, she'd done so aggressively, trying to get rid of Sasha. To Hannah, that wasn't a friend, that was a controller and a manipulator. Something they definitely had to remedy. In the meanwhile, she'd let Mickey squirm until she apologized and meant it. She would eventually. Because Hannah really did believe she wanted the best for her, she was just too hardheaded to realize it couldn't or wouldn't be her way.

Hannah crawled in her truck and drove to a nearby small Mexican restaurant. She parked and honked at Casey who was sitting at a table on the crowded patio. He waved but didn't look overly excited or happy. She hoped it had nothing to do with the girlfriend.

But it seemed these days that all the two of them could talk about was how to get their girls. And poor Casey was a mess.

Hannah entered the restaurant and bought a bottle of Sobe, a veggie burrito, and chips and salsa. She joined Casey on the patio and sat in a plastic chair. Casey looked like death warmed over. He was picking at a bowl of tortilla chips.

"Okay, I know you must be having a bad day because you haven't even touched the bottle of Tapatío." He always had to have hot sauce. Even if the salsa had plenty of fire, he'd add it to it. The boy had taste buds of steel.

He groaned and continued to pick.

"Didn't you get something for dinner?"

"Not hungry."

"Casey, you have to eat."

"How can I when the woman I love won't speak to me?"

"Again?"

He shrugged. Apparently, his girlfriend had decided to keep the baby, but she again claimed she wanted nothing to do with Casey.

"You still think she's seeing that other guy?"

"Yeah. She won't forgive me, Mom. I tell her I want the baby and that I don't think she should get rid of it, and she freaks on me. Then she's okay with me for a while and then bam, she decides to keep it but hates me again for it. I can't keep up."

"Sounds like she's scared."

"I just wish she'd decide to be with me. So we can build a life. I'll take care of her and the baby. You know I will."

Hannah of course knew that he would. And he would probably have to. But she didn't care for the way his girlfriend was treating him. The last thing she should be doing was seeing another guy.

"Be careful what you wish for, Casey. You may end up getting it."

"What's that supposed to mean?"

She took a bite of her burrito. "I'm saying that it isn't all peaches and cream. It's hard. It will be hard. And if she doesn't help—"

"You think I can't do it?" He shoved his chips away.

"Of course not, Casey. I'm just warning you. It's not a life I wish for you is all. Not so young."

"Yeah, well, it's too late isn't it?"

She reached for his hand and rested hers softly on it. "Casey, have you ever wondered if the baby is really yours?"

His face contorted. "What? Are you serious?"

She looked at him with all the love and concern she had. It didn't seem to help. He shot up out of his chair and looked down at her and spoke with a voice she'd never heard before. One strangled on rising tears.

"How dare you," he said. "How dare you." He walked away and slammed the patio gate behind him, causing the other patrons to look.

She sat quietly and watched him go. She'd scared him, offended him. But she'd had to do it. She didn't trust the girlfriend, and the way she was behaving was suspicious. Casey was giving her money to help her, and Hannah wondered if the other guy was too. She could be playing them both. Part of her wished the girl was playing Casey, that way his life wouldn't be disrupted. But it would destroy Casey. His young heart was so raw and new and fragile. It would take him a while to heal. But she would rather him have to heal than to be trapped in a loveless marriage with a child that might not even be his own.

It wasn't that she didn't like Abby; she'd been pleasant enough. There was just something about the situation that didn't sit right with her. Why would she end things with Casey when he was willing to do whatever it took to support her and the baby? And why go to another guy? Was he as willing as Casey to care for her and the baby? It seemed unlikely. She wished she could question the girl more. Sit with her one-on-one to get some answers. Casey, she knew, would have a fit if she tried to do so. For now, she had to wait it out. She'd planted a seed of doubt and questions in Casey, and it had to be enough. Hopefully, it would be enough to get his mind going.

She finished half her burrito and sat to stare into the sun. The heat of the day was seeping into her skin in an hypnotic effect, and any other day it would lure her to relax and sleep. But today, given her situation with Sasha and Casey, it was doing little to dull the sharp edges of her thoughts. She knew she needed to talk to Sasha, to try to explain, but she wondered what good it would do. She'd told her the truth and it had sounded bad enough. How could she lessen that pain? It was what it was. She'd gone rock climbing with a woman who was interested in her. Innocent, yes. Justifiable, yes. But it had hurt Sasha and made her see a reality she didn't want to see. A reality she wasn't ready to see. That had been plainly written all over her face. And yet despite her hurt, she'd done the noble thing. She'd told Hannah to go. Said that she didn't want to hurt her anymore.

That alone had shocked Hannah. Sasha had matured. It seemed they both had. Neither wanted to hurt the other, nor hinder their happiness.

But what was maddening was that their happiness probably depended upon them finding each other again.

It just obviously wasn't the right time.

When would it be?

She didn't know.

Would it ever be?

She sipped her warm drink and rose to leave the table. That, she didn't know either and it was damn near killing her.

CHAPTER THIRTY-ONE

Did you meet her?" Katherine asked as she popped her head into Sasha's office. Her young eyes were wide and her mouth was open with a broad smile. "She's here and she's so cool." She popped back out, and the next coworker came along and did nearly the same thing.

Sasha tried to concentrate once again on her paperwork. The office was all abuzz with the arrival of the new news anchor. Sasha had heard of course, all about the new hire, but her mind was elsewhere, as usual.

She glanced at her calendar. It had been nearly a month since she'd allowed herself to think of the name Brandy. And she'd been pretty proud about that. Perseverance and self-control could indeed go a long way if one tried. However, her mind still mulled and ached over Hannah, which wasn't good, but things had been getting better. The pain wasn't as piercing, and out of sight, out of mind really had helped as well. Each and every day for two weeks, she had hesitated while holding the phone ready to call her. But each time, she'd talked herself down and found something else to do. It hadn't been easy, and her dreams at night were uncontrollable, but she felt that she was making headway. She had to. Hannah's happiness depended upon it. Hannah needed time and she should've known it all along. And she definitely should've known it when she'd tried to touch her chest that night in the Jeep. Hannah still wasn't ready, regardless of what she said. So Sasha had done the right thing from the beginning by putting space between them.

"Have you met her yet?"

Sasha glanced up to see Dennis in her doorway. He had his arms crossed, and he didn't look nearly as happy as the others seemed to be with their new arrival.

"No, I've been busy here. Have you?"

He leaned on the doorjamb. "Yeah, she's okay I guess. A bit hotsy totsy if you ask me."

"Oh?" She was surprised to hear him speak that way about a coworker. Usually he was Mr. Nice Guy.

"You know, a bit stuck up."

Sasha laughed. "You got all that from a hello?"

"That's all it took."

Sasha stood, knowing she did indeed need to introduce herself before the rest of the crew ate the woman alive. She smoothed down her skirt and eased into her flats. Thankfully, her swelling was under control once more and she could fit comfortably in her shoes. Soon, she'd be back to heels. She breezed past Dennis with a smile and headed to the boardroom where lunch was being served in celebration and welcome.

People were scattered about, eating from small plates, chatting and laughing. A deep, throaty laugh caught her attention from near the corner. Gavin, who had his back to her, turned, revealing a tall redhead with a gorgeous smile. Her laugh was infectious, and she had the small group around her nearly in tears.

Sasha smiled as well, wondering what the joke was. She was about to ask when the woman caught her gaze and locked in. Her green eyes danced, and a perfectly groomed eyebrow shot up in obvious interest.

"And who might this be?" she asked, causing the rest of the group to turn.

Gavin embraced Sasha with a half hug and pulled her in. "This is Sasha Bashton. Sasha, this is Heidi Malone."

Heidi shook her hand firmly and then ever so slightly, tickled her palm with her middle finger. Sasha blushed and Heidi seemed pleased, assuming her message was received.

"Welcome aboard," Sasha managed. "We're thrilled to have you."

"Thank you. I'm thrilled to be here." She winked. "I have to say, I've never had such an enthusiastic welcome before."

"Oh?" The group dispersed for food, and Sasha found herself alone with Heidi. "Where were you before?"

"Dallas. How about you? Have you been here long?"

"Oh gosh, yes. Years."

"You know, I believe Gavin told me about you. Bragged is more like it. You're marketing, right?"

"Yes." She searched her face and fought standing on her tiptoes to be eye-to-eye with her. She also couldn't stop thinking about that press of her finger into her palm. Was she aware she had done it? Did she know what it meant?

By the curl of her lips and the way she studied Sasha, she seemed to know exactly what it meant.

"Gavin thinks very highly of you, to say the least."

"Gavin is wonderful. You will love working for him."

"I don't know about that, but I'm sure I'll love working with you."

Sasha blushed again. She was flirting. Actually flirting. Sasha knew she should say something or excuse herself. But she was captivated by her long, curly locks, her mesmerizing eyes, and her playful mouth. The woman was drop-dead gorgeous.

"I'm sure I'll love working with all of you." She grinned.

She was clever. Very clever.

"Sasha, did you eat?" Dennis asked, interrupting.

Sasha eyed him hard, upset at being interrupted with something so silly. He made it sound like she needed a mother or a constant reminder to do things. Where did he get off?

He seemed to sense her thoughts. "It's just that it's going fast and I know you need to stay fueled."

"I'm fine, Dennis."

He nodded quickly and moved away.

"Boyfriend?"

Sasha gasped. "God no."

"Wannabe boyfriend?"

"He seems to think so."

"It's kind of sweet." Heidi grinned.

Sasha scoffed. "No, it's not. Trust me."

"Why do you need such care, Sasha?" She raised that eyebrow again. "Are you delicate?"

"Hardly." Was she? Is that how her coworkers saw her now? The thought made her cringe. She straightened and motioned toward the table. "Shall we?"

Heidi grabbed a plate. "Oh, we shall." She began picking up finger foods. "Let's eat in my office," she said.

Sasha glanced at her from across the table. Should she? Then she saw Dennis lingering in the corner, watching her. "Sounds good."

She followed Heidi back to her office and fought gaping at the gorgeous view. She'd been given a corner office, and the view of downtown was spectacular. She'd always envied those in this office. Now it seemed she would be envying Heidi.

"Please, make yourself comfortable." Heidi sat behind her desk. "Pull that chair up if you like."

Sasha set down her plate and did exactly that. They were now both sharing the desk.

"So what's the story on the boyfriend?" Heidi popped a red grape in her mouth, and Sasha couldn't help but watch her chew.

"Dennis? Oh, he's silly really. Has a bit of a crush I think."

"Mm." She nodded. "And there's no other men on the forefront?"

Sasha took a small bite of pasta salad. "No."

Heidi seemed pleased.

Sasha decided to turn the tables. "How about you? Any women on the forefront?"

Heidi swallowed some of the same salad and grinned. "No, as a matter of fact."

"Surprising."

"Is it?"

Sasha nodded.

"And you…"

"No, there's no one." But it hurt her chest to say so. And she knew it was obvious by the way she felt the pain constrict her face.

"Uh-oh." Heidi sipped her iced tea. "You going to tell me? Or do I have to dig it out of you?"

"It's just—nothing. I was in a very long relationship that ended some months ago and it's been—difficult."

Heidi was watching her closely. "Who in their right mind would let you get away?"

Sasha laughed. "It was actually me. I did the breaking up."

"Again I say who would let you get away?" She played with another grape before easing it into her dark red lips.

Sasha was speechless. "Maybe you should ask her that. I can be a pain in the ass I suppose."

"Trust me, if I saw her, I'd be too busy sizing her up to ask her how she could've been so stupid."

Sasha winced. Hannah was far from stupid.

"Sorry. Too far."

Sasha shrugged. She was no longer hungry, but she pushed the food around on her plate.

Heidi was watching her closely. "I know there are rules about dating and so forth, but I'd almost leave for another network if it meant I could buy you dinner sometime."

The flush came again, and Sasha fought rubbing her cheeks. "I'm not sure that's a good idea."

"Neither am I. In fact, it's probably a terrible idea. We will most likely end up in bed ravishing each other, and then where would that leave us?"

Sasha felt the pang of pleasure between her legs as she stared into her fiery eyes. "I don't know. Where would that leave us?"

A knock came from the door.

"In," Heidi said.

Dennis poked his head in, and Sasha nearly groaned in anger. He looked directly at her as if she'd been caught with her hand in the cookie jar.

"You have a phone call."

"I'm at lunch. They can leave a message." Why the hell had he answered?

He closed the door. Sasha palmed her forehead. "I think I might actually have to do something about him."

"He's got it bad. And he doesn't like me." She sat back and crossed her legs.

Sasha laughed. "No, I'm afraid he doesn't."

"He knows I'm competition."

"You think?"

"Oh yes. He has me pegged. He has you pegged. We will have to be careful."

"Will we?"

"If you agree to go out with me, yes."

Sasha stood and grabbed her plate. "We'll have to wait and see." While she desperately wanted to say yes to dinner, she knew she needed to take her time and be sure. She didn't want another Charlie on her hands.

"You're going to make me wait?"

Sasha flashed her own grin. "Absolutely."

Heidi drummed her fingers on her desk. "I like it."

Sasha turned and left, so wet she was nearly afraid to walk. But she managed to hold her head high and get through the door, leaving Heidi gawking after her.

When she returned to her desk, she found the written message from Dennis about the client phone call. Just as she'd suspected, it wasn't anything that couldn't wait. She decided to nip the problem in the bud. She called him in.

"Sit," she said when he stood in the doorway. "But first close the door."

He did so and sat like the chair might bite. "What's up?"

"Well, that's what I'd like to know, Dennis. What's up?"

"What do you mean?"

"I want to know why you're shadowing me all the time and acting like a nosy, pesky mother hen."

He reared back as if he'd been slapped. "Mother hen?"

"Do you have another word for it?"

"It's called caring. I simply care about your well-being. But I can see it's obviously not appreciated."

She held up her hand. "Don't get me wrong, Dennis. I appreciate your caring. But the shadowing, etc, it's a bit out of hand. I'm fine, as you can see."

He scrunched his face. "You're not always fine, Sasha. I can tell. So don't pretend like you are."

She sighed. "I am fine, Dennis. With my new medication, I'm feeling much better. Now, granted that can change and it most likely will at some point. But for now, I'm okay. And I'm a big girl. I can care for myself you know. Been doing it for years."

"You don't do a very good job. And I know you don't ask for help when you need it. Instead you pretend."

She shook her head. "I don't understand, Dennis. Why does this matter so much to you?"

He glanced away.

"I care," he finally said.

Gooseflesh broke out on her arms. She knew it was more than a friend and a colleague simply looking out for her. It was something more, that was becoming more and more obvious. Something a bit…creepy. And she wasn't sure how to handle it. So far he hadn't acted out of line. Not anything she could complain about really.

"Can you back off a little on the caring then?"

He stared into her. "Sure." His jaw flexed.

"Thank you."

"Is that all?"

"Yes."

He stood. "Just so you know, Heidi Malone is a predator. She'll use you and break your heart."

Sasha blinked with surprise.

"I'm sorry?"

"She will. I looked into her. She goes through women like underwear. She—"

"Dennis, that's enough. You can go."

"But—"

"Go, now, please."

He turned on his heels and marched from the room. He slammed the door behind him. Sasha rested her head in her hands.

What the hell was that?

She leaned back in her chair. He'd looked into Heidi. Why? What for? Things were getting beyond creepy. She picked up the phone and dialed Heidi's desk.

"Malone."

"Heidi, hi, it's Sasha."

"Wow, so soon? To what do I owe this pleasure?"

"I wanted to talk to you about Dennis."

"Oh?"

"He just told me he looked into you."

There was a brief silence. "Oh? What exactly did he mean by that?"

"I'm not sure. He just warned me to stay away from you. Said you were a player of sorts."

Throaty laughter.

Sasha laughed a little herself. "It does sound ridiculous doesn't it?"

"No, Sasha, he's absolutely right."

"He is?"

"I don't have a good track record I must admit."

"You don't?"

"No, I don't. And it's not that difficult to find out. I have a bit of a reputation when it comes to dating."

"So, you're not upset?"

"I'm upset that my personal life is being discussed by a stranger, yes. But he is telling the truth. Perhaps you should listen to him."

Sasha smiled and spun in her chair. "Like I told him, I can take care of myself."

"Oh, is that so?"

"Yes."

"Well, I'm glad to hear it."

"He wasn't."

"Maybe you'd better watch out for him rather than me."

"That's what I'm thinking. I told him to back off."

"Good."

Silence. Sasha grinned and it burned her cheeks. "So how about drinks on Friday? Sort of a welcome to Phoenix get-together?"

"Oh, I'd love to, but honestly, I'm already beat and I have so much unpacking to do this weekend, I'm afraid I won't be much company with my mind on all I have to do."

Sasha laughed softly.

"What's so funny?"

"You hardly sound dangerous."

"Oh, give me time, Sasha Bashton, give me time."

They both laughed and Sasha's other line rang. "Listen, I've got to go. Talk later?"

"I look forward to it."

"Great."

She ended the call, took the incoming call from Katherine, and got busy getting back to work. But as she worked, her gaze kept falling on the door and her conversation with Dennis. Just what was he up to? And more importantly, what did it mean for her? She rubbed more gooseflesh from her arms as she focused on her dual computer screens.

Hannah would know what it meant. Hannah would know what to do. Hannah had always said she was too nice to people, too friendly when she shouldn't be. It drew people without boundaries. Maybe she'd been right. Maybe she'd been too friendly with Dennis.

But she couldn't call Hannah to run it by her.

She'd solve this one on her own. She only hoped she could.

Chapter Thirty-two

Hannah could hear the smacking of her shoes against the pavement as she slowed her run to a walk and lowered the volume on her earphones. She was listening to a song about what a woman wants to hear, and she just couldn't take it anymore. The lyrics had struck home and plucked the messy strings of her heart until the song sounded strange and wickedly slow.

She popped the earbuds from her ears and bent to catch her breath. She had only run two miles, but today that seemed to be more than enough. She staggered up her driveway to the garage door and entered her code on the keypad for entry. When the wall of cold slammed against her insides, she jerked and then sighed into it. She pulled open the fridge, grabbed a water, and sank onto the couch. She eyed her watch and noted it was way too early to wake Casey. Just as well, he wasn't speaking to her anyhow. Neither was Mickey.

She laughed and sipped her water. She seemed to be on a roll with those closest to her. Her venting her feelings so freely was new to them all, and apparently it was going to take some getting used to on all their behalves. But strangely, she didn't feel all that guilty about it. She knew she couldn't keep hiding her feelings. It wasn't healthy and it had driven her to drink. Those around her would have to understand that.

She felt her phone vibrate from within her pocket. She fumbled for it and was surprised to see it was a text from Brandy.

She wanted to know what her plans were for the day. Hannah sat up and considered her response. She had the day off and nothing better to do than sit around and feel sorry for herself with no one to talk to. She could handle the cold shoulder from Mickey, but not Casey. That was nearly unbearable.

She needed to get out. Do something. Anything.

Before she could answer, Brandy sent another text asking about breakfast. Hannah laughed as she suggested Hannah cook for her.

Hannah shrugged. Why not? It was nice out now. They could sit on the back patio and enjoy the rabbits and hummingbirds. She smiled as she told her to come over in an hour, sending her her address. She rose and headed for the bedroom. She was glad Brandy was reaching out, considering how they'd left things last time she'd seen her. She'd had to call and explain the situation to her, to which Brandy said she completely understood. She even suggested that they might not want to double with Mickey anymore until things were smoothed over. Hannah had agreed. She just didn't know when that would be. But at the moment, she didn't care. She hadn't heard from Mickey and it was just as well. She wasn't ready to talk or to forgive. Mickey was just too headstrong and aggressive in her opinions on Sasha and Hannah and Hannah and Brandy.

Hannah stripped and stepped in the shower. She couldn't help the excitement she felt in knowing Brandy would soon be over. Despite their pending friendship-only status, she noticed that her body tingled as she washed. So much so that she groaned when she soaped between her legs, stroking her engorged flesh with her slick fingers. Her legs trembled and she nearly climaxed where she stood. Instead, she forced herself to stop and leaned against the wall as the water sloshed from her taut body. She wanted the excitement to remain, wanted to harness it for as long as she could. She hadn't felt this alive in ages.

She killed the water and stepped from the shower. She recalled the last time she'd felt so aroused. It had been before her surgery.

She'd been on the couch with Sasha late at night. Casey had been at a sleepover with friends. Sasha, who normally was not the aggressor, had began whispering in her ear and stroking her inner thigh. And when her tongue had come out to rim her ear, Hannah had lost it and crawled atop her to devour her mouth. They'd kissed wildly and fumbled with each other's clothes. Sasha had torn off Hannah's mesh shorts and grabbed her ass, maneuvering her onto her bare thigh. And that's where Hannah had lost it. She'd been so hot, so turned on, she'd rubbed herself against her skin and come instantly, crying out and spasming on top of her while Sasha pinched her aching nipple and dug her other hand into her ass cheek, encouraging her to ride it as long as she could.

Hannah shivered at the memory. She rubbed the steam from the mirror and leaned forward. She could see the raw desire in her eyes, feel it in the beat of her heart. A part of her wondered if Sasha would be lying seductively on the bed as she reentered the bedroom. But she shook the thought away. She had to focus. Brandy would be there soon.

She touched the red on her cheekbones, then allowed her fingers to fall to the scars on her chest. She lightly grazed them and her breath shuddered. She could still feel, could still react, but there was no center for release. No bunching of nerve endings. There was nothing. She dropped her hands. There was no time. She couldn't sit and stare at herself and wish things were like before.

She combed her hair, brushed her teeth, and dressed. Then she sprayed on the cologne Casey had given her, the one she'd never worn for Sasha, and she hurried into the kitchen. She began pulling out pans and spatulas but then realized she didn't know what Brandy preferred to eat. So instead, she forced herself to sit at the table and sip some orange juice. Patience had never really been her strong point, and it was driving her insane at the moment. But she forced herself to wait. Maybe if she'd done more of that for Sasha instead of just assuming, she wouldn't be alone.

She tried to think of the last time she'd asked Sasha what she preferred or what she really wanted when it came to simple things.

Had she ever really waited and asked? Had she ever truly put her needs ahead of her own? She thought back to how when shopping together Sasha always wanted to meander and look around, while she wanted to get in and out. She'd often leave her, buy what was needed, and then find her to tell her it was time to go. Why had she done that? Was time really that precious that she couldn't take a half an hour and explore a store with her partner? She inwardly cringed at the memory. There were so many things. So many times where she was so caught up in herself, that she just didn't enjoy the little things. The things that made life whole.

She rubbed her forehead and turned as she heard Casey emerge from the hallway. He looked like death warmed over, and she knew he hadn't been sleeping well. She'd found him on the couch several nights in a row, hair mussed, arm slung off the side.

"Morning."

He grunted.

"How are you?"

Another grunt. He yanked open the fridge and downed some orange juice from the container.

"Casey, I wish you wouldn't do that. Damn it."

"Why? It's just you and me."

"Because it's gross and inconsiderate. And because I have a friend coming for breakfast."

He paused, juice bottle held just below his mouth. "A friend? Since when?"

"Since now."

"Not Mickey I take it."

"No."

He screwed the lid back on and shoved the bottle back into the fridge.

"What about Sasha?"

He was looking for a fight; she could feel it.

"Sasha and I aren't together."

"Bullshit." He laughed with sarcasm. "You two fight it, you always will. But you'll be miserable apart. Take my word for it."

"Casey, I can't really go into this right now."

"Of course not. Not when it's something important."

"Excuse me? We always talk about what's important. It's you who's shut me out."

"Right, right. Couldn't possibly be because you're in your own little world, could it?"

"What are you talking about?" But she held up a hand to stop herself. "You know what? I'm not doing this, not now. I have a friend coming. I'm allowed a friend. Hell, I'm allowed a wife if I wanted her. So don't go trying to make me feel guilty."

He laughed again. "The guilt is all your own, Mom. I'm just simply spilling the truth. Funny how an eighteen-year-old kid can see what you and Sasha refuse to see. This adult shit, as you call it, is laughable. Especially if it means living with your head in the sand." He marched back into his bedroom and slammed the door. When he emerged five minutes later, he was dressed in sweats and sneakers and had his earphones dangling from his neck.

"Where are you going?"

"Out."

"Casey, wait."

"No. Have a nice time with your new friend."

He slammed the front door.

Seconds later, the doorbell rang. Hannah ran to the door and pulled it open, breathless and worried that Casey had been rude. Brandy stood looking back at the driveway as Casey drove away, peeling out and leaving smoke behind him.

"I'm so sorry," Hannah said, shaking her head.

Brandy faced her with a soft smile. "He seems—nice."

Hannah belted out a laugh, and Brandy joined her as she stepped inside.

"I mean I know I make quite a stir with first impressions, but that one just about beats them all."

"Please ignore him. He's having a bad day."

"Already?"

"'Fraid so."

Brandy smiled again and leaned in to kiss Hannah on the cheek. It caused Hannah's face to burn.

"You smell good," Brandy said as Hannah took her hand and led her into the kitchen.

"So do you." She noticed the light airy scent to her neck and the freshly shampooed scent of her thick hair. But mostly she noticed her kind eyes and easy outfit of cargo capris and a loose fitting white blouse. Somehow the clothes hugged her body just right, as if they'd been tailored for her. Everything with Brandy seemed so easy and flawless. And at the moment, easy was more than welcome.

Brandy swung onto a barstool and glanced around at the kitchen. It was nicely decorated in reds and tans, Sasha's doing.

"I can't take any credit for any of this," Hannah said. "It was all Sasha."

"She has good taste."

"Yes, she does."

"So I take it that was your, what, son?"

"Casey, yes. He's going through a rough patch. Please forgive him. We argued just before you arrived."

"No explanation needed. He's a handsome guy."

"He is."

"Like his mama."

She gave Hannah a wink.

Hannah pushed off from the bar. "Unfortunately, I can't offer you juice because he chose to drink from the container this morning. He's becoming quite the cave man here lately."

"Oh, no worries. I'm more of a coffee girl."

"Right."

Hannah snapped her fingers and got to it, turning on the coffee maker. "What would you like for breakfast?"

"Honestly? You."

Hannah froze and fumbled with replacing the lid on the coffee maker.

"Sorry, too much? I couldn't help it."

Hannah stood very still with her back to her. She didn't know what to say. The words had penetrated like they had years ago with Sasha. They'd gone straight to her center and caused it to throb.

She heard Brandy move. She was coming closer. Hannah knew she should move. Speak. Do something, anything. But she couldn't. She was frozen in her awakening desire.

"I can't help myself, Hannah." She touched her hips and whispered in her ear.

Hannah moaned and nearly buckled.

"I look at you and I feel you. I know how badly you need it. Want it. But you'll never bring yourself to say so."

Hannah closed her eyes. "I—"

"Shh, just let me. I promise I won't get all mushy afterward. I won't ask you to marry me. I won't even expect a movie date. Just let me please you. Let me take you far away."

Hannah dropped the container of coffee and Brandy turned her and took her mouth ferociously. Hannah made a noise of sheer helplessness as she fell into her, kissing her back like she was dying of thirst and Brandy was the river of life. Brandy grabbed her face, held her still, and pulled away to look into her eyes.

"Come with me," she said. She took her hand and led her to the living room. They both stood breathless as Brandy went to tug off Hannah's shirt. Blood was rushing to Hannah's clitoris, and her head was spinning, but she still managed to grab Brandy's hands to stop her.

"Wait."

"What is it?"

"I—I've had surgery. A double mastectomy. I don't want—I can't"

"Okay." Brandy stroked her face. "I get it."

She kissed her again. Lighter, softer. Her hands went lower to Hannah's waist. She popped a button to her shorts.

"Is this okay?"

Hannah nodded. "Yes."

They locked in a kiss again, and Brandy eased her from her shorts. When she straightened again, she palmed her flesh through her wet panties. She licked her neck and rubbed the heel of her palm against Hannah's cleft, causing her to gyrate along with her movements.

Hannah clenched her eyes and her breath hitched. The pleasure was shooting up through her like thick, molten lava. She couldn't take much more.

Brandy seemed to sense her mounting pleasure, and she slowed and then dropped to her knees. She pushed Hannah onto the couch and eased her legs apart. She fastened her mouth to her and nibbled through the fabric of her underwear. Hannah came up off the couch and knotted her hands in her hair. The sensation was so good her eyes rolled back in her head. Yet it wasn't quite good enough. It was just enough to get her there and then disappear again. Again and again, Brandy played her like this. First nibbling, then sucking and then holding her clit firm between her teeth. All through her panties. Hannah was crying out, yanking on her head, gripping the couch, thrusting her hips. Sweat broke out on her brow and body. She wanted it. Needed it.

Like she never had before.

"Please," she begged. "Please."

"Please, what, lovely?"

"Lick me."

"Where?"

Hannah struggled for words. "My pussy. Please."

Brandy groaned and pulled the panties to the side. She snuck out her tongue and flicked her clit. Hannah nearly choked with pleasure.

"Please," she rasped. "Now. Hurry. Please."

She clenched her eyes. Felt Brandy flick her again, this time bringing her just to the brink and then backing off again.

"Open your eyes," Brandy said.

Hannah blinked them open.

"Watch me lick you." She flicked her again, up and down and side to side. "Is that what you want?"

"Yes. But—"

"But what?"

"More."

"Like this?"

She flattened her tongue and licked her from her hole up to her clitoris, again and again, until Hannah was hoarse and thrashing.

"More," she pleaded.

Brandy laughed. "Like this?" She took her flesh into her mouth and worked it, sucking while thrusting with her tongue. Hannah screamed and pulled herself up, shoving herself into her face until her legs burned and her muscles cried out for mercy. She pushed into her face until her feelings fell into numbness, carrying her to a place where only pleasure existed and pain was merely a stepping stone to get there. She thrust until she fell to the floor and writhed like a crazed beast with Brandy still attached to her.

She fucked her until a part of her was lifted up, shattered, and gone, evaporating into a mist.

She fucked her until she was completely still, heart careening, insecurities gone, and life was coming at her from new angles.

She fucked her until she let go of it all.

And then she curled into her and cried.

Chapter Thirty-three

Sasha was curled up on the couch watching *The Break-Up* when her phone rang. Bonnie was out on a date, the house was hers, and she was intent on enjoying a movie. But the current one was depressing her to no end. She eyed her phone, placed it face down, and then picked it up again. Could Heidi really be calling her this late on a Friday night?

She decided to answer, almost as if making sure the call were real and not her imagination.

"Hello?"

"What are you doing this fine evening?" Heidi asked with her smooth, deep voice.

Sasha couldn't help but grin. "I'm watching a very depressing movie while pretending I like this plain air popped popcorn."

"Ah. So nothing too exciting then?"

"Hardly. What are you up to?"

"I, my dear, was just getting ready to open a bottle of wine. Care to join me?"

"I don't know. It's really late."

"Don't tell me you'll turn into a pumpkin."

"No," she laughed. "Not quite."

"Then come. Bring your jammies. We'll get tipsy and build a pillow fort. Make it a night."

"A pillow fort? Gosh, how could I say no to that?"

"You can't. I'll text you my address. Don't forget your jammies. I would like it too much if you had to wear one of my T-shirts."

Heidi ended the call and Sasha rose to pack a bag. She'd already soaked in the tub and dressed in her pajamas. Now all she needed to do was to throw a quick overnight bag together. As she did so, she thought over the request. Sure it seemed a little odd and a little forward to invite her to spend the night. But they'd really hit it off as friends, and the thought of spending the evening with her excited her. Anything was better than her current situation. And Bonnie had been bugging her to get out more. Was she excited to be asked out for a wine-soaked slumber party of sorts? Or was she excited at the thought of spending a wine-soaked evening alone with Heidi? In the dark. Amidst soft pillows and blankets.

"Both," she said as she zipped up her bag. "And there's nothing wrong with that." She hurried downstairs, wrote Bonnie a note, and slipped into her sandals. She left the front light on and locked the door behind her. A text came from Heidi as she slid into her Jeep. It gave the address and the directions and a final note.

Can't wait for you to come.

She laughed a little wondering what all it implied if anything. Regardless, her blood grew hot beneath her skin and she turned on the AC to keep herself cool. Heidi was one hell of a good-looking woman. Not to mention successful, witty, and funny. The fact that she was a lesbian had been icing on the cake. And now she was interested in Sasha? Could her luck get any better?

She grinned again and ran her fingers through her hair. Then she reached in her purse for her lip gloss and sprayed on a light perfume. Whether this was considered a date or not, she was going to put her best foot forward. Just as she always did.

She drove in silence, too anxious for the radio and too keyed up to think about anything else but her destination. Heidi lived on the outskirts of Scottsdale, and Sasha found the night quiet and dark with yellow lights illuminating beautiful front doors and large stucco homes with flagstone accents and perfectly manicured front lawns. She turned off her AC and eased down her window. The air was bordering on refreshing but still warm enough for her to feel sweat form on her upper chest. She knew it was mostly nerves, and she willed herself to breathe and relax. But she came to a stop in front of the house with the correct number before she could do so.

"Okay, this is it. You're here." She pulled carefully into the front drive and parked behind the garage door. She rolled up her window and grabbed her bag and exited the car. She mumbled to herself the entire walk to the front porch.

And just as she rang the doorbell, she realized she was in her damn pajamas of all things. What had she been thinking? She could've at least put on a pair of nice jeans and a shirt. Made a little more effort. She palmed her forehead and the door unbolted and opened.

"Well, don't you look adorable?" Heidi said, standing there in a maroon satin robe and bare feet. "What are those? Cowboys?" she asked, referring to her pajamas

"Cowgirls."

"Of course." She smirked and opened the door farther. "Come on in, darlin'."

Sasha stepped inside and fought the blush that was rushing madly to her face. Heidi continued to check her out as she closed the door behind her.

"I literally just finished unpacking an hour ago. And I'm so happy I could dance a jig."

"I can imagine." Sasha followed her farther inside. "Your place is…wow."

"Thanks, I had a lot of work done. New paint, new floors, new window treatments. And the kitchen was completely gutted and redone. I like to flip houses as a hobby so it was a little hard to say no to this place. I just had to do it. Now, I'm glad I did."

"It looks fantastic." She stood in awe, taking it all in. It made her think once again about getting her own place and decorating it herself. But no matter how many times she thought about it, she just couldn't bring herself to do it. It seemed so scary, so final. But then again, what was she afraid of? Wasn't final what she needed?

"Wine?" Heidi called from the kitchen. She'd taken Sasha's bag and purse and placed them in the large living room. Now she was holding up a glass of white wine.

"Thank you." Sasha took the glass, planning on only sipping it. She enjoyed wine too much to say no.

Heidi carried her own glass and the bottle and sat on one end of the couch. Sasha followed and sat on the other end. She sank comfortably into the lovely cushions.

"Goose down?"

"Yes."

"Very nice."

"I like to be comfortable."

Sasha smiled and sipped her wine. It was divine.

"Like it?"

"Oh, yes." But more than that, she was liking her view. Heidi had crossed her legs, showing off her beautifully sculpted calves and moist looking skin. And the way she held her glass…so careful and seductive, circling the rim with a single fingertip.

Heidi seemed to be aware, and she placed her glass on the end table and leaned toward her with her arm strewn along the back of the couch.

"So how have you been?"

"You see me nearly every day. I'm fine."

"I see you at work. I want to know how you really are. No bullshit."

Sasha shrugged. "Okay, I guess. My health is…" She hesitated. She never liked discussing her health. It still made her feel exposed and weak somehow. She really liked Heidi, and she was afraid being totally honest would scare her away. But then again, if they dated, she'd see it firsthand. This was her life now, like it or not. She couldn't pretend like she did at work. A brave face only went so far.

"It's up and down. I take it week by week. I never know when I'm going to just crash and feel horrible or when I'll be fine. And I understand a lot of people can't handle that."

"Are you trying to scare me away?"

"I just want to be honest."

She took a slow sip of her wine. "Thank you for that. But you needn't worry. I think I can handle it."

"You think that now, but…"

"How do you feel this evening?"

"I'm well. I feel good." Really good. The wine was helping.

"I apologize for not even asking if you were okay to come over. I just got so excited at being finished with the house, I couldn't wait to have you over."

"No apology necessary. I was just as excited at being invited."

They both sipped their wine. In the far distance, as if a gentle tease to her ear, Sasha heard Debussy playing. It relaxed her further and she swore the moment couldn't get any better after a long workweek pretending she was okay and all smiles.

"I love Debussy."

"Really?"

"Oh yes."

"I heard you were more of a rocker." She raised an eyebrow.

Sasha laughed. "God, what else have you heard? Wait, don't answer. I don't want to know."

"So are you going to tell me then? Are you a rocker?"

"Well, let's see I have Led Zeppelin for my ringtone and I'll listen to anything by Greta Van Fleet."

"What about Jet?"

"Love them as well."

"I think I can paint a good picture now. How about we play something by Greta Van Fleet? You can give me a taste." She winked and called out. "Alexa, play Greta Van Fleet."

"Playing Greta Van Fleet," the home speaker system answered.

"Alexa, turn it up." Heidi looked to Sasha with a smirk. "Sing."

"What?"

"Come on, get up and sing."

"No way," Sasha said, laughing.

Heidi stood and held out her hand. "You feel good, right? Let's take advantage. I'll dance with you."

Sasha allowed herself to be pulled into a stand. Heidi began to dance.

"Come on, woman, dance with me and sing that song."

Sasha hesitated but then started to move. The song was "When the Curtain Falls," and she knew every word. She moved faster and began mumbling the words.

"Louder."

Sasha closed her eyes. She sang louder as her body moved. Soon the song completely overtook her and she was moving like there was no one else left in the world but her. The wine fizzed her mind, and her skin heated. She felt like floating away, and she danced as if she could. The earth around her fell away, and she was free, completely free. She smiled and opened her eyes. Heidi was sitting back on the couch watching her, seemingly captivated.

But Sasha didn't stop. She kept going. She moved closer to her. She was empowered now with music and rhythm, and they were humming in her blood. She was fearless.

The song came to an end, and Heidi commanded the speaker to stop. She never took her gaze away from Sasha's.

"Come here," she said.

Sasha went to her. Heidi took her hands and pulled her down on top of her. Sasha straddled her as Heidi held her face.

"I want to kiss you, Sasha."

Sasha struggled for breath, the fearlessness still radiating from deep inside. "So kiss me then."

Heidi pulled her in and stopped with her lips a breath away from Sasha's. They danced that way, breathing and teasing. Then Heidi grabbed her torso and tugged her in hard as she took her mouth in a deep, fierce frenzy, one that Sasha answered with a ferocity of her own.

They both moaned in approval with twisted tongues and hungry lips. Heidi tasted of the sweet wine, and Sasha feared she'd never be able to get enough. She pulsed against her, thrusting her hips as Heidi pulled on her ass.

"I want to fuck you," she said with strain to her voice.

Sasha sucked in a breath as Heidi attached her lips to her neck. "So fuck me."

Heidi leaned back and looked in her eyes. "Yeah?"

"Yes."

Heidi tore off Sasha's shirt. Her eyes widened at the sight of her breasts. She inched forward and flicked her nipple with her tongue. Sasha grabbed her head and hissed, and Heidi did the same to the other nipple causing them to harden so fiercely they pierced the night. Then she groaned, forced Sasha to stand, and tore down her pajama bottoms. Sasha stepped out of them and allowed Heidi to tear down her underwear. As soon as she stepped out of those, Heidi grabbed her hips and pulled her atop her once again. She ran her hands up and down her thighs and then teased the folds of her center with her fingers, causing Sasha to jerk and groan. Heidi held her gaze and teased farther in, sliding into her wetness.

Sasha moved into her and took hold of her wrist, guiding her. She clenched her eyes and sighed as Heidi's fingers sank deep inside and began to move.

"Fuck me, you feel so hot and tight."

Sasha bucked her hips and dug her fingers into Heidi's shoulders. She knelt and kissed her, capturing her talented tongue, sucking it into her mouth as she gyrated against her.

"I can't wait to fuck you," Sasha said.

"Right now it's all about you." She pumped her hand. Harder, faster. Sasha began to call out. "I want to watch you dance on top of me. Fuck my fingers with your beautiful body. Writhe into the night like a moving goddess. God damn, you are beautiful."

Sasha reared back. "Mm, you're fucking me so good. Oh God, help me, it's so good."

"Yes, Sasha, fucking take it. Take it all in. I'm going to give until you beg me to stop."

"Don't ever stop."

"I won't."

"Ever. Oh God, it's so good. Oh God. Oh fuck." She laughed wickedly and stared down at her. "You have the most glorious fingers."

"They're all yours."

"They're mine."

"Yes. Ride them, baby."

"I am. Oh God. Ah, fuck. Don't stop. Don't stop. I'm coming. Oh God, I'm coming." She bucked uncontrollably. "Ah Jesus, I'm coming so hard. Can you feel me coming? Coming all over your sweet, sweet fingers."

"I feel you, Sasha. I feel you."

"Oh yes. Oh God." She fucked and bucked and finally screamed into the silent night, letting it all out, every last bit. She moved and spasmed and Heidi was telling her she was beautiful, but she couldn't quite make sense of it.

And then she fell against her, barely able to breathe. Sweat coated her body and her heart beat like a wild animal's.

Heidi held her tightly. Whispered in her ear. Sasha still couldn't make sense of it. The world was completely muffled around her. Smeared. Blurry. Oh Jesus, she'd just been fucked so good. So good she couldn't think or move.

"Thank you," she managed. "I so needed that. Thank you, thank you."

"No, thank you. That was incredible. You are really incredible."

Sasha lifted her head from Heidi's shoulder. "The whole thing was pretty fucking incredible. And so are you."

They kissed. Soft. Languid, enjoying the fine wine of each other.

"Shall I get the pillows for the fort?"

"Oh yes, please. I've been looking forward to the pillow fort. Honestly, I think I could collapse anywhere though."

Heidi eased out of her, kissed her, and then tapped her leg. Sasha stood carefully on wobbly legs. She slipped back into her pajamas as Heidi excused herself to go retrieve the pillows and blankets. Sasha sat and curled up on the couch. She finished her wine and looked up at the ceiling. Her chest felt clean as she breathed, like she'd just ran a mile. She smiled to herself and watched as Heidi returned, arms full.

"Need help?"

"No, no, I want you to relax. I got this." She set the load down and disappeared again. Then she returned with another armload full. "One more," she said, disappearing again. When she came back with the final armful, she was all grins. "There." She got busy unfolding the blankets and maneuvering the pillows.

"What are you? Like an expert?"

Heidi laughed. "Sort of. I have nephews."

"How sweet."

She laughed, hands on hips. "I'm anything but sweet." She stood before Sasha and knelt to place her hands on her thighs. Her eyes danced and her lips parted in what looked like anticipation.

Sasha swallowed hard and felt her pulse race in her neck. "Seem pretty sweet to me," she said softly.

Heidi knelt closer. "You sure? Because looks can be deceiving." She inched closer, paused, and then lightly tugged on her lip before pulling back.

She left Sasha breathless.

"Come," she said, taking her by the hand. Sasha stood alongside her, feeling a bit like a child. Heidi swept her arm outward. "Welcome to your pillow fort, Madame."

Sasha followed her to the opening of the blankets. Inside the dim fort, she could see a layout of pillows and more blankets. It looked like heaven on a cloud.

Heidi took her glass. "Crawl inside," she whispered. "There's magic in there."

Sasha heated from her breath against her neck and knelt to crawl inside. She noticed the freshly laundered smell of the linens and the muffled noise around her. She made herself comfortable and relaxed against the pillows. It was warm and soft and safe. She wanted to close her eyes and drift away.

"How is it?"

She watched as Heidi's robe dropped to the floor just outside the fort. Then she knelt once more and crawled inside wearing nothing but a maroon teddy. Her amber scent was stronger, tantalizing and mysterious. It caused Sasha's insides to burn once again.

"I like the pajamas, but I was hoping not to see them again so soon," Heidi said, getting settled in next to her. She lay on her side, propped up on her elbow. She crossed her ankles, and Sasha so badly wanted to stroke her long, smooth looking legs.

"I'm more concerned about you right now."

"You are?"

"Mm, yes."

Heidi grinned. "Wait, one last touch." She reached behind her and switched on a weak flashlight. "To keep the monsters at bay."

Sasha cracked up. "And here I thought you were going to be the one protecting me."

"Oh, but I am. This is just my sword of sorts."

"I see."

Sasha moaned and relaxed farther into the pillows. "I haven't felt this good in a very, very long time."

"I'm glad." Heidi leaned toward her and stroked her face. "You should feel good every day, Sasha. I'm so sorry for what you go through, with your health."

Sasha tried to smile, act like it was no big deal, but her emotions got the better of her.

"Thanks. That means a lot."

"I mean it. And I want you to know you aren't alone. I'm here; your friends at work are there for you. We all want the best for you."

Sasha wiped a stray tear. "You all talk about it?"

Heidi paused in her movement. "Some days it's kind of hard not to. When you're not feeling well. We worry."

"Oh God."

"No, don't be embarrassed. You have a lot of people who care about you." She grinned. "Dennis especially."

Sasha grabbed a small pillow and hit her with it.

Heidi looked shocked at first, but then her eyes flashed and she took the pillow from her and hit her back. Sasha laughed and wrestled her for it but couldn't win. She just wasn't strong enough. Eventually, she gave up and sighed with laughter.

"Okay, okay, you win."

Heidi stilled. She stared deeply into her and tossed the prize pillow aside. Then she crawled on top of her and straddled her.

"Please tell me I didn't hurt you."

"Of course not. Don't be silly." But Sasha was lost in the way she felt atop her. The way she looked atop her. The way her red curls were strewn about her face, the way her chest was moving with rapid breaths, the fabric of her teddy showing winks of her taut breasts.

Sasha felt her own breathing hitch at the mere sight of her.

"Kiss me," Sasha demanded. "Hold me down and kiss me."

Heidi straightened in response to the words and pushed back her hair. "Are you sure?"

"Yes."

"Because once you touch me, Sasha, I won't be able to control myself. I think I could come all over you right now with just the slightest of movement."

Sasha placed her hands on her bare thighs and sucked in a hiss of air at the feel of her hot skin. She bucked.

"I don't want you to control yourself."

Heidi took hold of her hands and placed them above her head. She held her there for a long moment, and they locked eyes.

"I've been wanting this for weeks," she said.

"Me too."

"The way you dress, the way you smell. You drive me insane." She licked her neck, then all the way up to her jawline. Then she teased her lips.

Sasha welcomed her once again with teases of her own tongue.

They kissed as they had before. Madly, deeply. With Heidi thrusting on top of her.

"Oh God, I'm so close."

Sasha whispered in her ear. "Lie down. On your back."

Heidi stilled and then moved. She crawled from her and got settled, her back against a plethora of pillows.

Sasha sat up and maneuvered slowly between her legs. She lightly kissed her way up and then spread her apart, causing Heidi to gasp for breath.

Sasha teased her glistening flesh by blowing on it.

"Sasha, I'm going to come. I swear to God, I'm going to come."

"Mm, not without me tasting you you aren't."

She teased her swollen clit, then licked it up and down fully. Heidi went insane, grabbing Sasha's head, trying to hold fast to her. Sasha attached to her, feeling her trembling flesh quiver in her mouth. Heidi exploded in a tantrum of screams, gripping her head, sitting up, forcing her to remain.

Sasha groaned into her, loving every last second.

"Sasha," she said. "Fuck, Sasha, give it to me." She collapsed back onto the pillows and laughed all deep and throaty. Sasha positioned on top of her, sank her fingers into her tightness and began to thrust. And as Heidi cried out and clawed at her back, Sasha closed her eyes and enjoyed the pleasure she heard streaming from a woman. Something she hadn't heard in a very long time.

Chapter Thirty-four

Hannah drove in silence through the rain, enjoying the tapping of the frenzied drops against the windshield. She had an inner peace inside she couldn't quite grasp, but at the same time she felt solemn. She struggled not to get lost in the dance of the rain and the swipe of the wipers. She turned on the air to battle the humidity and hoped the icy flow would help to spark her insides. She was headed to meet Brandy, and she didn't want to ruin their date. Truth was they'd been having a great time together, even if they hadn't been intimate again since the fateful night five days ago. But Brandy hadn't pushed. In fact she had been completely understanding.

It was her empathy and understanding that kept Hannah sticking around. She didn't want to lose her just because she was struggling to overcome her fears. The sex had been great, better than great, and obviously something she'd needed. She just hadn't liked the confusion and guilt that had flooded her afterward. But she had enjoyed falling asleep in Brandy's arms on the couch. The feel of a woman holding her had been long missed. Something she hadn't realized until that moment. She'd not only neglected Sasha in the past, she'd neglected herself.

She pulled in the center of several large commercial buildings and parked in front of the rock climbing center. Brandy's car was already there, and thankfully, it was only her. She still hadn't seen Mickey since their last argument, and she had no plans to call her anytime soon. Brandy had tried to talk to her about it, but she'd avoided the topic. She still felt betrayed and burned by what Mickey had done.

She grabbed her bag of gear and hustled through the rain to the front door. Cool air surrounded her as she headed inside. The industrial carpet had a wet smell to it near the door, and a few people were hesitant to step outside. As if they'd melt once the rain touched them. Hannah saw Brandy from across the room on a wall toward the back. She was helping a young boy remove his gear, and she clapped him on the shoulder with a smile as they finished. Hannah couldn't help but warm at the sight. And she couldn't help but warm at the sight of Brandy. She had on black yoga pants and a bright blue tank that showed off the power in her arms and shoulders. With her locks of auburn hair pulled back in a thick ponytail, she was turning more than one head as people meandered throughout the facility.

Brandy saw her and hurried to her.

"Hi." She planted a wet kiss on Hannah's cheek and touched her face.

"Hi back." Hannah blushed even though she was getting used to her touch and attention.

"Your second time, huh? Can't believe you came back. Proud of you." She squeezed her hand and led her to the rock wall. They sat on a nearby bench where Hannah removed her sneakers.

"I wanted to give it another go. Conquer my fear completely." She'd hated the way she'd felt the first time. Even though she'd beaten the wall, she'd been shaky and terrified. And with what Mickey had done, she really hadn't had time to downshift and enjoy the fact that she'd made it to the top. Today, she hoped all that would change.

"I understand completely."

"I figured you would." She smiled at her. "It's why I'm here. You're my rock, so to speak."

"Glad to be of service."

They stood after Hannah put on her climbing shoes, and Brandy helped her finish getting ready. When she was all set and strapped in, Hannah stared up the wall and took a deep breath.

"You can do it, Hannah. I've got you."

Hannah looked back at her and nodded. Then she began. As she worked her way slowly upward, she cleared her mind and freed herself from every other anxiety and worry she had. She used her mind and her muscles, sometimes grunting and straining, other times problem solving and conquering. When she reached the top, she grinned, breathless and with arms and legs shaking. She didn't look back down. She knew how high she was. Instead she slapped the wall and enjoyed the whooping from below. She'd done it. Properly this time. With the right mentality. She felt wonderful.

When she reached the bottom, Brandy embraced her, and Hannah swept her off the floor.

"I feel fantastic," she said.

"You should. You did great."

They stilled and Hannah got lost in the happiness she felt and the happiness she felt Brandy truly had for her. She kissed her, and as their mouths melted together, Hannah felt something ignite deep inside her. It was desire.

"I think I want you," she whispered.

Brandy lightly kissed her jaw. "You think?"

"No, I know."

"Are you sure?"

"One is usually very sure about whether or not they want to ravish someone."

"Oh, ravish is it?"

"Yes."

Brandy's eyes sparkled. "I guess you are sure then."

"Can we get out of here?" Hannah's heart was racing and her blood was pumping hot. Endorphins were screaming through her, and hot on their tail was her growing want and need to feed on

Brandy. She tugged her closer and inhaled her scent. She wanted to nip her neck, stroke between her legs.

"Whoa, whoa there." Brandy pulled away. "I have a class in half an hour."

"Can you cancel?" But Hannah shook her head. "No, nevermind. I'm being ridiculous."

"You are just feeling is all. Nothing wrong with that, Hannah."

"I'm—" She palmed her forehead. "I don't know—out of control at the moment."

"It's okay."

She shook her head. "I've got to get out of here."

"No." Brandy took her by the hand, and after she helped her remove her harness and gear, she had her sit on the bench. "I have a feeling you always tend to run. Well, I'm not going to let you. You're going to sit right here and watch me teach. And then we can leave after that."

Hannah tried to stand, but Brandy eased her back down.

"Okay? Just calm down, feel the feelings, and watch the class. I really don't want you to leave."

Hannah took in a deep breath. Her head spun, but she started to slowly still and refocus. Brandy was right. She was so used to running from her emotions. She didn't know what it felt like to actually sit still and face them. Her body shook with what, she wasn't sure. Desire, adrenaline, acceptance. She hugged herself and nodded to Brandy.

"I'll stay."

Brandy kissed her cheek and began gathering and organizing for her class. Every once in a while she'd give Hannah a glance and a smile causing Hannah to feel like she'd made the right choice. Soon, her body followed her mind, and Hannah relaxed. She realized she was thirsty and she crossed to the juice bar and ordered a crancrazy. The tartness of the cranberry blend rewoke her senses, and she sat on a stool and watched the rain come down outside. Thunder growled in the distance, and she laughed, knowing any other day she'd probably growl along with it. But something was happening to her. She wasn't sure if it was all the exercise or spending time with Brandy, but she was awakening inside. Good days were outnumbering the bad. She was smiling more, even while alone. And the past few nights she'd found herself laughing at the television. She'd forgotten how good it felt to laugh.

Feeling this way surprised her, mainly because Casey was still avoiding her and she still had the issues with Mickey. But it didn't seem to stop her from growing and stretching, like a new plant reaching for the sunshine. Mickey, she knew she could work out and Casey, too. It would just take time. They'd have to wait and see what happened with the birth of the baby. She knew, though, that he was still trying to win Abby over. He was buying her baby supplies and bringing them home to wrap. On more than one occasion he'd brought home flowers. But things must still be the same, because Abby hadn't been around and Casey still seemed angry and sad. And it was awful watching her son bang his head up against the wall. Just awful. He'd lost weight, and she knew he wasn't sleeping well. But he wouldn't talk to her. He would just run every time she brought it up. Like mother, like son.

As she finished her drink, she saw several children hurry in with excitement. She stood and followed, discarding her drink along the way. They headed straight to the small beginners' wall where Brandy and another woman had moved to set up. The kids greeted them with high-pitched hellos and high fives. Hannah sat on a distant bench, gave Brandy a wave when she looked for her and sat back to enjoy the class. For once she let her mind and body relax and just enjoyed the show.

❖

Hannah drove home as quickly as she could in the continuing rain. The grin on her face felt plastered there, and it was the result of Brandy's teasing. After her class was over, she'd approached Hannah and told her she wasn't going to get to ravish her yet. First, she wanted more time with her over dinner. That she kind of liked making her wait. She'd said it was good for them to wait it out, to let the anticipation continue to build. Hannah had argued only briefly, scared that somehow her desire would vanish or fade. But as she drove home, she began to feel more and more confident that her feelings were solid.

She hurried into the house and showered and dressed. When she emerged into the kitchen with fresh cologne on, she ran into Casey who was on his way into his room with a bowl of macaroni and cheese. She noted the dirty dishes in the sink and realized again that he hadn't been cleaning up after himself.

She stopped him with hands gently resting on his shoulders. He looked at her but didn't hold her gaze. His eyes were sad, distant, and his normally well combed hair was askew.

"How are you?" She tried to get into his line of vision.

He shrugged. "Fine."

"You don't look fine."

"Yeah, well."

"Well what? Will you please talk to me?"

"What for? I'm the same. Trying like hell to get my girl back while you've all but given up on yours and moved on."

"What do you mean?"

"Mom." He finally met her gaze. "I've seen your new chick. I came home the other night to find you spooning with her on the couch. And FYI, your bare ass was sticking out of the blanket. So the next time take it to the bedroom, okay?"

She flinched. "Oh, Casey, I'm so sorry. We just—I—"

"Save it. You got carried away. That I understand. But please, try to keep it in your pants until you reach the bedroom."

"I will. I mean—it won't happen again."

"Is she nice at least? You know, nicer than Sash?" He looked so hurt she had to look away. What had she done? God, how could she have? Falling asleep like that for Casey to walk in on?

"She is. Nice I mean."

"Better than Sasha? Because I don't believe anyone is better for you than Sasha."

She shook her head, feeling so guilty she could cry. "No, not better, just different."

"Yeah, well, I couldn't replace my girl like that."

"Casey—"

He sidestepped around her. "You better go. You're going to be late for your date."

"How did you know?"

He gave a nod toward her. "You're all dressed up and smelling good. I know good and well all that isn't for Mick."

"Casey?" She called after him. "I'm just trying to do the right thing here."

"The right thing…I don't know, Mom. Seems debatable to me." He turned and walked down the hallway to his room. She heard the door slam behind him.

"Shit." She wanted to go after him, but she knew he was closed off now and she was going to be late. She grabbed her keys from the wall hook and got in her truck and took off. Her mind reeled the entire way to the restaurant. Surprisingly, she didn't think about Sasha and Casey's comparison or the guilt he'd tried to lay on. Instead she thought of his well-being only and what all she could do to help him.

When she entered the popular Mexican restaurant, she had to get her bearings and focus to look for Brandy. She found her at a table near the patio, an iced tea already in front of her. Hannah sat with a sigh.

"Sorry, I'm late."

"No worries. I haven't been here long." She pushed back her hair and smoothed down her tan linen blouse. The turquoise stones in her necklace played with the color in her eyes. She winked at Hannah and reached for a chip to dip in salsa.

"You look amazing," Hannah said.

Brandy chewed and then leaned a bit forward. "So do you. And you smell good enough to be on the menu."

Hannah laughed and held up her menu. She tried to decide on a meal, but she just kept flipping pages, unable to concentrate.

She pushed out another sigh.

"What's wrong?" Brandy asked.

"Hm? Oh, I just had a run-in with my son. Apparently, he saw us sleeping on the couch the other night."

"Oh no. I thought—I was under the impression he wouldn't be home."

"I kind of thought that myself. I'm just grateful he didn't come home…earlier."

"Mm, me too. Is he okay? He isn't upset is he?"

"He is, but not totally because of that. I just need to talk to him some more."

She reread the menu and decided on a taco and enchilada combo. She knew her nerves were too worked up to eat it all, but she wanted a taste of both. She set it aside and also ordered an iced tea when the waitress came. But when the waitress moved, Hannah caught sight of someone familiar. She did a double-take and then burned so hard and fast she thought she'd combust. Sasha was standing at the bar with a woman.

"What? What is it?" Brandy turned. Turned back. "Is that? Isn't that the woman from the news?"

"Yes. It's who's with her that I'm more concerned about."

Brandy turned again, and that's when Sasha caught sight of them. Hannah wanted to sink lower and vanish, but she didn't. She sat very still and stared at the salsa. Meanwhile her heart pounded in her throat while the rest of her went numb.

She could see Sasha and the woman approach from the corner of her eye.

"Hannah?" Sasha said softly.

Hannah forced herself to look at her. She tried to swallow but couldn't. She coughed and had to sip some tea. Sasha stood looking at her with surprise, looking gorgeous in a bright yellow dress. Her date was equally attractive in dark dress pants and a matching vest. The two of them were complete knockouts.

"Sasha, hello."

Sasha seemed to struggle for words. "It's good to see you."

"You too. You look well."

"I'm doing okay in that department." She smiled, and Hannah felt it was genuine. "You look good as well."

"Thanks." Silence befell them, and Brandy spoke.

"Hi, I'm Brandy. Hannah's friend." She stuck out her hand.

Hannah felt a fool. "Of course. I'm sorry. This is Brandy. Brandy, this is—"

"Sasha." Sasha shook her hand. "And this is my friend Heidi."

Heidi grinned and shook both their hands. When she took Hannah's she paused with a hard squeeze. "Pleasure, Hannah."

Hannah dropped her hand. "Likewise."

"Well, we won't keep you," Sasha said, her eyes only on Hannah. "Just wanted to say hello."

Hannah swallowed hard this time and nodded. "Great to see you."

"Take care, Hannah," she said softly. Heidi, who was smiling at Brandy, winked and led her away.

Hannah didn't stare after them. But she didn't look at Brandy either.

"I would ask if you are okay, but it looks as though you aren't."

Hannah grabbed her tea again and took several swallows. Then she cleared her throat and forced a smile.

"I'm just a little shell-shocked I guess. I haven't seen her in a while."

Brandy reached for her hand. "She's very beautiful. Very nice."

"Yes, she is."

"I can see why you're so torn up."

"I'm okay. I think." She squeezed Brandy's hand.

"You sure? We can go if you need to."

"No, no, no. I'm okay. I want to stay. Really, I want to be here. With you."

Brandy studied her as if to make sure. "Okay then. Let's order."

They placed their order and ate through light conversation. Hannah did her best to respond and ask questions in return, but she found she rarely could pay attention to the answers. Her mind was on Sasha and the way she'd looked so surprised and then hurt. It had only been a quick flash in her eyes, but Hannah knew her so well, she just knew she'd seen it. She desperately wanted to call her to be sure, to check on her, but she couldn't. Sasha had moved on, and seeing her with Heidi had solidified that. She knew they were more than friends. She could tell by the wicked grin Heidi gave as they'd walked away. By the press of Heidi's hand on her back, gently ushering her out. It was a sign of protection and possession. And if she were being honest she'd have to admit the sight hurt her. But did either one of them hurt badly enough to do anything about it?

She straightened to attention as the waitress brought the bill. She quickly snatched it and paid, much to Brandy's protest. But Hannah insisted and they stood and headed toward the door. Hannah almost pressed into the small of Brandy's back just as Heidi had, but she stopped herself, unsure. She'd only ever done that to Sasha. An hour ago, she would've done it, but now, things were different once again.

Brandy seemed to sense the change in her mood. She turned when they reached the door.

"Are you going to go home?"

Hannah was surprised by the question. She hadn't been thinking ahead since she'd laid eyes on Sasha.

"I—I wasn't planning on it." She didn't want to be alone. Not now.

Brandy seemed surprised by her answer. "Oh? Would you like to come to my house?"

Hannah took her hand. Despite what she'd seen, Brandy's hand was still warm and soft. She was still there and she was still beautiful. Maybe the change was all in her mind.

She nodded and she climbed in her truck and followed Brandy to a nearby subdivision where the homes were small, elongated, and close together. Hannah popped a mint and hopped from the truck. She met Brandy in the garage and they walked inside. A small poodle mix greeted them with jumps and excitement.

"Roxie, down," Brandy said.

"Oh, she's okay. Don't worry about it." Hannah bent to pet her, and Roxie assaulted her with kisses. Hannah laughed. "She's precious." She straightened. Brandy was watching her closely.

"You passed the dog test," she said. "Impressive."

"Who couldn't love her? She's a white ball of love."

"You'd be surprised."

Heidi offered her a drink, but Hannah declined. Instead she made herself comfortable on the sofa and took in the warm look of the home. Brandy's style was a bit bohemian with items that seemed to be collected from varying places, even countries.

"I like your place. Very colorful."

"Thanks. I love to travel, and I tend to bring things home." She was standing at the entryway while Roxie joined Hannah on the sofa. After a few more kisses, she settled on her lap.

"I'm going to go change," Brandy said.

Her voice had lowered and she sounded husky.

Hannah noticed her heavy lidded eyes, and she moved Roxie so she could stand. A million thoughts ran through her at that moment. Sasha, Heidi, Casey, love, lust, regret, guilt, jealousy. She fisted her hands at her side and willed them all to go away. She had a beautiful woman standing before her, and she was slowly starting to unbutton her blouse.

"I want to come with you," Hannah said. "I need to come with you."

Brandy held out her hand. Hannah took it and walked down the hallway. The bedroom was delicately lit with a small lamp burning. A red shawl was draped over the shade cascading a pink light. A colorful quilt covered the bed, and a Buddha statue sat on the dresser, keeping guard.

Brandy encouraged her to sit on the bed while she stood before her.

Hannah's breathing became short and shallow, and Brandy touched her face, placing a kiss on her forehead. She continued to open her blouse.

"I don't care why you want me," she said. "I'm just going to go with it."

Hannah started to speak, but Brandy stopped her with a finger to her lips.

"I want you too, and maybe not for the noblest of reasons. I'm terribly jealous of your reaction to Sasha, and I know that isn't right. But we are both here. We are attracted to each other and we both need and want this."

She let her shirt fall to the floor. Next she removed her shorts and kicked off her sandals. She stood before Hannah in nothing but a white thong.

Hannah took in her beautiful body, her creamy looking skin and the peak of her nipples.

"Touch me," Brandy said. "Touch me here." She brought Hannah's hands up to her breasts and sighed as Hannah stroked their center, causing the nipples to stiffen beneath her palms. Brandy licked her lips and then lowered Hannah's hand. "And touch me here." She slid Hannah's hand into her panties and they both made noises of delight and pleasure when Hannah found her slick and ready.

She closed her eyes and rocked into Hannah. "Yes, touch me there. Slowly." She guided her hand by gripping her wrist. "Mm. That's it. Stroke my clit. You feel it getting bigger? You feel it respond to you?"

"Yes."

"God, you feel good. You and those long fingers."

She rocked faster. Touched her breast. Hannah followed suit, running her palm over her nipple while she stroked her.

"Now," Brandy said. "What do you want to do?"

"I want to taste you," Hannah said.

Brandy stilled her hands and stepped back to slip out of her panties. She lightly touched herself, reaching down to stroke her center through a small patch of hair. She crawled on the bed and rested her head on a pillow. Then she called to Hannah by curling her finger at her.

Hannah kicked off her shoes and moved onto the bed after her. Unable to resist, she started at her ankle and kissed her way up to her thigh. As she neared her center, Brandy opened her legs and placed two fingers alongside her clit.

"Lick me," she said. "Lick me between my fingers. While I touch myself."

Hannah burned at the sight of her stroking her glistening flesh. She lowered herself, wrapped her arms around her thighs, and pressed her tongue to her clit. She moved it up and down in rhythm with Brandy's movements while Brandy called out in pleasure and struggled to keep her hips still.

"Oh my God. Yes. Oh, please. Like that. God yes."

Hannah pulled her closer, pressed harder, firmer. Soon, Brandy released her flesh and gripped Hannah's head. Her hips began to move, fucking Hannah's face.

"God yes, oh my God, yes. My clit. Oh shit. My clit."

Hannah kept on, giving all she had. She shook her head back and forth, sucked her between hard licks, then circled around her clit to let the pleasure build once again. She did so until Brandy was writhing beneath her, clawing at her hair, scratching her scalp, and screaming into the pink light. When she came, it was strained and silent with her arching her back up off the bed, mouth open and muscles quivering. She pulsed like that for what seemed like an eternity and then fell back to the pillows and struggled for air.

Hannah watched, mesmerized, with her cheek against her thigh. She crawled up next to her and held her, held her through more spasms and sighs until she completely stilled and groaned into her. Hannah held her and closed her eyes and forced herself to enjoy the moment. But like water building behind a dam, all the previous thoughts rushed back in and Hannah felt a tear run down her face.

Brandy smoothed the tear away.

"I'm sorry," Hannah said.

"You don't need to be. I already know. I saw it in your face when you saw her. You're still in love with her."

Hannah's voice hitched as she fought crying.

"It's okay, Hannah."

Hannah couldn't speak; she just held her tighter. Brandy snuggled farther into her.

"Shh, it's okay. I understand. Just close your eyes and relax."

"I can't do this again," Hannah finally said. "I just can't."

"Then let's just enjoy this moment together. You're safe here."

Hannah closed her eyes and breathed deeply. She knew she'd never be able to sleep. But for that moment, she held on tight because she feared if she let go, she'd be lost forever.

Chapter Thirty-five

Sasha checked the message light on her phone for what felt like the hundredth time that day. But the light remained unlit and the phone remained quiet. Frustrated, she sat back in her office chair and propped her feet up. Her ankles were only a bit swollen, but she wasn't taking any chances. While she felt fine physically, she didn't emotionally. Her nerves were snapping and firing on overload, and the silence was killing her. For days, she'd waited for Hannah to call. After running into her unexpectedly at the restaurant, she was sure by the look on her face she'd call her. But to her dismay, she hadn't. She knew she should be relieved at this point in their separation, but she wasn't. She desperately wanted to talk to her, to feel her out, to cautiously see if she'd had the same feelings Sasha had.

She ran her hands through her hair as she pushed out a breath. She'd just thought she'd been shocked and jealous when she'd mistaken Casey's girlfriend for Hannah's. But now, after seeing what she was sure was the real thing, especially after the phone call with Mickey, her insides were eating her alive. She could hardly eat, sleep, or function without feeling distracted. People were having to repeat things to her at work. And Bonnie. Bonnie was beside herself, convinced she was only going backward in her progress.

But she felt what she felt; she couldn't control it.

And now she was sure Heidi had noticed too. They hadn't spoken in three days. Not even at work. Heidi was always busy and she wasn't returning her calls.

"Damn phone."

Sasha plucked her cell from her purse and checked it even though she knew it was useless. As suspected, she had no calls. She pressed her lips together, glanced through her office window, and seeing no one, she found Hannah's name and called. Her pulse galloped as she waited through three rings. On the fourth ring, she was ready to end the call, but Hannah answered.

"Sash?"

Sasha gasped. She couldn't speak. Couldn't react.

"Sasha, are you okay?"

She heard the rising panic in Hannah's voice. "Hi, Hannah. I'm fine. Just an accidental call. I'm so sorry."

"Oh." The disappointment was evident in her voice.

Silence.

"Are you doing okay?"

Sasha felt like she needed to put on a show. "Oh yes, I'm fine. Doing well. Just busy busy."

"Yeah."

More silence. "Well, I guess I should let you go then."

"Yep, I'm late for a meeting."

"Bye, Sasha. Take care."

"You too. And I'm sorry about the call."

"You can call me anytime. Never worry about that. Good-bye."

She ended the call, and Sasha sat with the phone pressed to her ear listening to silence. A quick knock to her door broke her trance.

She put her feet down and grumbled, tired of the intrusions.

"What is it now, Dennis? I told you I'm fine." He'd been hounding her all day, asking if she was okay.

But it wasn't Dennis who entered. It was Gavin, her boss. "Sorry, were you expecting Dennis?"

"No, no, you're fine. Please, come in."

He entered and pulled out a chair. "May I sit?"

"Please."

He cleared his throat. "How have you been feeling, Sasha?"

"Pretty good overall."

He shifted. "You sure?"

"For the most part. May I ask why you're asking?"

"I'm just checking in." He sighed. "Honestly, I've been hearing rumors. About you and Heidi."

Anger flushed her face. She could take one guess as to who was spreading those rumors.

"Dennis?"

"I'm not at liberty to say. I do, however, have to ask if the rumors are true. Are you two seeing each other?"

"We have been, yes. Outside of work, on our own time."

He steepled his fingers. "Although that may be true, the rumors have already been spread and people are talking. As you know, we can't afford that kind of disruption in a newsroom."

"Understandable." Was this why Heidi was avoiding her? Had Gavin already spoken to her? She had to talk to her.

"I take it I can assume you'll put an end to any outside relationship you may have with her?"

Sasha blinked. "Are you serious?"

"Yes."

"Dennis spreads a few rumors and we have to stop seeing each other?"

He shifted again. "You know it goes deeper than that, and I don't want you two to have to deal with HR. Heidi assured me things would be taken care of. I was hoping you could too."

"I—" Sasha was speechless. She burned again with anger, this time at Heidi. "I'll be sure to take care of it."

He seemed to relax. "Very good. Now on another note, I was wondering, given the current situation, if you wanted to take some of your vacation time now?"

She blinked again. "Now?" She had three weeks coming, but she'd assumed he wouldn't want her to take it all given her time off for illness. "What about all the sick time I took?"

"That was sick time. You had so much saved up, it covered it."

"So you want me to take a vacation, now?"

"I thought it might be for the best. Give everyone a chance to move on and get refocused."

"Gosh, Gavin, you're kind of coming out of left field with all of this."

"I know. Which is why I want you to take tonight to think about it. You won't miss anything here. I've made sure your team can cover it."

She laughed. "I'm not being phased out am I?"

"Absolutely not. You know how I feel about your work. And I've promised to always be up front with you."

"You have, yes."

"And you with me."

"Yes."

He stood. "You can take two to three weeks, whatever you fancy." He walked to the door and turned to face her. "Thank you, Sasha, for not putting up a fight. I appreciate it more than you know."

"Sir? Can you have a talk with Dennis? Tell him to back off. I'm afraid he's become quite obsessed."

He stroked his jaw. "Already taken care of. I've put him on a different team. He won't be bothering you anymore."

"Thank you." She sighed.

"I see more than you think." He winked, then opened the door to walk out.

She grumbled again at Dennis and crossed her arms. True, they weren't technically supposed to be fraternizing as coworkers according to HR, but still, she'd thought they'd done a damn good job of keeping it quiet.

Now she was angry and thoroughly embarrassed.

She eyed the clock and realized to her surprise it was already well after six. She gathered her things and headed for her Jeep. She had one destination in mind.

Heidi's.

Chapter Thirty-six

It took Sasha over an hour to get to Heidi's house in northern Scottsdale. She spent the drive going over and over what she was going to say, and she still had no idea. She knew she didn't necessarily want things to end, but she didn't see any other choice. She also was worried about how Heidi felt about the whole thing. She'd been avoiding her, and she wondered if it was because she was somehow upset with her. Like she was blaming her for the rumors. Dennis was her responsibility, and she would understand if she blamed her for his behavior. All she could do was apologize and hope things worked out somehow. Ending it, with the way she was currently feeling, would be detrimental. She knew thoughts of Hannah would come rushing back, and all the progress she'd made would be destroyed.

Deep in her heart, she knew that wasn't a healthy reason to keep seeing Heidi. She knew she was wrong. But she was desperate. Damn near panic. She pulled along the side of the house and noted a Mercedes in the driveway. Did Heidi have company? She sat and debated what to do. She'd driven all this way; she might as well get out and at least try to have a quick conversation with her. She exited her Jeep and walked up to the front door. It was dusk and the front lights kicked on as she stepped up to ring the bell. Noises came from inside. Voices. She smoothed down her blouse and skirt.

She heard laughter just as the door opened. Heidi's eyes widened.

"Sasha."

"Hi."

"Hi."

There was more laughter, and tanned arms wrapped around Heidi's robe from behind. A face appeared over her shoulder.

"Is it the Chinese food?"

Sasha took a step back. The woman smiled and held firm to Heidi. Heidi patted her hands and whispered to her. Then she stepped outside and closed the door behind her.

"What are you doing here?" she asked softly. She crossed her arms and searched her eyes.

Sasha took another step back, completely shocked. It was as if she'd been struck. Smacked hard in the face.

"Who is that?" She tried to sound strong, but her voice shook.

Heidi didn't bother to look back. "A friend."

"I see that."

"Look, Sasha—"

"Is she why you've been avoiding me?"

Heidi shifted her weight and looked to the ground.

"And here I thought you'd been devastated by what happened at work. Upset that Gavin wanted us to end things. Silly me."

"I was upset over that. It was really shitty. But honestly, Sasha, the way you've been acting since we ran into your ex, well, it's been noticeable. I just don't think you're ready to date."

"What? This is news to me."

"I told you I'm not into serious relationships. I like to have fun. And since you saw Hannah, we haven't had any fun."

Sasha stared at her in disbelief. Had she missed something? She thought they'd been exclusive.

"So—you've what? Been seeing other people the whole time?"

"That's not the point, Sasha"

Sasha scoffed. "You know damn well it is."

Sasha wiped an angry tear. Her throat burned with raw emotion.

"Sasha, I care about you. We had a lot of fun for a time. But with Gavin and HR, it just felt like it was time to end things."

"You could've filled me in."

"I didn't think it was wise to approach you at work. I felt like we were under a microscope."

"You could've called." She shook her head.

"Don't cry. Please don't cry." Heidi took a step toward her, but Sasha backed up.

"Fuck you, Heidi. Just—fuck you."

"Sasha," she called after her. But Sasha hurried to her Jeep and climbed inside. She started the engine, peeled out, and sped down the street. When she reached the end, she pulled over and bawled her eyes out. Not because she was heartbroken. Not because she felt betrayed. But because she now had to face the ultimate truth. And that absolutely terrified her.

Chapter Thirty-seven

Hannah was tossing and turning in the dark when her phone rang. It had been ringing for a while, but she'd had trouble pulling herself from a dream. She'd been dreaming about Brandy. About how they'd both cried when they mutually ended things. While it had hurt, it had hurt worse to try to pretend with her.

She focused in the darkness, saw the late hour on her clock, and bolted upright. It was nearing one in the morning. Knowing the news couldn't be anything good, she fumbled for the phone and finally managed to answer.

"Hello?"

"Yes, is this Mrs. Carter?"

"This is Ms. Carter." Her pulse raced. Something was wrong, something was very wrong.

"I'm calling from the emergency room at Valley General. Your son Casey was involved in an automobile accident."

Hannah's whole world spun. "What? Is he okay? Oh my God, is he okay?"

"He's just arrived in the emergency room. He's awake and asking for you."

She stood and fell, tripping over her slippers. "I'll be right there." She scrambled to turn on the light and then yanked on a pair of jeans and a tank top. She slid into her sneakers, shoved her phone in her pocket, and ran through the house to the garage.

"Please, please, please," she said as she drove. She realized the last time she'd felt this way was when Sasha had been unconscious and rushed to the hospital. It was a feeling she'd hoped she'd never have to experience again.

Fighting tears, she managed to find a nearby parking spot and hurried into the waiting area of the emergency room. She approached the woman behind the counter and spoke to her through plate glass.

"My son is here. Casey Carter. He was just brought in."

She busied herself on the computer and looked up. She pressed a button and the door swung open.

"He's in curtain eight."

"Thank you."

She headed back and wove between medical staff and curtained sections. Noises came at her, talking, crying, coughing. A code was called over the loudspeaker, and her panic went into overdrive. She found curtain eight and glimpsed Casey in a bed, hooked up to cords. She stopped dead in her tracks when she saw the woman with him, holding his hand.

It was Sasha.

Hannah entered the room slowly. Casey tried to smile.

"Mom," he said. "Hey."

This time tears did drip down her face. "Hey."

She glanced at Sasha who also looked as though she'd been crying.

"What's going on?" Hannah asked, taking his other hand. His left leg was elevated and his ankle wrapped. His lip was swollen and stained with blood. His hand shook inside hers.

"I was hit," he said. "Guy ran a red light."

She touched his face and noted bruising along his left side. "Where do you hurt?"

"My ankle…it was trapped. My ribs and my lip."

"They gave him something for the pain," Sasha said.

"Yeah, it's not so bad now," Casey said.

The curtain scraped along the rod. "Knock, knock," a large man with a goatee said as he entered the room. "Time for Mr.

Carter here to have his scan." He popped the brakes on the bed and wheeled him out.

"Can I go with him?" Hannah didn't want to let him out of her sight.

"We'll be back in a jiff," the man said.

Hannah sighed and paced. Sasha sank into a chair.

"How—what are you—"

"The hospital called me when they couldn't reach you. Remember I'm on his emergency contact card in his wallet."

"Oh. Right."

Sasha wiped her eyes and ran her hand through her hair. She, too, looked as though she'd hurriedly dressed and rushed over.

"He was in a lot of pain when he first came in," Sasha said. "Scared me to death."

Hannah chewed her nail. "Well, is he okay? I mean what have they said?"

"They suspect he has a broken rib or two, and his ankle is broken. They want to scan his head to make sure he's okay there. Overall, they said he was very lucky."

Hannah pushed out a long breath of relief. She plopped into a chair and rested her head in her hands. Thank God, he was okay. Just thank God.

She looked up at Sasha. "Thank you. For being here."

"There's no need to thank me. He's my son. I raised him with you. You know that."

"Yes. Still, thanks. It's nice to have you here." She couldn't think of anyone else in the world that she wanted there at that moment.

"I'd do anything for you two. Anything at all."

Hannah felt like crying again, and she realized just how close her emotions were to the surface. She stood.

"I need to step out for a bit."

Sasha nodded.

Hannah wove between people and came to a bank of snack machines. She dug in her pocket, found some money, and bought two coffees. She sipped hers slowly and took her time heading back. She found Sasha sitting and staring as if she were lost in thought. She handed her her coffee and returned to her seat.

Sasha lit up. "Thank you so much. Just what I needed."

"You're most welcome."

"You don't have to do that, you know," Sasha said.

"Hm?"

"Run every time you feel something. You've done it for years, and I'm letting you know you don't have to."

"I—" But Hannah chose not to argue. Sasha was right. Though she'd gotten better, she still needed to do better. "I guess I've always been afraid to," she confessed. "I always tried to be strong. For you and Casey."

"Running isn't strong, Hannah. Staying and going through something with us is strong. And you are strong, Hannah. Casey and I both know so. You're so hard on yourself."

Hannah felt tears threaten again, and she thought about leaving once again. She gripped the armrest.

Sasha was watching her. "See, you're feeling something right now. Tell me, Hannah. Let me in."

Hannah shook her head. "I—"

"Here we are," the man with the goatee said as he backed Casey's bed into the room. Casey opened his eyes and tried to smile, but it obviously hurt his lip. "He was a rock star." The man patted his hand and left them.

Hannah and Sasha both rose to stand next to him. "How you feeling?" Hannah asked.

"Like I got hit by a car."

She and Sasha laughed softly.

"Well, at least you haven't lost your sense of humor."

"Never," he said. But then his eyes clouded and he looked beyond them.

Sasha squeezed his hand. "Casey? What is it?"

He spoke as he continued to stare off in space. "It's over," he said.

"Sorry?"

"What's over, Casey?" Hannah asked.

"Abby and me." He looked at Hannah. "You were right. The baby isn't mine."

His face crumpled and he began to cry softly. Hannah knelt and held him as best she could, her heart aching for him. She hadn't seen her son cry in years, and it was ripping her heart out.

He stopped and took in ragged breaths. Hannah straightened and found Sasha crying herself, with a look of defeat on her face. Casey saw it too.

"I'm sorry I didn't tell you sooner, Sash. I was just so worried with you being sick and all. I didn't want to put this on you too."

"It's okay, hon. I get it. I just hate that you've suffered this much. It's too much to have on your shoulders at this age."

"Wait, you know?" Hannah asked.

"He told me a few weeks ago."

Hannah knew they'd been keeping in touch, mostly with phone calls and texts. Sasha and Casey had always been very close. So why she was surprised that Sasha knew just as much as she did, she wasn't sure. Maybe it was because in her keeping her distance from Sasha, she'd assumed Casey would too. But that was ridiculous. They'd been a family. Would always be a family.

"Abby was the reason I was out so late. The guy she's been seeing called and told me, and I—I didn't believe him. So I drove to her place and we argued. But she finally admitted the truth. The baby isn't mine and she doesn't want me in her life anymore."

His face threatened to crumble once again. Sasha soothed him by stroking his face.

"I'm so sorry, Casey," Hannah said.

They all cried as Casey released his pain. "I did so much for her. I wanted us to work so bad."

"Shh, it's okay. It's okay."

"I was probably driving too fast when that car hit me. I was so upset."

A tall man entered at that moment and stood at the foot of the bed. "Sorry to interrupt."

Casey grew quiet. He seemed to recognize him. "Doctor."

"Well, you're very lucky, kiddo. No head trauma."

"Thank God," Hannah whispered.

"You've got some bruising to your ribs, and like I said earlier, your ankle is fractured. But overall, you came out pretty clean. I'm sending you to an orthopedic surgeon for the ankle. In the meantime, I want you to rest up. You'll be sore for a good while. So take it easy, okay?"

Casey nodded.

"Thank you, Doctor," Hannah said.

"A nurse will be in to give you further instructions." He gave a nod, wished Casey the best, and disappeared.

Sasha looked to Hannah. "I can bring him home if you want to get a head start. I'm sure you'll need to get things ready for him if he's going to be on crutches."

"Yeah, I think I want to be on the couch, Mom. It'll be the easiest."

"Good idea." She knelt and kissed his forehead. "Anything else you want me to do? Anything at all? You know I'll give you the world." It was what she used to always say to him when he was little and upset.

Casey gripped her hand. He looked from her to Sasha and back again.

"I need you both to do something."

"Anything," Sasha said.

"I want you two to work things out." Hannah reared back a bit and looked to Sasha who appeared equally shocked. Casey continued. "You're both so unhappy, and don't try to argue that fact with me. Mom, you're miserable. Sasha, you just told me yourself how you feel alone. You're both so ridiculous. Suffering while you deeply love each other. Who does that?"

Hannah met Sasha's gaze. She had tears in her eyes.

"You want to do something for me? Love each other. Without barriers. Love each other like I truly know you do."

Sasha hitched a breath. Hannah tried to steady her breathing.

"That's it. That's what I want," Casey said. He looked to Hannah. "Mom, you can go now. Sasha, you can help me get ready to leave."

Hannah released his hand and stepped away. She paused at the curtain and looked back at Sasha. She smiled through burning tears. Sasha returned it.

❖

Hannah brought the mug of steaming coffee to Casey and then adjusted the pillow for his ankle.

He groaned and winced, then sipped the coffee. "Ah, thanks. This is so good." He'd just woken up, and he still looked sleepy with messy hair and a wrinkled shirt. His lip was still swollen and looked dry.

"I guess coffee wasn't exactly the best drink to give you with that lip," she said as she settled down on the chair across from him. "You want something else instead?"

He shook his head. "Juice will just sting in another way. This is good." He set it down on the end table. "I'll let it cool a bit though."

Hannah watched him as she lifted her own mug from the coffee table. "You want mine? It's cooler than yours."

"Nah, I'm good."

He snuggled into his blanket.

"Ready for some breakfast so you can take your painkiller?"

"No, not yet. I need to wake up first. I still feel loopy from last night's dose."

Hannah settled back against the chair. She'd finally calmed from the night before and had been able to get a couple hours of sleep. Casey had completely crashed thanks to his pain medicine. It was nearing noon.

"So have you called her?" he asked.

"Hm?"

"Sasha. Have you called her?"

"Was I supposed to?"

He looked frustrated. "Yes. I asked you to work things out."

Hannah laughed a little. "Casey, we just saw her."

"Right, and it's time to see her again."

"Casey—"

"Look, you don't know how good you have it. You two, you're something special, but you're too dumb to admit it. I know you see it. I know you feel it. Now do something about it."

She stared at him, lost for words. "She's seeing someone."

He shook his head in defiance. "No, she's not. I asked her. She thought the same about you. I cleared that up as well."

"You did?"

"Yes. You're welcome. Now you have no excuse."

"How did you—"

"Please, Mom. You've been moping around here acting like it's the end of the world. You may still be working out, but your loneliness has been more than evident. And I know you think about Sasha because you have the family photo album next to your bed. You've been brooding."

"I've just been—"

"Lost. Alone. Heartbroken. I know those feelings. I've been fighting them for months. That's what you don't get. You've got your love right in front of you. She's there. Waiting. Suffering just like you are because she friggin' loves you." He pushed out a breath, and the doorbell rang. Hannah looked to him in confusion.

"Aren't you going to get it?"

Hannah stood and hurried to the door. She had no idea who it could be. She hoped like hell it wasn't Abby. What nerve. She pulled open the door and stared in awe. Sasha stood holding a big basket of goodies, squinting in the sun.

"Hi."

Hannah struggled to speak. "Uh, hi."

Sasha smiled shyly.

"Ask her in!" Casey yelled.

"Of course. Please, come in." She opened the door farther and Sasha entered. "Here, let me take that." Hannah took the basket and followed her inside. Casey grinned as best he could from the couch as Sasha bent to kiss him.

"How do you feel?" she asked.

"Groggy," he said. He saw the basket. "What's that?"

Hannah set it on the coffee table.

"I brought you some goodies. Your favorite snacks, magazines, movies. Even a book or two."

Casey's eyes lit up. "I see Slim Jims. Thanks, Sash."

"You bet, sweetie."

They stood in silence, and Hannah could feel the awkwardness in the air.

"It was nice of you to come by to see Casey. And the basket is wonderful. So thoughtful."

"She's not here just to visit," Casey said. "She's here to stay."

"Sorry?" Hannah searched both their faces.

"He didn't tell you, did he?"

"I asked Sasha to come stay with us last night on the way home from the hospital. I'm going to need the help and you need to go to work." He shrugged. "So it's just easier if she stays here."

"I can't believe you didn't tell her," Sasha said. "I should've known by the look on her face when she opened the door." Sasha looked thoroughly embarrassed. "Maybe I should go."

"Absolutely not," Hannah blurted. They both looked at her with surprise. "I mean…it's a great idea. Of course you can stay."

"You're staying," Casey said. "We insist."

Sasha threw up her hands. "Okay then."

"Good, it's settled," Casey said. He reached out for their hands. When he grabbed them he smiled and said, "I finally have my family back. It's about time."

Hannah flushed and didn't say a word. But inwardly, she couldn't agree more.

CHAPTER THIRTY-EIGHT

Sasha stumbled in the front door and cursed below her breath. She quietly closed and locked the door behind her and then carried her satchel and another bag farther into the house. She'd left the accent lights on in the kitchen so she was able to see without needing further illumination. She moved closer to the couch and saw that Casey was still asleep. She breathed a sigh of relief.

She'd left him an hour ago to pick up her work satchel and a few other things from Bonnie's. At the time, Hannah still hadn't arrived home from work so she'd been a little uneasy in leaving Casey. But his medication really knocked him out, and he seemed peaceful and undisturbed. As she moved back through the kitchen toward the hallway, she caught sight of Hannah's lunch bag. She'd made it home.

Sasha continued on into her bedroom. She stopped at the door. Three candles were lit, dancing light upon the walls, and an enormous bouquet of flowers sat on the dresser. On the bed was a basket similar to the one she'd given Casey. She walked in, set her bags down, and sifted through it. She found many of her favorite things, candies, lipsticks, perfume, bath salts, books. She smiled and palmed her cheeks. She picked up the note left next to the basket.

A little something for you. For all your help.

Love, Hannah.

Sasha examined every goodie inside the basket, then she reread the note. She walked to the dresser and inhaled the flowers. There were two dozen dark pink roses. Her favorite.

She glanced back over everything and smiled. Her heart fluttered, and she knew she couldn't wait until morning. She headed back down the hallway across the house to the other wing. She saw a light on under Hannah's door. She knocked softly. There was no answer. Hannah must've fallen asleep. She cracked the door, wanting to get a look at her while she slept. She crept inside and stiffened when she saw Hannah's bed empty. At that moment, Hannah emerged from the bathroom soaking wet, wearing nothing but a towel. She stopped and let out a noise of surprise. Her hand went to her heart.

"Sasha, oh my God."

"I'm so sorry. I just—I just came to—I thought you were asleep and I—"

Hannah stared at her. Sasha stared back.

"I wanted to thank you for the gifts and the flowers." She caught the scent of Hannah's masculine shower gel, and her body reacted, nearly buckling her knees.

"You deserve to be spoiled too. It's what I should've been doing all along. Getting you things you love, doing nice things, taking you to nice places."

"You think that's what I wanted?"

"I think it's what you needed, yes. Me showing you how much I care. How much I love you. An ongoing seduction."

Sasha took a step toward her. "Hannah, that's not the kind of seduction I need. What I need and what I wanted…well, it's what you've been doing the last few months. Being there for me, showing up, being so kind and attentive to my feelings. That's been the greatest seduction of all."

She saw Hannah tremble. And she could barely tear her eyes away from the way the water glistened and highlighted her muscles. But Hannah was silent. Still. And obviously cold.

"I'll go so you can dry and dress. You're freezing." She turned to leave, but Hannah stopped her.

"No, wait."

Sasha stilled, her back to her.

"I didn't shiver because I'm cold."

"No?" Sasha felt her knees weaken again. She knew she couldn't turn and see her like that again without going to her. She just couldn't.

"No. I'm shivering with desire, Sasha."

Sasha still didn't dare turn. She knew she wouldn't be able to control herself, and she knew how sensitive Hannah was with her body. She had to respect that, even if it was killing her.

"Turn around, Sasha," Hannah said.

"You know I can't."

"Yes, you can."

"I can't. I want to touch you, Hannah. All of you."

"Sasha, turn around."

Sasha swallowed hard and turned. Hannah looked heavily into her eyes and dropped the towel.

Sasha inhaled sharply at the wet etchings of her muscles and at the red scars on her chest. She walked to her, heart pounding so fierce she felt her pulse in her ears.

"My God, you're so beautiful," she said as she stood before her. A tear slipped down Hannah's cheek as she took Sasha's hands.

"Touch me," she said. She gently rested her hands on her chest.

Sasha lightly skimmed the backs of her fingers over Hannah's scars. She shuddered once more.

"So beautiful," Sasha said. She closed her eyes and leaned in to kiss her. Hannah was shy at first, only meeting her halfway. They breathed upon each other in a tease, touching lips ever so slightly and then backing away again. At last, Sasha moaned and tugged her toward her. She looked into her eyes and then took her lips in hers and made her hers once again.

Hannah made a small noise and fell against her, allowing Sasha to conquer her and stake her claim with her tongue. She steadied herself by wrapping her arms around Sasha, running her short nails up and down her back.

Sasha groaned at the sensation and pulled away. She licked her lips and felt herself lose total and complete control. She lowered herself and ran her tongue along Hannah's marks. When Hannah responded with a sigh, she went lower, tracing the line in her abdomen down to her center. She fell to her knees in worship and parted her legs. She looked up at her.

"I have dreamt about this moment thinking it would never come again."

"Me too."

"May I taste you, Hannah?"

Hannah closed her eyes then opened them again. "Yes."

Sasha snuck out her tongue and slowly licked the length of her clit. Hannah shook and she grabbed her head, knotting her hair in her hands. Sasha wrapped her arms around her and took hold of her ass. She pulled her tighter to her and sucked her clit into her mouth, just like Hannah loved.

Hannah cried out and whimpered, and Sasha bobbed her head, sucking her off as slow and deep as she could. Hannah pulled her hair and whispered sweet nothings, begging her not to stop. When her knees trembled, Sasha knew she was close, and she pulled away with a smack. Hannah stared down at her with wide eyes. She still made noises even though Sasha was an inch away, looking up at her.

"I love you, Hannah," she said.

Hannah blinked hard and long, as if she couldn't speak. "I love you, Sasha."

Sasha stood and kissed her deeply. She backed her to the bed and eased her down. Hannah slid up to the pillows, and Sasha leaned over to the bedpost and removed two scarves. She grinned as she tied them to Hannah's wrists.

"What are you doing?"

Sasha straddled her and tied her to the bedposts. "Don't you remember my long time fantasy?"

"Oh no."

"Oh yes. I'm going to tie you up and pleasure you until you beg me to stop. Climax after climax."

"I'm not sure I can take it."

"Oh, you can. I'm going to go painfully slow. I'm going to give you all the pleasure I've been dying to give you for years, Hannah Carter."

She kissed her once more and then made her way down her body. She parted her legs and settled between them.

"I only have one request."

"What's that?"

"When you come, I want you to say my name. I want you to say my name all strangled and strained with pleasure, just like you do in my dreams."

Another tear slipped down Hannah's face. "I'm sorry I kept you at such a distance."

"Shh, no apologies, no sadness. Only you and me and pleasure. Only you and me and love." She kissed Hannah's thighs, licked her clit until she squirmed, and then took her in her mouth once again. She sucked her until Hannah bucked into her. Until Hannah cried out, until Hannah nearly pulled the posts from the headboard. She sucked her so hard she could taste her desire, her tears, and her come. When Hannah finally strained and her mouth fell open with no sounds and the veins in her neck slithered beneath her skin, Sasha sucked and pulsed with her tongue, giving her an orgasm she'd never forget. She did so with all the love and devotion she had inside her. She gave her everything she had. And as Hannah fell back and moaned her name softly, Sasha relaxed against her thigh and stroked her abdomen with her fingertips.

"That's how much I love you, Hannah," she said.

Hannah squeezed her with her legs. "I believe you," she said.

"Do you?"

"Yes. And I can't wait to show you how much I love you."

"You already have, Hannah."

"Oh, but I have so much more to show you. So much more."

"Really?"

"Absolutely."

Epilogue

Sasha zipped up the back of her favorite red dress and turned in front of the mirror.

"You look amazing, Sash," Bonnie said as she came to stand behind her. "Any idea what's going on?"

"Not a clue. Hannah hasn't given away anything and neither has Casey. He used to always be good for a hint or two. But he just smiles and shrugs." She finger combed her hair and reapplied her lipstick. She'd spent the afternoon at Bonnie's at Hannah's request. All she'd said was go to Bonnie's and get ready. And be sure to put on that little red dress.

"So mysterious. How romantic."

"I know." Sasha sighed and faced Bonnie. "You wouldn't believe how romantic she is. She's spoiling me rotten."

"And now this," Bonnie said. "I'm dying to know what she's up to."

"I told her I don't need anything fancy. I just want her love."

Bonnie hugged her. "I'm so happy for you. God, I'm going to miss you."

"I'm going to miss you too." The day before had been hectic as she and Hannah moved her things back to the house. Her muscles still ached from carrying boxes. Not to mention what they'd done to celebrate later that evening. Sasha had spent the first night back in their room, sleeping soundly in their bed, in Hannah's arms. She almost pinched herself when she'd awakened that morning.

The doorbell rang, and Bonnie jumped up and down with excitement. "Oh my God, she's here."

Sasha smiled. "Thanks so much for supporting me in this, Bons. It means so much."

"After all you've told me she's done these past months, I definitely think you're making the right move."

They embraced again and Bonnie teared up.

"Don't cry or I'll start."

"Sorry." She laughed and wiped her tears. "Go, go." She pushed her toward the stairs. Sasha headed down and took a deep breath and closed her eyes before opening the door.

"Hi."

Sasha opened her eyes. Her heart fluttered and her hand went to her heart. Hannah was standing there in a dark pantsuit, holding a dark pink rose.

"Hi."

Hannah handed her the rose and then bowed and swept her arm to the side to show the black stretch limo waiting at the curb.

"Oh my God. Hannah. What is all this?"

Hannah took her hand and led her to the car. The driver opened the door and they both crawled inside. He closed the door after them.

"This is all for you," Hannah said. She leaned in and kissed her delicately on her cheek. Sasha could smell her familiar cologne, the one she'd worn for years, the one that drove her crazy with desire. She crossed her legs as her center tingled.

"I told you, I don't need all this." But truthfully, she was excited and completely overwhelmed.

"I know, but this is what I need. I need to do this for you. For us."

"Just what exactly is all this? Where are you taking me?"

"Someplace you'll never forget."

"What about Casey? Is he okay?"

Hannah grabbed a bottle of champagne and poured her a glass. "He's going to be fine. Mickey is going to stay with him."

"Stay? How long are we going to be gone?" She took the glass and stared at Hannah in awe.

"A week."

"A week?" She laughed. "I don't know what to say. This is unbelievable."

"Mickey owes me big time, and Casey fully supports this whole thing. He even helped me plan it."

"He did, did he?" It had been like old times again in their home. Warm, loving, cozy. Exchanging inside jokes and witty banter. Watching movies together. Eating dinner at the table. She'd never been more content.

"Uh-huh." Hannah leaned in again and tilted her chin. "Have I mentioned how incredible you look?"

"Not yet." Sasha smiled playfully.

"How about I just show you then?" She kissed her.

Sasha's head spun at how light and gentle and soft it was. As if she were a delicate flower.

Hannah took the glass and set it aside.

"I didn't even take a sip," Sasha said, not minding at all.

"Later," Hannah whispered. She kissed her again. Warm, soft, seeking. Her hand moved up her leg and her mouth found Sasha's neck. Sasha moaned and uncrossed her legs. She was beginning to throb, and as Hannah's hand moved closer to her center, she felt desire begin to soak her panties.

"Oh, Hannah," she groaned. "What about the driver?"

"We have a while until we arrive at the airport." She nibbled her ear. "So just relax and feel me."

"What about my clothes? Hannah, I didn't pack a bag."

"I packed two for you. They're in the trunk." Hannah pushed closer and stroked her inner thigh with her fingertips.

Sasha couldn't help but struggle for breath. She gripped Hannah's blazer and opened her legs farther.

"Where are you taking me, Ms. Carter?"

Hannah finally found her and she pressed into her aching flesh through her panties. Sasha made a noise and bit her lower lip. She stared into Hannah's eyes.

"It's a surprise."

"Tell me."

Hannah played her with her fingers.

"I'll give you a hint. There's a beach."

Sasha panted. "A beach? Mm. Where?" Her hips bucked. "Tell me."

"That's all the information you're getting from me." She slipped her hand into her panties, and Sasha threw her head back and groaned. She tightened her grip on Hannah's blazer as her hips continued to move.

"Oh Jesus, Hannah. What are you doing to me? It's madness."

"I love you, Sasha." She kissed her jawline and teased her ear. "And I can't wait to see you running toward the ocean in that dress. I know it's a moment I'll never forget." She quickened her hand, stroking her hungry flesh.

Sasha looked at her. Tugged her in farther. "Oh God, I love you too, Hannah. Make me come, baby. Make me come in your hand."

They kissed. Mouths fusing wildly. Hannah kept stroking her, framing her flesh with her fingers. Squeezing and stroking.

"Come for me, Sash. Come."

Sasha clenched her eyes and moved her body as quickly as she could. Fucking Hannah's hand. "I'm coming for you, baby. Oh God, here I come." She threw her head back and groaned long, slow, and loud.

"That's it, Sash. Oh God, I love it when you come."

Sasha's voice faltered and her body moved uncontrollably. She rode the orgasm like a wild woman, demanding every last bit. Hannah kissed her neck, kissed her jaw, and encouraged her to fuck until she could take no more. When she stilled she fell against her chest and struggled for air. Hannah held her in her arms in silence. Eventually, she spoke.

"Do I have you now, Sasha? Will you stay with me forever?"

Sasha stared into her. "Yes, Hannah. I will. Just promise me this isn't the last seduction." She smiled to let her know she was teasing. Hannah tugged her close as if she'd never let her go.

"Oh no, baby. This is only the first. The first of many."

Sasha laughed. "I'm only kidding, Hannah. You know I don't need all this."

"I will never stop trying to seduce you, Sash."

"Then just give me you."

"I will, hon. I'll give you me and so much more."

Sasha snuggled into her and closed her eyes.

She smiled and wiped a stray tear.

She had her woman.

She really, truly had her.

And most important of all, they had forever.

THE END

About the Author

Ronica Black lives in the desert Southwest with her menagerie of animals and her menagerie of art. When she's not writing, she's still creating, whether drawing, painting, or woodworking. She loves long walks into the sunset, rescuing animals, anything pertaining to art, and spending time with those she loves. When she can, she enjoys returning to her roots in North Carolina where she can sit back on the porch with family and friends, catch up on all the gossip, and relish an ice cold Cheerwine.

Ronica is a two-time Golden Crown Literary Society Goldie Award winner and a three-time finalist for the Lambda Literary Awards.

Books Available from Bold Strokes Books

Accidental Prophet by Bud Gundy. Days after his grandmother dies, Drew Morten learns his true identity and finds himself racing against time to save civilization from the apocalypse. (978-1-63555-452-6)

Create a Life to Love by Erin Zak. When sixteen-year-old Beth shows up at her birth mother's door, three lives will change forever. (978-1-63555-425-0)

Daughter of No One by Sam Ledel. When their worlds are threatened, a princess and a village outcast must overcome their differences and embrace a budding attraction if they want to survive. (978-1-63555-427-4)

Fear of Falling by Georgia Beers. Singer Sophie James is ready to shake up her career, but her new manager, the gorgeous Dana Landon, has other ideas. (978-1-63555-443-4)

In Case You Forgot by Fredrick Smith and Chaz Lamar. Zaire and Kenny, two newly single, Black, queer, and socially aware men, start again—in love, career, and life—in the West Hollywood neighborhood of LA. (978-1-63555-493-9)

Playing with Fire by Lesley Davis. When Takira Lathan and Dante Groves meet at Takira's restaurant, love may find its way onto the menu. (978-1-63555-433-5)

Practice Makes Perfect by Carsen Taite. Meet law school friends Campbell, Abby, and Grace, law partners at Austin's premier boutique legal firm for young, hip entrepreneurs. Legal Affairs: one law firm, three best friends, three chances to fall in love. (978-1-63555-357-4)

The Last Seduction by Ronica Black. When you allow true love to elude you once and you desperately regret it, are you brave enough to grab it when it comes around again? (978-1-63555-211-9)

Wavering Convictions by Erin Dutton. After a traumatic event, Maggie has vowed to regain her strength and independence. So how can Ally be both the woman who makes her feel safe and a constant reminder of the person who took her security away? (978-1-63555-403-8)

A Bird of Sorrow by Shea Godfrey. As Darrius and her lover, Princess Jessa, gather their strength for the coming war, a mysterious spell will reveal the truth of an ancient love. (978-1-63555-009-2)

All the Worlds Between Us by Morgan Lee Miller. High school senior Quinn Hughes discovers that a broken friendship is actually a door propped open for an unexpected romance. (978-1-63555-457-1)

An Intimate Deception by CJ Birch. Flynn County Sheriff Elle Ashley has spent her adult life atoning for her wild youth, but when she finds her ex, Jessie, murdered two weeks before the small town's biggest social event, she comes face-to-face with her past and all her well-kept secrets. (978-1-63555-417-5)

Cash and the Sorority Girl by Ashley Bartlett. Cash Braddock doesn't want to deal with morality, drugs, or people. Unfortunately, she's going to have to. (978-1-63555-310-9)

Counting for Thunder by Phillip Irwin Cooper. A struggling actor returns to the Deep South to manage a family crisis, finds love, and ultimately his own voice as his mother is regaining hers for possibly the last time. (978-1-63555-450-2)

Falling by Kris Bryant. Falling in love isn't part of the plan, but will Shaylie Beck put her heart first and stick around, or tell the damaging truth? (978-1-63555-373-4)

Secrets in a Small Town by Nicole Stiling. Deputy Chief Mackenzie Blake has one mission: find the person harassing Savannah Castillo and her daughter before they cause real harm. (978-1-63555-436-6)

Stormy Seas by Ali Vali. The high-octane follow-up to the best-selling action-romance, *Blue Skies*. (978-1-63555-299-7)

The Road to Madison by Elle Spencer. Can two women who fell in love as girls overcome the hurt caused by the father who tore them apart? (978-1-63555-421-2)

Dangerous Curves by Larkin Rose. When love waits at the finish line, dangerous curves are a risk worth taking. (978-1-63555-353-6)

Love to the Rescue by Radclyffe. Can two people who share a past really be strangers? (978-1-62639-973-0)

Love's Portrait by Anna Larner. When museum curator Molly Goode and benefactor Georgina Wright uncover a portrait's secret, public and private truths are exposed, and their deepening love hangs in the balance. (978-1-63555-057-3)

Model Behavior by MJ Williamz. Can one woman's instability shatter a new couple's dreams of happiness? (978-1-63555-379-6)

Pretending in Paradise by M. Ullrich. When travelwisdom.com assigns PR specialist Caroline Beckett and travel blogger Emma Morgan to cover a hot new couples retreat, they're forced to fake a relationship to secure a reservation. (978-1-63555-399-4)

Recipe for Love by Aurora Rey. Hannah Little doesn't have much use for fancy chefs or fancy restaurants, but when New York City chef Drew Davis comes to town, their attraction just might be a recipe for love. (978-1-63555-367-3)

Survivor's Guilt and Other Stories by Greg Herren. Award-winning author Greg Herren's short stories are finally pulled together into a single collection, including the Macavity Award nominated title story and the first-ever Chanse MacLeod short story. (978-1-63555-413-7)

The House by Eden Darry. After a vicious assault, Sadie, Fin, and their family retreat to a house they think is the perfect place to start over, until they realize not all is as it seems. (978-1-63555-395-6)

Uninvited by Jane C. Esther. When Aerin McLeary's body becomes host for an alien intent on invading Earth, she must work with researcher Olivia Ando to uncover the truth and save humankind. (978-1-63555-282-9)

Comrade Cowgirl by Yolanda Wallace. When cattle rancher Laramie Bowman accepts a lucrative job offer far from home, will her heart end up getting lost in translation? (978-1-63555-375-8)

Double Vision by Ellie Hart. When her cell phone rings, Giselle Cutler answers it—and finds herself speaking to a dead woman. (978-1-63555-385-7)

Inheritors of Chaos by Barbara Ann Wright. As factions splinter and reunite, will anyone survive the final showdown between gods and mortals on an alien world? (978-1-63555-294-2)

Love on Lavender Lane by Karis Walsh. Accompanied by the buzz of honeybees and the scent of lavender, Paige and Kassidy must find a way to compromise on their approach to business if they want to save Lavender Lane Farm—and find a way to make room for love along the way. (978-1-63555-286-7)

Spinning Tales by Brey Willows. When the fairy tale begins to unravel and villains are on the loose, will Maggie and Kody be able to spin a new tale? (978-1-63555-314-7)

The Do-Over by Georgia Beers. Bella Hunt has made a good life for herself and put the past behind her. But when the bane of her high school existence shows up for Bella's class on conflict resolution, the last thing they expect is to fall in love. (978-1-63555-393-2)

What Happens When by Samantha Boyette. For Molly Kennan, senior year is already an epic disaster, and falling for mysterious waitress Zia is about to make life a whole lot worse. (978-1-63555-408-3)

Wooing the Farmer by Jenny Frame. When fiercely independent modern socialite Penelope Huntingdon-Stewart and traditional country farmer Sam McQuade meet, trusting their hearts is harder than it looks. (978-1-63555-381-9)

A Chapter on Love by Laney Webber. When Jannika and Lee reunite, their instant connection feels like a gift, but neither is ready for a second chance at love. Will they finally get on the same page when it comes to love? (978-1-63555-366-6)

Drawing Down the Mist by Sheri Lewis Wohl. Everyone thinks Grand Duchess Maria Romanova died in 1918. They were almost right. (978-1-63555-341-3)

Listen by Kris Bryant. Lily Croft is inexplicably drawn to Hope D'Marco but will she have the courage to confront the consequences of her past and present colliding? (978-1-63555-318-5)

Perfect Partners by Maggie Cummings. Elite police dog trainer Sara Wright has no intention of falling in love with a coworker, until Isabel Marquez arrives at Homeland Security's Northeast Regional Training facility and Sara's good intentions start to falter. (978-1-63555-363-5)

Shut Up and Kiss Me by Julie Cannon. What better way to spend two weeks of hell in paradise than in the company of a hot, sexy woman? (978-1-63555-343-7)

Spencer's Cove by Missouri Vaun. When Foster Owen and Abigail Spencer meet they uncover a story of lives adrift, loves lost, and true love found. (978-1-63555-171-6)

Without Pretense by TJ Thomas. After living for decades hiding from the truth, can Ava learn to trust Bianca with her secrets and her heart? (978-1-63555-173-0)

Unexpected Lightning by Cass Sellars. Lightning strikes once more when Sydney and Parker fight a dangerous stranger who threatens the peace they both desperately want. (978-1-163555-276-8)